WAITING ON A WITCH

FOLK HAVEN
BOOK 6

LAUREN CONNOLLY

WAITING ON A WITCH

Moira looks forward to settling in a small town, building a magical library, and finding her animal familiar. She does *not* look forward to babysitting a monster.

Moira has always been the responsible–bossy–one in her family of witches. But that's okay, as long as her siblings are safe, and she can live her dream of running a library full of mystical books. Plus, with her brothers and sisters grown and mated to loving partners, Mor can finally focus on herself.

Until she realizes one of the statues in her backyard is actually a monster frozen by a curse.

Bo made a mistake and pissed off the wrong dragon, which landed him trapped by an enchantment for over a decade. Now he's free, only to discover the world has moved on without him. What's a monster to do?

Well, when a beautiful witch offers you a job in her magical library, it seems like the choice is pretty easy...

ISBN-13: 978-1-949794-40-3

For the all the bossy bitch witches.

CONTENT WARNING

This book contains scenes with eyesight issues, captivity, toxic parental relationships, unwanted sexual advances, blood and gore, violence, and dismemberment.

PROLOGUE

Once upon a time, a witch decided to build a library of magical books. She traveled the country in an RV with her younger sister, seeking out texts about mythical creatures as well as abandoned grimoires.

Soon, the sisters had so many books that there was no room to sleep in the camper. The two witches were tired of traveling. They wanted to find a place to stay.

A place where the books could be shared with others.

A place to call home.

There were whispers of a small town in northern Georgia, tucked away in the Chattahoochee National Forest, near the foothills of the Smoky Mountains. In this town, supposedly, more mythical creatures lived there than humans.

The town was called Folk Haven.

The witches arrived, and through deals and persuasion, they bought an old Victorian house, perched on the edge of a lake. The house used to belong to a dragon, and some of the creature's magic lingered in the walls.

But this only made the house more to their liking.

Soon, all the books were on shelves, and the Folk Haven Public Mythic Library was open.

However, no place was perfect. Folk Haven had its own secrets and prejudices.

And sitting next to the magical library was a collection of metal statues that intrigued the elder sister. The inanimate objects had so many emotions clinging to them that they almost felt alive.

Then, one day, she realized that one of them was ...

1

Mor

"BREAKING a curse is starting to feel like a family tradition," I murmur as I trudge through the woods toward the statue garden that sits beside my library. My three siblings and my brother-in-law follow close behind.

When my sister and I first moved to Folk Haven—a small town in northern Georgia, known among mythical creatures as a safe place to build a life—I expected to spend most of my days sorting books and helping others with their research. That was why I'd spent so much time collecting magical texts. I'd wanted to simply be a keeper of knowledge.

But now I'm the third witch in my family with the self-assigned task to free an unfortunate soul from a curse.

"Yes. Exactly." My brother Anthony jogs to catch up with me, his arms full of a pewter cauldron. "I was thinking that, too, and it's freaking me out. Like, when is a mythic, trapped by an evil enchantment, going to stumble into *my* life and need me to save them? Is someone going to try cursing Zara?" He names the harpy and veterinarian he fell in love with not long ago. The two of them met when she rescued him from a snake.

Turns out, the reptile was Anthony's familiar, so he was never actually in any danger. Witches tend to find an animal companion at some point in their life, and the creature acts as a comfort and protector.

Of the four Shelly children, I'm the only one who hasn't encountered mine yet.

I'm also the only one without a partner.

"Being mated to you is curse enough, I'd say," Broderick offers, smirking at his twin, then dodging away with a bark of laughter as Anthony tries to kick him.

Sometimes, I forget they're grown men. Around each other, they slip back into teenage antics.

"Do you think the creature will try to kiss you?"

I halt in my tracks and turn to stare at my sister, Ame. All of us Shelly siblings have rich red hair, but where my brothers and I are tall, she's relatively short. And while I have plenty of curves, Ame is on the slight side. In general, she gives off an air of vulnerability, though in practice, she's got some impressively powerful magic.

Still, everyone in her life seems to have the unconscious urge to protect her. My need to keep her safe is only surpassed by one other.

Her mate, my brother-in-law, Jack.

The werewolf, who claims my sister as his, holds her hand now and carries most of the spell ingredients in a large satchel over his shoulder. He's the strongest of our lot, and he volunteered to transport the heaviest load.

"Why," I ask Ame, my voice tight with trepidation, "do you think the creature will try to kiss me?" An unbidden image of cold metal lips pressed against mine flashes through my thoughts, and I shudder.

Once they're free, they shouldn't be metal, I remind myself.

The sculpture is not actually made of iron, but is in fact a living mythical being, and they have been trapped for who knows how long. From the day I moved to Folk Haven two years ago, the beast has stood frozen. A massive figure, snarling with a mouthful of razor-sharp teeth and a body that appears to be an uncomfortable blend of fur and scales.

Even though I'm willing to free the creature, it is not something I'd like to lock lips with.

"That's what Jack did." Ame points at her handsome mate.

When we first came upon the man a handful of years ago, he was trapped in the form of a black cat. I thought he was only a cat, but Ame sensed the feline was more than he appeared. Eventually, after searching for years through our collection of grimoires, my sister discovered a way to break his curse. A spell I plan on using tonight.

But this is the first I'm hearing about his reaction to being freed.

"You went from cat to man and immediately tried making out with a stranger?" Anthony asks, frowning at the wolf.

"Not a stranger. Ame." Jack speaks in a flat tone, not caring in the least about what any of us thinks of him. Ame's opinion is the only one that matters. "I'd do it again."

"In the future, I consent," Ame adds, smiling up at Jack.

He leans down and kisses her.

I huff a sigh and turn back toward my destination. In theory, I'm very happy for my sister—all my siblings in fact—and their fulfilling love lives. But the PDA is getting to me.

A reminder that *I* haven't gotten any in a while.

Not even private displays of affection.

But that does not mean I want some raging creature unshackled from a curse to immediately try a lip-lock.

"You're coming for protection, Jack," I call over my shoulder. "That also means unwanted romantic advances. Do not let whoever this is kiss me."

The wolf grunts an affirmation, not one for a lot of words unless he's talking to my sister.

"Ophelia didn't try to kiss me," Broderick sighs. "I would have let her in a heartbeat."

Ah, yes, the other Shelly sibling who freed someone from a curse, only to fall in love with them, thereby making this into a pattern.

The same sorcerer who had cursed Jack to be a cat also enchanted a firebird named Ophelia into the form of a rabbit. Broderick took the lead on freeing her. Then he promptly insulted her—on accident—and it took months for her to speak to him again.

Now they're dating, and he's besotted, and there's more of that PDA I have to deal with.

"Don't worry." Anthony pats Broderick on the shoulder. "She fell for you in the end."

He sidles up to me as I spy my first statue through the break in the trees. His shoulder nudging against mine is a good distraction from the heaviness of emotions pulsing in the air. "I'm sure whoever this is will be grateful for your help, then head on their way. No getting handsy."

I huff a laugh, then roll my shoulders and rub my eyes to try and ease the tension ratcheting up in my body.

The cloud of tumultuous emotion we're approaching only seems to affect me even though my siblings have emotion powers of their own. Under normal circumstances, I can fully block out the emotional registers of others, or I can mute them until all I see is a vague collection of colors in their aura.

But when emotions are high, they hit me like a weight, hurt me like a migraine. If I can't block them, I have to experience them as if each were my own.

We break from the trees and step into the statuary.

The moon is dark tonight, which means the sky is a blanket of stars. My night vision is decent, but I flick on my flashlight because this is delicate work, and I need to check the spell as I set things up. In the flare of light, the shadowy art pieces seem to come to life. Or maybe that's just how they were crafted. Each figure appearing on the verge of movement.

I step around a Pegasus rearing toward flight and navigate to the only statue here that will truly move tonight.

As long as I cast correctly.

For a long time, I was too uncomfortable to visit this statue garden. The strong emotions drenching this place make approaching it hard for me to handle. My magic and mind are under constant bombardment, the mysterious emotions threatening to overwhelm me.

I thought the effect was from grief. Dimitri, the dragon who previously owned our house and crafted all these designs, lost his wife—his mate—just before moving to Folk Haven.

Emotions have a touch of magic to them. They can tie themselves to a place or object.

That's often how ghosts come about.

And if you're a witch like me, constantly aware of the emotional auras of those nearby, lingering feelings can also register.

But none were ever so strong as those in the statue garden.

Turns out, that's because they weren't leftover feelings.

All the pain and rage and remorse and fear belong to this creature, held prisoner in an all-encompassing cage of metal.

"Anyone having second thoughts about letting our metal buddy loose?" Anthony asks. "Looks like they could do some damage."

"Most everyone in Folk Haven can do damage," Ame points out. "That doesn't mean they deserve to be trapped."

"I checked with Levi and Selena." I name the monster and witch, respectively, who sit on the town's Mythic Council. "There's no record of a monster being imprisoned. They claim the town has never done that. They attempt to use less painful methods to deal with any problems."

Like Ame's magic, which can be utilized to persuade people. She's worked spells to have people want to leave Folk Haven behind forever.

"And Jack has agreed to act as protection if it gets violent," my sister reminds us.

All five of us turn to stare at the statue's snarling mouth.

"My bet is on attack first, talk later," Anthony mutters.

"Do you want to leave?" I snap at my brother, already on edge because of the bombardment of emotions and the pressure of working a large spell I've never done before.

He pouts. "No. I don't want to be left out of family activities."

"Then stop nitpicking. I've had months to consider this, and I'm doing it."

I finally faced my fear this past summer, venturing into the statue garden, and that was when I realized this terrifying creation was actually a living creature.

But I couldn't simply grab a spell book, waltz back, and free him.

This is a delicate process, requiring some rare ingredients and a helpful boost from the cosmos. Today is the autumn equinox, and I plan to channel the power of the season to supercharge my spell.

Our group takes the next hour to set up everything for the curse breaking.

Lighting bonfires and burning the herbs I've gathered.

Drawing chalk circles, filled with spell words in the witch language.

And something new—marking the statue with a tracking symbol. I have to climb up on the creature's shoulder to reach the spot behind their ear where I want to draw it. This puts my face next to theirs, so close to their saffron-colored fury that pulses like a heartbeat.

"You'll be free soon," I whisper to them. "We're here to help."

There's no response in their aura, and I wonder if maybe they were frozen in the last emotion they felt.

"Please don't kill us," I add before climbing back down.

Preparations complete, I kneel in front of the grimoire, watching as my three siblings pierce the skin of their thumbs with the sharp blade of a dagger. They've agreed to be power sources while I work the spell.

I tug off my sweatshirt, shivering, as I'm left in only leggings and a sports bra. Broderick and Anthony flank me, each pressing a hand to the bare skin of my shoulders, while Ame settles her palm on the middle of my back.

They speak the words to share power, and I can't hold back a yelp of surprise at the amount of magic flowing into me. My veins buzz with the excess strength.

Is this how my parents felt when they took from me?

I shake my head to clear away the toxic memory and focus on the grimoire open in front of me.

My veins are flush with power, and I'm ready to do some badass magic shit.

"Take of my body. My blood to break." Now it's my turn to cut my palm, spilling blood over my feverish skin. "A curse before me," I say in the witch's tongue, "break it."

This spell work was agonizing for Ame when she cast it on her own and still painful for Broderick when he had my sister and my help.

For me though, backed by three witches, there's almost no discomfort.

Or maybe it's the nature of the curse we're breaking. The other two were cast with twisted magic by a sorcerer.

This is ... different.

The metal turns a scorching red, as if sitting in a furnace. The glow lights up the clearing, pulsing like a heartbeat.

Then it begins to melt, dripping off in rivulets that hit the ground with steaming hisses.

More and more molten metal spills away, revealing what was encased beneath.

Dark fur, bisected by violet scales. A body that appears to have been mashed together in odd amalgamations. A dramatically sloped spine shudders and flexes. A heavy jaw jerks.

A throat lets out a long, low snarl.

Jack returns with one of his own, but the sound is a simple warning.

The beast thrashes, and we all jerk back. All except for Jack, who steps forward, now wearing his wolfman shape. I'm not sure when he shifted, but I'm glad he took the initiative. This is the best form he has for fighting.

Turns out, a protector isn't needed though because, the next moment, the creature topples forward, landing in a quivering heap on the ground.

Then the melting starts again, only this time fur and scales morph into skin.

In the space of ten deep breaths, a man appears.

And the tapestry of his emotions temporarily blinds me.

2

Bo

Pain. Fear. Anger. Desperation. Remorse. Panic.

Loop. All on a loop.

But also frozen. No sense of time.

In my cage, I am not exactly aware of the world around me. That is the only way my mind can fathom what happened to me. I was locked away somewhere. Aware that I am alive. Aware that I can't move. Aware that the world goes on around me.

But I'm not awake.

I am lost in a painful fog that froze my limbs and left me cold and angry.

And scared.

I am terrified that this is all there is left.

But then the world returns in a new kind of hot agony. I gasp in a breath, realizing I haven't inhaled in ...

I don't know how long.

Because I don't know what happened while I was in that prison. And I don't know why I'm out now.

The last clear memory I have is the creak of an old staircase under my feet as I tried to move stealthily through the dragon's house. The wood shouldn't have made a noise. I was good at creeping. It was one of the reasons I'd felt hope when I took on the task.

For her.

I thought I could keep her safe.

I thought I could do something meaningful in my life. That I could be important to one other in this world.

But the house knew I was inside. Or the dragon did.

Because after the stairs sounded an alarm, the world around me shifted and burned. I smelled scorching hair, and I heard the ring of metal and my own shout of fearful surprise.

Then I was cold.

Now the chill is gone.

I'm covered in sweat. Weak. Limbs shaking.

I blink, and the night is too bright. My eyes burn in the light of multiple campfires as I try to take in the world around me.

Will I face Dimitri? Will he be in his dragon form, ready to devour my insignificant life? Because I might be fearsome in my beast shape, but I am no dragon.

Or will another monster be in front of me? The one who had set me on the task that left me in that prison. Will he deem my effort unworthy?

Do I dare hope that she will be in front of me? Will she tell me that I saved her?

Or will she tell me that I failed?

When I whip my head upward, wrenching the screaming muscles in my neck, I find none of those I expected.

There's a woman before me, but not the one that I long to keep safe.

This one is a stranger.

Skin is pale as the moon. Fiery curls cascading around her flushed cheeks, lit by flickering fires of the same shade. Eyes locked on mine and seeming to spark with magic.

Magic.

Is she going to use the magic against me?

Am I in a new danger that I do not even know about?

"Where ... what ..." The words tear at my unused throat, and I don't know that they are worth speaking. Will these people tell me anything?

"Hello." The pale woman stands slowly, her fingers holding a bit of black fabric. When she pulls it over her head, I realize it is a sweatshirt. "My name is Mor. Mor Shelly. You were trapped in a curse, and I just broke it for you." She holds her hands up in the universal sign of not intending any harm.

I have no response, still struggling to comprehend the situation.

"This is my sister, Ame. These are my two brothers, Anthony and Broderick." She points to more people who surround her, each of them with hair as flaming as hers. "And that is Jack." She waves at a wolfish figure, crouched at the side of the smallest woman. "He is part of our family. He is a werewolf, and we are witches."

She imparts all these pieces of information in a clear, concise tone. Almost as though she knows the more facts I have, the more grounded I will feel in this situation.

I appreciate this effort she makes for me. Her words solidify the world around me as much as my fingers digging into the earth and the grass beneath my knees.

Mor reaches for the ground and grips a blanket, which she extends between us. That's when I realize nothing covers my naked form. Hurriedly, I take the offering and wrap the soft material around my body. And because I was never able to stop it, a blush of embarrassment creeps over my skin. The fact that I am embarrassed in this moment is ludicrous. There is so much more that I should be concerned with. And yet my sensitivity to being vulnerable around anyone still rears its head.

"Can I ask what your name is? Do you remember it?" the witch prompts me.

My mouth opens, and it takes me two full breaths before I even recall that important piece of information about myself.

"Bo." I cough, my throat feeling as though it needs to defrost as I attempt to regain my words. Speech is all I have. "My name is Bo."

"Hello, Bo. Do you have any idea what happened to you? How you got cursed into the form of a statue?" The witch in front of me grimaces, the expression almost apologetic. "It's probably hard to talk about. But we just want to make sure you're safe. That the danger is not still near."

"Dimitri," I rasp. "His house. It cursed me."

The witches all exchange a look, and I cannot read what's on their faces, but it has my hackles rising.

"Is he here? Is he nearby?"

Will the old dragon be furious to realize that his prison on me has been broken? How long was I trapped in there? A day? A week? More?

Will a month of immobility make up for the wrong I did him?

"He's not here," Mor says, and a small knot of tension eases in my chest.

"Are you from Folk Haven?" One of the male witches asks this question, leaning forward, as if he means to move closer to me, but he stills his steps when I flinch away.

I do not like the fear that courses strong in my veins. I'm not a stranger to fear, but this level has reached new heights.

"Yes." I scan their faces again. Each one unfamiliar. Even the color of their hair would have them standing out in this town. "But you're not."

Mor tilts her head to the side, her eyes narrowing. "We are now. We all have lived here for two years. We bought the house that used to belong to Dimitri Novac. The dragon passed away."

"He passed? When?"

Dimitri was just alive. Glaring down at me from the top of the staircase as his house bound me in metal.

"I did nothing to him."

Nothing other than take a step into his territory.

"We know. He died of natural causes. Three years ago."

"Impossible. That's ... impossible."

Three years?

How long ... how long was I trapped in there? Three years is not possible. I would've died.

Or maybe not.

Magic does not always follow the rules, but the rest of the world does.

"Are you telling me that I was trapped for three years?"

The werewolf gives the slightest flinch at my question. As if the words were a blow to him.

"I don't know." This answer comes from the witch in front of me. From Mor. She remains on her knees across from me, her astute eyes seeming to both look at me and look at the air around me. "Like I said, even though we live in Folk Haven now, we're new here. But your statue has been in this garden since we owned the home. I don't know if you have been in prison for three years, but you have been for at least two."

Two years. Three years.

What if my efforts were not considered enough payment? What could he have done to her with me being away for years?

"Do you know ..." My need for the answer is so desperate that it cuts off my throat. The moment I ask the question, I might learn the devastating truth. "Georgiana. Have you met a Georgiana since you've been here? Do you know ... is she okay?"

The witch in front of me appears confused, and my stomach bottoms out at the thought that she might not have even heard of the woman.

"The siren? Georgiana Stormwind?" Mor glances at her siblings, then back to me. "As far as I know, she's alive and well."

Relief rushes like ambrosia through my body. Georgiana is safe.

But I can only enjoy that information for a short moment when my mind presses in on the facts I've been given.

Georgiana is alive and well.

I was trapped for years.

Strangers are the ones who freed me, and the siren is not here with them.

Dimitri is dead.

What in the hell dimensions has happened?

3

Mor

THE MONSTER'S emotional grid is a frantic jumble of glowing threads that pulse and flash and reach for me as I try to untangle them. I pluck apart the obvious emotions while doing my best not to let them weave into my own feelings.

Fear. Confusion. Pain. Anger.

White. Sage. Neon blue. Tangerine.

What I'm keeping a special eye out for is amber—for aggression.

Someone can be angry and not lash out. I would fully expect him to be furious after being trapped for however long. But that doesn't automatically mean he's dangerous.

The freed mythic is tall despite his hunched shoulders, with wild brown hair that falls partly over his eyes, but cannot hide his strong features. When his fingers flex, I spy what I'm almost certain is webbing between the digits. He gives off a sense of heaviness, matched by the thickness of his limbs. Even his neck is large, so much so that I doubt he could be taken down by a choke hold.

If he decides to fight, this mythic will be a force.

Let's hope he's a pacifist.

"I know this is all disorienting," I say in my calm, no-nonsense voice. "But we can take as long as you need. Answer every single question you have. Are you hungry?"

Without food for years, he should be dead, no matter what manner of creature he is. But that statue magic seemed to keep him preserved.

He stares around the forest clearing, meanwhile pressing a hand against his stomach, as if checking.

"We have all kinds of food back at the house." I gesture toward the library, the roof visible just over the treetops.

He follows the direction of my hand, then jerks back, stumbling away.

Flashes of white flare bright.

Pure, unfiltered fear.

"No! I'm never going back there!"

And I'm too late to fix my mistake because Bo whirls on his heel and dives into the forest. Disappearing among the trees and leaving the blanket behind.

"Me follow?" Jack asks in his wolfman shape, voice a broken growl, his eyes on the dark foliage.

After considering his offer, I shake my head. "I think chasing him would only make it worse."

Hurrying over to my bag, I pull out a rolled-up paper. Unfurling it reveals a map of Folk Haven and Lake Galen. I draw the necessary symbols in the corners, speak the tracking spell, and mentally direct my power into the paper. After a moment, a small glowing dot appears.

I breathe a sigh of relief.

"The tracking spell is working."

Now that I've activated it, it's only good for a handful of hours. But this way, we can find Bo without hunting him through the woods.

"I'll handle this," I tell my siblings, grateful for their help up to this point, but feeling the urge to have as few people following Bo as possible.

"You shouldn't do it on your own," Ame says.

"I won't. I've got some backup on standby."

After the Ophelia incident—where she burst into a giant fiery bird and flew away across the lake—I thought it best to alert the Mythic Council and town police that I would be freeing another cursed mythic.

They're all expecting me to check in tonight.

After disinfecting the cut on my hand and wrapping a quick bandage around the wound, I dig my phone out of my pocket, tapping on a familiar name in my Contacts list.

"How did it go?" Levi asks the moment we connect. He's the monster council member and the most likely to have to oversee our new town resident.

"He's upset. Confused. And he ran. But I didn't sense violence." I start jogging through the woods, trusting my siblings to clean up the spell site. "I'm tracking him. Are you with Samantha?" I name the Folk Haven chief of police.

"Yeah, you're on speaker."

"We're in my cruiser." Samantha speaks directly to me. "Half a mile from your driveway toward town."

"I'm going to drive myself. Meet me on the road and follow." I glance down at the map, surprised to see his dot in the water.

Is he part water mythic?

"Looks like he's swimming now, but on his way toward the Of the Claw section." Which you'd have to pass through to reach the Monster section. Not that I have to voice that for us all to know.

"Do you know his name?" Levi asks.

"Bo." I climb into my truck and place the phone on the mount. "That's all I got so far. Ring any bells?"

"No, but I'm sure Moira will know." He names his mate, the

only real estate agent in Folk Haven and from one of the founding families.

"That sounds familiar to me," Samantha says just as I pull onto the road and spot her headlights behind mine. "But I can't place it."

"I think ..." I swallow, feeling a sudden wave of worry for the mythic I shouldn't feel responsible for. "I think he was trapped for a while."

This is not the world Bo knows anymore.

4

Bo

I KEEP to the woods as I navigate from Of the Wing territory to Monster territory. Using roads and bridges would have added more than a mile onto my journey. Desperation to prove the witch wrong about how long I was gone spurs me to dive into the closest point of the lake and swim across.

One benefit of my webbed fingers is, they catch the water and propel me forward faster than most mythics in their human shapes. Soon enough, my bare feet dig into the steep red-clay bank, and I scramble from the water and break into a sprint. Twigs scrape at my bare skin, spiderwebs cling to my face, and dead leaves stick to my wet feet, but I don't care.

I need to get back to the trailer. Need to find my father, even if our conversations never go anywhere. He'll at least prove that I haven't been trapped for ... gone for ...

Years.

I burst through a stand of trees and find myself in a yard with a house sitting not far off.

No. This can't be right.

There aren't supposed to be any homes here. This stretch of land has always just been woods.

Shaking the confusion from my mind, I keep running.

Finally, I come upon the steep hill that leads to the back of our trailer. Kudzu vines trip me, their tangled lengths stretching higher than I've ever allowed the weeds to grow on our property.

Kudzu spreads fast, I remind myself. *This doesn't mean anything.*

Then I see it. The trailer.

Or what's left of it.

In a field of tall grass sits the dilapidated carcass of the only place that ever came close to being my home.

Dad and I were never the decorative type with manicured lawns and colorful ornaments. But we mowed. And used the power washer on the siding. We were handy, fixing most anything that went wrong with the double-wide.

He never would have lived in a place with a partially collapsed roof and patches of siding peeling off. He would've fixed the rotten front steps and weed-whacked the kudzu climbing up the back walls.

A groan creeps from deep in my chest as I stumble toward the property wrecked by time.

Years.

The door hangs lopsided on its hinges, and the wood around the lock is splintered, like someone kicked it in.

That happens when a place is abandoned.

I ease my way into the trailer. Everything is dark, and the light switch does nothing when I flip it. The smell of mold and damp wood linger in the air, along with stale beer and smoke.

As my eyes adjust, I see whoever forced their way in left signs. The orange plaid couch sits shoved up against the far wall, stuffing and springs showing from rotted material. Empty beer bottles and cigarette butts litter the floor. A broken bong rests on its side. The small TV we'd watch foot-ball on is gone.

The refrigerator door hangs open, showing black spots on the no-longer-cold surface.

Abandoned. Forgotten.

The floor creaks under my steps, the carpet releasing puffs of dust as I make my way farther into the trailer. The door to my bedroom is gone, replaced by a shower curtain stapled in place. When I push it aside, I wrinkle my nose in disgust at the smells of bodily fluids. A mattress lies on the floor, empty condom wrappers littered around it.

Everything else, all signs of my life—of my existence—are gone.

Driven by a sudden urgency, I charge to the closet, fingers reaching to scrabble along the paneled wood until I brush the piece that doesn't fit exactly right. I pry the board loose and reach into the cavity, cobwebs clinging to my fingers.

It's still here. A shoebox.

One thing of mine remains, and I could sob in simple relief.

I pull the box free, only to drop it. A knee-jerk reaction to the dark stain covering the sides.

"No," I groan. "Gods, please no."

I flip off the top, and I wish my vision weren't so good in the dark because then I wouldn't be able to see that all the money I'd hoarded away to start a new life is coated in black mold. The smell of decay is thick and choking. The paper money flakes off, disintegrating with the lightest touch, eaten by dampness and time.

Years.

I have nothing.

Lights flash through the window, and the sound of tires on gravel announces I have a visitor.

Why would anyone bother coming?

My life is a rotten mess of nothing.

Despite the callous ways others have treated the place I grew up in, I'm careful when I set aside my box of molded dreams. Maybe somewhere else in this picked-over trailer, there's something I can rebuild with. But my confusion and pain and helplessness overwhelm my ability to form a plan.

I shuffle back the way I came, eyes on my bare feet as I step on the worn carpet. The sight of the decay around me is too much to take in a second time.

Outside, a pickup truck drives over the forest of weeds that choke the gravel drive. I never would've let them get out of hand like that.

Years.

Once again, I'm naked, having lost the blanket gifted to me in my frantic retreat. And there are no clothes left in my home. I shield myself with my hands, a hot blush engulfing every inch of my flesh when I realize the red-haired witch is climbing out of the truck.

"Hey, Bo," she says, her voice casual, as if this were a run-of-the-mill night. "Want some sweatpants? I have a pair I meant to give you."

"Yes, please."

I keep my eyes down as she approaches. In her hands, she cradles the pants as well as a flannel shirt.

"Thank you, ma'am."

"I get that the whole *ma'am* thing is supposed to be part of your Southern charm," she says conversationally, her back turned while I pull on the clothes. "But it always just makes me feel old. You can call me Mor, okay?"

"Yes, ma—Mor," I stutter, still stuck in my manners.

"Are you dressed?"

"I am."

She turns around, and I brace for pity on her beautiful face. But all I spy is curiosity.

"Is this where you lived?"

"This isn't how it looked," I hurry to tell her, wanting her to know I wouldn't live in a run-down mess.

"Of course not. You've been away for a while." She waves behind her. "Can I introduce you to someone? He's here to help."

I square my shoulders and nod. Then I flinch when I realize another car is pulling up behind the truck.

A cop car.

Sweat gathers beneath my pits and down my back, and I shove my hands into the pockets of the sweatpants, as if that'll hide how they ball into nervous fists.

Mor steps in close to me, her face concerned now. "We're all here to help, Bo." She holds out her hands, palms up, and I see a bandage wrapped around her left one that's stained red. "You're not in trouble."

Yes, I am.

Even when I didn't mean to cause trouble, I was still in it. That's what being a monster in Folk Haven means.

Only this time, I also did something wrong. Doesn't matter if I was trying to save someone.

"Your hand," I say to distract myself from law enforcement approaching and to divert the witch's attention from my shamed expression.

She glances at the wrapping and shrugs. "Some spells like blood."

I frown. "You bled ... for me?"

Mor steps in close, capturing my eyes and holding them so I can't duck away from her stare. "I did. And I'm here to help until you don't need me anymore, okay?"

She can't mean that. I don't even know how to take such a generous offer.

I just nod.

When the cruiser comes to a stop, two individuals step out. From the driver's side is a blonde white woman, dressed in a police uniform. From the passenger side is a tan man with black hair and the most intense stare I've encountered. He's not in a uniform, but his neat business attire is intimidating in its own way.

"Bo, this is Chief Samantha Reedsy. She's currently the head of the Folk Haven police, and she is a mermaid." Mor gestures at the new arrival, and the woman offers me a nod.

I try not to show my surprise. The police chief I knew was Bryant, a griffin who pulled me over more than once when I ventured into town after dark. I tried to stay off his radar as best I could.

"And this is Levi Abadi. He is the monster representative on the town's Mythic Council. I figured you might want to talk with him."

"There's …" I shake my head, as if that'll make the words make sense. "A monster representative?"

"Hello, Bo." The monster—Levi—steps closer with his hands loose at his sides. "Yes. We do have representation now. We have for a few years."

"That's …" I drag my fingers through my hair, tugging on the strands, as if the pain will calm the turmoil in my mind.

Years. I was stuck in that statue garden for *years*.

"This is a lot to take in, I'm sure." Levi's voice is gentle but firm, reclaiming my attention. "Is there anyone we can call for you?"

"I-I lived here." I jerk a thumb over my shoulder at the decaying trailer home.

If my dad isn't here, I don't know where he'd be.

Did he even care that I had gone missing?

Did he even notice?

"What's your last name, Bo?" Mor asks.

"Folan." I glance up in time to watch Mor and Levi look at Chief Reedsy.

Her brows dip in thought. "I swear I've heard that before. But I can't place it."

Gods. Gone a few years, and it's as if I never existed in this town.

As if I never existed at all.

"You asked about Georgiana earlier," Mor says. "Do you want us to get in touch with her?"

Hope burns in my cold chest at the name of the one mythic who would remember me.

I shouldn't contact her. I should leave her out of this. We've always been a secret.

But she'd want me to call her, wouldn't she? If I've been missing this long, she has to wonder where I've been.

Does she think I abandoned her? Left her to her own fate?

Calling Georgiana might be the best move. She can explain —to me at least—what happened after the last night that I can recall, and I can reassure her that even though this has shaken me up, I'm alive.

"Yes, ma'am. Please."

5

Mor

When I first approached the Mythic Council about releasing an unknown mythic from a curse, I talked to Selena, the witch representative. She visited the statue garden, studied the figure, then told me the being was most likely a monster and therefore Levi's responsibility when no longer trapped.

So, I called him, and Levi and Selena told the rest of the Mythic Council about my plan—I assume at their monthly meeting or maybe even in a coded email of some kind.

But they all knew.

Moira, a selkie and the Of the Fin representative.

Juan, a werewolf and the Of the Claw representative.

And Georgiana, a siren and the Of the Wing representative.

She knew this curse breaking was happening. Did she know the freed mythic would ask for her?

Whether or not she did, when Levi gets her on the phone and says a mythic named Bo is asking for her, we all hear the clipped, "I'm on my way."

While we wait, I head back to my truck and rummage

around in the passenger seat. My siblings might have gone into their curse breaking with only the basic planning, but I've always been the prepared one. Bossy, some might say. In addition to clothes, I've got a whole load of other supplies that I left on the front porch, which I retrieved and shoved them into my truck before following Bo, and I grab the bags now before returning to the monster, who looks entirely too lost and confused for my comfort.

"Are you thirsty?" I ask Bo. "I've got water, coffee, and Gatorade."

He blinks down at me, and I can't help comparing the snarling form he was frozen in to this soft-eyed look of contrition.

"Water, please."

I hand him the bottle.

"Thank you, ma'am."

I snort. "It's going to take some time to break you of that habit, huh?"

The muted chocolate-colored splash of embarrassment seeps through his aura. I decide to give him a break from my ribbing. He uncaps the bottle and swallows the entire thing in three long pulls, the muscles of his neck flexing with each swallow.

"Impressive. I've got two more. Also some granola bars if you're hungry." I hold out the foil-wrapped snacks. "And the blanket if you're cold." I hold up the fluffy knitted number I made myself. Nothing better than turning on an audiobook and settling in with a nice big knitting project.

"You're very kind," he murmurs, as if it's a secret.

Which isn't too far off. I'm not exactly the caregiver type, though I did basically raise Ame since our parents were ... let's just say, if I never see Helena and Alistair Shelly again, it'll be too soon.

So, I know *how* to take care of someone. But I'm not the type to seek out wounded birds in need of a new nest. I'm not baking cookies for neighbors or volunteering at retirement homes.

But when I do have a charge, I take my responsibilities seriously. And Bo is mine.

Well, not *mine*, mine.

Bo was trapped as a statue on my property for far too long, and I feel a certain kind of duty to make sure he gets back on his feet in the community.

But I'm not about to claim him as my mate. That's for my siblings, not me.

Thank the gods he didn't try to kiss me.

"Glad you think so." I smile up at him. "Doesn't hurt to have a good reputation around here."

He gazes down at me, and I can't read his expression. I'm also trying my hardest not to read his emotions because the guy has already bared plenty of himself tonight. He deserves a bit of privacy.

But I guess Levi has other priorities. "Bo, can you tell us what you last remember? Before the curse was broken?"

The man at my side stiffens, his hands freezing on the granola bar he was in the middle of opening.

"I—" His voice is strained. "I remember the house."

"The library?" Levi asks.

Bo's browse dip in confusion.

"The house that used to be owned by Dimitri Novac," I explain. "I own it now. I turned it into a library."

Bo's face clears, and he nods. "Yes, that one."

"What happened at the house?" This question comes from Samantha.

Bo frowns. "I ... I can't ..." He coughs repeatedly, rubbing his throat, as if that'll soothe the reaction.

I hand him a second bottle of water, which he drinks as quickly as the first.

"That's okay," Levi says. "If you don't remember yet, we can come back to it later. But do you know why you were at the house?"

That's a good question. Nowadays, mythics of all kinds come by to browse the collection of texts I have. There's a reason for people to visit. But from what Delta—Dimitri's daughter and the woman who sold the property to me—has said, her father was a recluse. Not one for visitors.

And why would a visitor be cursed?

A prick of wariness tugs at the back of my mind. The reminder that I don't know anything about this monster, and just because others we have freed from curses were innocent, that doesn't mean Bo was.

The only thing that keeps me from scuttling away in self-preservation is the general vibe of the monster's aura. Before I shuttered my magical sight, I didn't pick up a single ounce of hostility.

When we came upon him this time, his aura was swamped in a navy blue, speckled with tan.

Loss.

Loneliness.

"I can't say," Bo mutters in response to Levi's question.

Before we can pry further, there's the rumble of an engine through the trees. Down the weed-choked drive comes a luxurious BMW SUV, and I shield my eyes against the blinding flash of LED headlights.

Bo grunts next to me, doing the same until the driver shuts the lights off and climbs from the vehicle. Blinking spots out of my eyes, I begin to make out the trim figure of Georgiana Stormwind.

In the past, I've only ever seen the siren completely put together—with her blonde hair styled, makeup on point, and clothes chic and smooth. Now she's still Southern belle gorgeous, but with a *just rolled out of bed* vibe. A camel-colored peacoat is buttoned over a set of what appears to be silk pajamas, matching a silk wrap around her curls. The hands that clutch her collar are perfectly manicured. She even slipped on a set of heels for this excursion.

How she's not wobbling on the uneven ground is a magical move itself.

"Bo?" Shock quivers through her singsong voice. "Is that really you?"

The monster stares at the siren, his face slack. "Georgie?"

Georgie? Sounds like they were close.

Her mouth pops open in an O, and she steps forward, wide eyes on his face.

"You ... you're the same," she whispers. "You haven't aged a day."

Bo's gaze is locked on her, and I wonder if I should back up and give them room for some kind of reunion hug.

"How long has it been?" he rasps.

She blinks, long lashes brushing her cheeks, and something about her changes. It takes me a moment to realize I was unconsciously reading her aura and the colors have altered. What was once a combination of lime-green surprise and lemon-yellow eagerness now fades into peachy wariness with sparks of white fear.

Is Georgiana scared of Bo?

If so, why is she still leaning toward him?

As if hearing my silent question, she straightens her spine. "You disappeared seventeen years ago."

Bo sways on his feet, and I find myself reaching out, as if I'd be able to catch him if he collapsed from shock. In most cases, I've got a good chance of holding someone up, but Bo is a big man and might end up squashing me.

Then, what she just said registers in my mind.

Seventeen years.

That's a long fucking time.

When the silence stretches, Samantha is the first to break it.

"To be clear, Georgiana, you know this man? And he hasn't been seen in seventeen years?"

The siren crosses her arms over her chest and gives the police chief a solemn nod. "We were ... acquainted. Bo's father, Arvin, used to run a mechanic shop on the north side of town."

"Georgie—"

"Georgiana," she corrects with a sharp note in her voice, and the monster flinches.

"That's a while back, but we don't have a lot of missing person cases here. Would've thought I'd have come across it at some point on the job," Sam says, her voice cautious, wary of calling out a council member. "Do you know if one was filed?"

"I'm not sure." Georgiana looks in the direction of the chief, but doesn't meet her eyes.

Everything about the siren's stance is defensive. Distancing.

"You didn't look for me?"

I pride myself on being a firm, practical person. Not one prone to soft sentimentality.

But damn if the hopeless way Bo asks that question doesn't jab my heart.

"You were always talking about leaving." Georgiana waves a dismissive hand toward the road. "Everyone figured you'd gone. So did I."

"I wouldn't have. Not before I—" He lets out a strangled gasp, as if suddenly choked by a strong hand. He coughs, deep and rough, clearing his throat. His mouth works, as if trying to form words, but nothing comes.

Georgiana looks deathly white in the glow of Samantha's headlights. She also appears cold, standing straight and staring anywhere but the man.

"Bo was cursed." I gaze unflinchingly at The Council woman, unabashedly reading her aura as I speak. Something about this exchange sets off my warning bells. "Bo was stuck as a metal sculpture in Dimitri Novac's collection. For seventeen years, apparently."

There it is.

The bright flash of burnt orange.

Guilt.

"What happened to you was unfortunate." The siren speaks like a customer service representative who was trained not to admit fault. "I'm glad you came out unscathed."

Unscathed? Does she not see the emotional and mental wounds burning bright in the aura of the monster?

No, I guess she doesn't. That's just me.

"Things have changed in the last seventeen years. The monsters now have representation on the Mythic Council." She nods toward her fellow council member. "Levi Abadi currently holds the seat. He can help you reacclimate."

Simple as that, she dismisses Bo. Passing the guy off, as if her being the only person he knows means nothing.

I didn't have much of an opinion about the siren before tonight, but gods do I now.

She's a bitch.

And he just takes her cold words, standing in the ruins of what must have once been his home, his large figure wilting in the face of her frost.

"I need to get home," she says, more to the group than to Bo. "My husband will be wondering where I am."

There—another slight flinch in his broad shoulders at that word.

Husband.

My curiosity for this story is sharp, but I can guess at parts. A younger Georgiana meant something romantic to Bo. Maybe they dated. Maybe it was only a mild flirtation. But to him, it was yesterday, and to her, it was nearly two decades ago.

Still, she doesn't have to be so harsh about letting him know where things currently stand.

Or is it more than that?

Not just letting a man know she's off-limits.

Warning a monster that she's not interested.

I've always gotten the sense that Georgiana is largely supported by the more traditional mythics of this town. The ones who think magical beings should only partner with their same kind or with a human. The people who believe monsters should be looked down on for their mixed bloodlines.

What would Georgiana's political supporters say if they found out she once was involved with a monster?

The siren strides toward her SUV, but Samantha calls out after her.

"Council Member Stormwind," the chief says, using the title, as if reminding the siren of her responsibilities, "do you believe Bo Folan is a danger to anyone in Folk Haven?"

Georgiana's shoulders are tight to her ears for a moment, but then they sag just slightly.

"No." The siren's voice goes soft. "Bo is harmless."

Then she leaves as quickly as she arrived, silence falling in her wake.

I don't know what to do. My comforting skills have always been lacking, and I doubt another granola bar would fix this.

"Bo"—Levi breaks through the tension with his deep voice —"I thought you could come home with me tonight. Get some sleep in my guest room." He holds his hands out, palms up. "You don't have to figure anything out tonight."

I glance back at Bo in time to see him give one short nod, even as his eyes stay downcast.

Despite my resolve not to, I ease the grip on my magic, allowing the colors of his aura to glow in my sight.

The most pronounced color twists my gut.

Cobalt blue for devastation.

6

Bo

THE OFFICER DROPS us off at a beautiful home that did not exist in Monster territory seventeen years ago. Most houses in this area of the lake were smaller with a handful of exceptions.

One mansion in particular stands out in my mind, but I push those memories away as Levi leads me toward the front door.

"I ask that you step quietly. My mate is sleeping. And she's pregnant, so she needs as much rest as she can get."

"Yes, sir," I mumble, still feeling unsteady. Not from any weakness in my body. But because of the dismissal I just received from Georgie.

Georgiana.

After the first shock, she seemed almost angry to see me.

Seventeen years.

That length of time continues to blink like a strobe light in my mind's eye.

I could see the time on Georgiana. The siren is still beautiful, but her face is sharper, with a few lines around her eyes and mouth that she didn't previously possess.

She didn't look for me.

I rub the aching hole in my chest. A crater left by the only being I'd thought cared for me. The one I had given up so much of my life for.

"Are you hungry?" Levi's low voice pulls me out of my turmoil of thoughts.

"No. Thank you," I respond at the same level. The thought of food makes me nauseous.

He nods and waves me down a long hallway, lined on one side with massive windows. The glass is dark now, but I suspect, in the daytime, it would show off a sprawling view of the forest.

"You can stay here." He opens a door to a bedroom. "Sleep. We can talk more in the morning."

Talk. Ha. What words can be said to bring back the time I lost?

Still, I've never been good at projecting my dark emotions onto the undeserving. Levi Abadi has been nothing but gracious, opening his home to me.

"Thank you." I nod numbly. "Sleep would be good."

At least it would be if I thought I could get any. But once I'm alone in the largest bedroom I've ever seen, perching on a mattress that could easily fit three of me—which is no easy feat—my thoughts only grow louder.

Seventeen years.

"What happened to you was unfortunate. I'm glad you came out unscathed."

I have nothing.

I have no one.

All because I went into that house to take something.

All because of *him*.

My mind latches on to the memory.

The aristocratic voice laying out the task, as if it would be simple to achieve.

Go in. Find the item. Leave and deliver it.

Then Georgiana would be free of his influence.

But that wasn't how it went at all.

Did he know what would happen to me? Did he send me on that errand as a sick joke?

Is he still here?

I realize I have nothing else in my life. Nothing but an undeniable urge to take out all this pain and rage and devastation on the monster who sent me to my fate.

A beast who might very well still live in Folk Haven.

I shove off the bed, and on silent feet, I stalk out of the house.

With jerky movements, I strip the clothes from my body, knowing I'll need all my brute strength to face him—and even then, I probably won't live through this.

I don't care.

7

Sev

SOMEONE IS MAKING an awful racket at the edge of my wards. Terribly rude when I am on my back porch, staring into the abyss that I imagine Lake Galen to be.

I am not melancholy.

I refuse to use that label.

I simply lack the motivation to care about anyone or anything in the world at the moment.

Including myself.

The sensation shall pass, as it always does. But not if that terrible banging continues.

"Seems someone wishes to die today," I murmur to the cicadas as I push up from my rocking chair.

The wooden seat may appear simple, but the repetitive movement soothes me in a way little can.

My mate could soothe me. If only I could locate them.

Over two centuries old, and I still have not come across the one I am destined to partner with. A lesser mythic than me might start to doubt the existence of a fated mate.

But I am a spectacular being. The gods would not have overlooked me when making destined matches. They might only wait a stretch of time in order to properly fashion the perfect mate.

Someone who looks ...

Someone who is ...

Someone who will ...

Well, I'm not quite sure exactly what traits the mate of the most powerful monster to exist will possess. Most likely, they will be in great danger, and I'll use my wiles and accumulated treasures to rescue them, and they will fall lovingly into my arms to adore me for the rest of their immortal existence.

Immortal.

That. That is the task I should be focusing on. The preparation I should be making.

After my last plan failed, I should have immediately resumed plotting. Instead, I've been rocking and ruminating.

How dare this interloper interrupt my ruminating?

I stride with fluid grace, my silk robe billowing around my body as I reenter my house and approach the front entrance. There's no hesitation as I open the front door, seeing as how my wards will keep any unwanted guests from crossing the threshold.

Especially if they wish me harm.

As the monstrous creature snarling in front of me most surely does.

Even in the dark night, I see him clearly. Not quite wolf, not quite water creature. Fur blends with scales—sometimes seamlessly, other places awkwardly. Paws with elongated toes sport webbing and end in wicked sharp claws. The face is a terror—a snout sporting fangs that could pierce and tear flesh with ease and a heavy brow over eyes that are dark with promised violence.

I'm almost impressed by the display of fury.

I didn't think the cowed monster had it in him.

"Ah. Bosephus Folan. You're looking less stiff than the last time I saw you."

The monster roars, a deep, rending noise that might make a lesser mythic than me wary. But I have nothing to fear from this monster.

He is incapable of hurting me.

His surprise arrival is interesting though. I always suspected that I would know when Bo's curse was broken. That there would be a waver in the ether, alerting me to an enemy unlocked from their cage. Not that Bo had begun as an enemy. But I'm sure that's how he views me now.

But there was no doorbell buzz telling me a pissed-off monster was once again free to roam the world and setting his sights on me.

I suppose this makes sense though. Even though I had sent him on the errand that left him trapped, I didn't have a hand in the cursing.

"Been a long time." I stroll out my front door, unconcerned by the slavering beast before me. One that lets out another tree-shuddering roar at my flippant comment.

In a blink, monster has reverted to man, and I'm proud to realize I recalled close to exactly how Bo had appeared all those years ago. With as many decades as I have, certain things begin to fade.

"A long time?" He pants while the words come out between low growls. Sweat slicks his naked body, causing him to glow almost as bright as the moon he's reflecting. "Seventeen years!"

"You're right. Not nearly long enough. Would you like me to send you into an eternal slumber?" I wave my fingers, as if casting a spell. "At least that way, I could get some peace and quiet."

It is a jest though. I have no interest in quieting Bo more

than I already have. This is the most fun I've experienced in months. Maybe years.

"You knew where I was this whole time?"

Of course I did. I had sent him to Dimitri's house in the first place.

"You had the power to free me," he accuses.

I shrug. "Maybe. I've never tested myself against dragon hoard protection before."

False. The results are ... mixed.

"You should have—"

"Georgiana." I say the name at a normal volume, cutting him off at the knees.

Bo stumbles back a step and reveals too much vulnerability on his face.

Silly little monster.

"Have you seen her?" I press.

He swallows hard, eyes dropping. I'll take that as a soul-crushing yes.

"Your beloved siren is alive. She is well."

His head gives the barest nods for each of those facts.

"And she never once came to me in seventeen years to ask about you."

His shoulders bow.

Bo was never a fighter. Not truly, though that beast form of his could decimate if he ever properly utilized it.

"And in seventeen years, I've always considered her debt paid. Despite you failing to uncover what I wanted. An item I have on good authority is no longer in that house."

His shoulders dip more, likely with the loss of hope.

I savor his reactions.

The monster came to me all those years ago, desperate to save the woman he claimed to love.

His attempt at honor disgusted me. But more than that, his surety that the siren was his fated mate enraged me.

He thought he had found his mate?

He thought it was *her*? A woman so self-absorbed that I doubt she could've picked Bo out in a police lineup.

That is not matehood. And to hear Bo speak of his one-sided relationship infuriated me.

Still, out of the kindness of my heart, I didn't kill him. I simply allowed the monster a few years to consider his actions and those of the people around us.

"Seventeen years of imprisonment for her crime. When you came to me, you said you'd do anything for her. And so you did." I shrug. "I am not the one you should be mad at."

"You would have left me there forever if it wasn't for the witch breaking my curse," he snarls.

Interest sparks. "Which witch?"

The man scowls at me. "Why does it matter?"

"Come now, Bosephus. Share with the class."

He keeps his lips pressed tight together.

Protecting the mythic who freed him? How noble.

I roll my eyes. "I'll find out on my own then."

"Leave her out of your trickery," he snarls. "I'm not making any more deals with you. If you try to come after any more innocents, you'll face my claws."

That earns a chuckle from me. "My, we are deluded, aren't we?" I lean toward him, lowering my voice, as if imparting a secret. "Georgie wasn't exactly innocent, was she? And no matter what I do, you'll find you can't lay a claw on me, Bo Folan." I tilt my chin toward his hand. The one he sliced open for a blood vow the night he came to me in supplication.

"What do you mean?"

"I mean, I have your enchanted loyalty. No attacking me. And"—this time, I grin wide—"no slandering me."

"Slander?"

"No telling anyone about our little deal. About how you ended up as a yard decoration."

"It's not slander if it's true!"

I shrug. "No shit-talking then. Label the binding however you wish. Only know that, unless I decide otherwise, you cannot speak or write a word against me."

All wrath drains from the monster's face, leaving behind a blank look of hopelessness.

As I said, not a fighter.

"Come now, Bosephus. Don't be so glum." I wave a hand back toward Folk Haven. "The world is new. You're no longer tied down by that shrew. The way I see it, I did you a favor."

"You took everything from me," he whispers.

I grit my teeth, a flare of fury rising in the face of his self-pity. The jovial tone I've effected drips away as I hold his eyes with mine.

"You do not know what it means to have all taken from you, Bosephus Folan. But if you do not leave my territory, I will gladly show you."

Uncertainty flicks across his eyes as he hears the dark truth in my words. Then the monster turns his back and shifts into his beast form before stalking away to lick his emotional wounds.

I feel no pity.

For I know what it is like to lose all.

8

Mor

Normally, the sound of my cell phone ringing at six in the morning would wake me up. But that would require me to have fallen asleep. Even though last night was stressful and exhausting, when I finally lay down in bed, sleep evaded me. For the last few hours, I've just been staring upward at my skylight, watching the starry sky shift with the earth's rotation. Even though it's technically morning, sunrise is more than an hour off.

I reach to my bedside table and unplug the phone from the charger before I answer it. "Hello?"

"Morgana. Hello. This is Levi." The monster council member's voice is tight. "I know this is probably a long shot, but I just checked on our new guest, and it looks as though he left at some point in the night. Is that tracking spell still live? Did he happen to return to the library?"

I sit up straight in bed and glance around my room, as if this were the space Bo would appear in. But of course he wouldn't be here. I would be shocked to find the mythic in any room in the library after the way he reacted last night.

Still, I feel obligated to check.

"The tracking spell was one use only, and I haven't heard anyone trying to get in. I locked and spelled the front door." And yet I have the sneaking suspicion this house would be able to undo all of my physical and magical protections if it had the whim. "I'll check though. Can I call you back?"

"Yes. Please."

The moment after I press to end the call, I consider if it might have been a better idea to keep Levi on the line.

Ame and Jack are here, I remind myself.

They have a noise-dampening spell cast on their room, so I don't have to hear their bedroom activities every night, but the spell is one-way. If I scream about an intruder, they'll hear me just fine. Especially with Jack's werewolf ears.

I slip out of bed and pull on a robe, then press open the heavy door that reveals a winding narrow set of stairs. The old wood creaks under my sock-covered feet, though the steps shine like new in the warm Edison bulb lights I mounted on the walls.

My room is not the most practical choice. We had to bring all the furniture up piece by piece because of the dramatic angles. The stairwell from the first floor to the second at least has coffin corners to help with maneuvering.

Still, my room has the best view and gives me the romantic notion of living in an enchanted tower.

Or I guess it's not just a notion. The house is enchanted, and three stories makes a tower as far as I'm concerned.

I make my way through the quiet house that has been converted into a library. I flip on lights as I go, not sure how it would feel if I came across the newly freed monster in a dark room. And yet the thought of him brings nothing like fear to my mind. His nonhuman form is intimidating in shape and makeup, but the man himself, even frantic, never seemed particularly violent. There were no splashes of amber in his aura that I've spied in those of violent people.

He was a blend of sage, tangerine, and cerulean.

Confusion, anger, and sadness.

All understandable.

Despite the house being on the larger size, it doesn't take me long to navigate through the entire place and see no sign of Bo.

I call Levi back.

"He's not here, unless he's hiding. And a guy that size would have trouble concealing himself in this place."

I unlock the front door and step out into the cool morning, my feet chilly on the porch's wooden boards. There are the sounds of cicadas and bats in the darkened woods. The occasional owl hoot. A few early rising birds have begun to chirp. I dodge the random spiderwebs that were built overnight on the front porch, planning to sweep them away, like I do every morning.

Spiders love a lake house.

"I guess it was too much to hope it would be that easy," Levi mutters on his end of the line.

"If I had to guess, I'd say he went back to his trailer," I offer.

I don't know much about the guy, but the fact that he ran there first indicates it may be the only place in town where he feels safe. It may be the only place that's familiar to him after seventeen years.

"That was my next thought. I want to head over there, but I'm kind of dealing with something right now." He clears his throat. "Moira's pregnant—I'm not sure if I mentioned that— and she's having some pain. She might need to go to Dr. Grove." He names a newer doctor who moved to Folk Haven only a few months ago.

"Oh no. Sorry she's not feeling great."

I haven't spent too much time with the monster and his selkie mate, but I do know their coupling caused some stirring in the town. Even after living here for a few years, I struggle to understand the faction of town folk that are upset by inter-mythic mating.

Mythics mixing bloodlines might result in monsters, but we're all weird and magical anyway. I don't see why we need to divide ourselves.

"You should stay with your mate." I don't hesitate on my offer. "I'll go find Bo. I'll check on him."

Levi huffs a surprised breath. "You will? You've already done a hell of a lot for him, and I don't want you to feel obligated. But that would be a massive help to me."

I don't know that I feel obligated, but I have a sense of responsibility related to Bo. I am the one who freed him from his statue prison. I don't think he's going to cause any problems in town, but if he does, I am not excited about that potentially reflecting back on me.

Also, the melding colors of his aura stay imprinted on my mind. The mixture of loneliness and defeat struck something in my chest. I don't like the idea of Bo being alone in this town that he no longer knows. I've only started to feel like I'm finding a place here. That I'm not an outsider.

Maybe I could help Bo find a place too. Maybe that is a way I could give back to this town.

"I don't mind. If he's not at the trailer, I'm not sure what my next steps will be, but I can definitely swing by there and see if he's around. I can check in with him to see if there's anything I can do to help."

"That would be great. And do not hesitate to call me if anything becomes more complicated than checking up on him. And if you do find him, please tell him that he is welcome back into our home."

"I'll keep you updated."

I reenter my house and head upstairs, ending the call as I go. As I quickly work through my morning routine and get dressed, I brainstorm what to do about the library.

There is no one readily available to watch it while I'm gone. Ame and Jack will be getting up soon, and they'll each be heading off to their respective jobs. Ame to the veterinarian office, where she works the front desk. And Jack to Ramla University, where he heads the tech department. Broderick also has classes that he has to teach today, and I was lucky that Anthony was able to step away from his tailoring duties for the spell last night. As we approach the Halloween Ball, he's been working eighty-hour weeks just to make sure everyone who ordered a gown has one by the time the event occurs.

There is no one else that I have trained to help in any way in the library.

It's a position that I've known I needed to fill for a while. But things keep getting in the way, so here I am, having to set up a sign outside the front door, announcing that the library is closed for the morning. I shoot off a quick text to Ame and Jack, so they know where I've gone once they wake up to find the library isn't open. Then I climb into my truck and point my headlights toward the Monster section of Folk Haven, watching as the sun colors the sky above the trees as I drive.

The road around Lake Galen is winding, but there's only one main road, so it is easy to follow. It's the gravel driveways that shoot off from the pavement that are hard to memorize. But I recall the one I turned down last night when seeking out the missing monster.

The sun has started to crest above the trees when I pull up in front of the dilapidated trailer.

Somehow, it looks even sadder in the light of day.

Now, I can see the peeling, sun-bleached paint and the water-warped wooden steps leading to the crooked front door. The whole trailer sags in the middle, and I wonder how much longer the roof will hold out. I wouldn't feel safe going inside the thing.

But I don't plan on leaving until I've thoroughly checked for Bo.

I shut off the engine and climb out of the truck. The moment I open the door, I hear movement inside of the dilapidated building. And I really hope it is Bo and not some strange animal I'm about to encounter. Safe bet, I decide to make my presence known as opposed to stepping into that condemned building.

"Hey! Bo?" I call out. "Is that you in there?"

There's a pause in the rustling.

I pray to The Dark One that I have not alerted a wild animal to my presence. But then there's the sound of footsteps, and the door gets pushed open to reveal a dusty, daylight-illuminated version of the man I saw for the first time last night.

But unlike last night, he's kept his clothes with him. I'm glad, mainly because he seemed achingly embarrassed about exposing himself to strangers multiple times.

"Mor?" He blinks, his eyes adjusting to the sunlight.

"Hi. Yeah, it's me." I give a wave, then cross my arms over my chest. "Levi gave me a call when he realized you'd left."

I brace myself for him to get defensive on how we're tracking him.

Instead, he ducks his head, cheeks flushing. "Sorry. I should've left a note."

"You didn't have to. It's just ... we want to help."

A spark of sage confusion flits in the corner of my sight, slipping through the control I have over my magic.

"Why? Y'all don't know me."

Why do I want to help him? Hell, isn't this guy from here? Shouldn't he have grown up with that classic Southern hospitality?

"I guess I want to help because I'd hope someone would do the same for me if I were in your shoes."

I tilt my head, glancing behind him at the trailer. There's graffiti on the side, most of the windows are broken, and discarded beer cans litter the lawn. I get the sense, after a certain time of this place being abandoned, some delinquents decided to use this as their party space.

Gods, what must it feel like to find your home has been misused in such a way?

If I found the library had been mistreated in my absence, I'd go on a rampage.

But Bo merely seems to be attempting to collect the shattered pieces of his life. And I feel for him.

"That's kind of you," he murmurs.

"Do you need help?" I wave toward the trailer. "Cleaning up? Or looking for something?"

Bo glances over his shoulder, face lined with despondency. "There's nothing left for me here."

His words sound like they refer to more than just the place he used to live.

Without contemplating the move, I stroll forward and wrap my hand around one of his thick wrists, tugging him away from the reminder of his past.

"Let's get breakfast. Life always seems shittier when you're hungry."

And I have the overwhelming urge to remind Bo that he's alive and that's a good thing.

9

———————

Mor

"THERE AREN'T ANY BUTTONS?"

Bo stares at the iPhone I'm holding like I'm an alien wielding Star Trek tech.

I don't have any interest in children. Taking over the raising of Ame was enough for me. And she was a relatively easy person to deal with. But after that, I felt good to go on the child-rearing. Not particularly for me.

But now I have this monster standing beside me who has missed the last seventeen years of the world. And I can't help but feel like I have a toddler who needs to have the simplest concepts explained to him.

I remind myself that's not right. Bo is a grown man.

He just doesn't know what cell phones are exactly. At least not the most modern version.

And when his eyebrows shoot up in wonder when I use mine to pay for our bagels, that's not naivete on his part. That is just a man who has never seen Apple Pay before.

He is not a child. You don't have to mother him. You just need to explain a few things that he missed.

"Nope. The tech geniuses of the world have figured out how to make touch screens." I swipe through a few things and open up a couple of apps, just a preview. "It may seem daunting, but you'll pick up on how to use a smartphone in no time."

He looks doubtful, like a confused puppy.

I guide Bo to an empty picnic table. One of the sturdier-looking ones. He's a big man. Even still, he is easily able to fold his body into the seat.

"How old are you?" I ask without considering if the question might be rude.

"Do you mean before the statue incident?"

"Yes. I'm guessing your aging was frozen during the curse."

He grunts an acknowledgment. "I'm twenty-three."

Wow. He should be forty years old. Bo should be ten years my senior; instead, he is seven years my junior. That's so odd to think about. Also, he seems to carry himself with more reservation than the twenty-three-year-old men I've encountered. No cocky swagger or smirk of the youth. But I guess being trapped for over a decade and a half will change a person.

Or maybe he was this way before he was frozen.

"Did you attend Ramla?"

I believe the university has been around for longer than seventeen years. Hopefully, if he earned a degree, it's in a subject that has not changed much over the past few years. If he studied computer science, then he's got a lot of catching up to do.

"No." The word isn't harsh, but it also doesn't leave a door open for more questioning.

His eyes are on the scarred wood of the table in front of us, and I watch as he digs a thumbnail into a crack. With his fingers pressed together as they are, I spy no sign of the webbing that I noticed earlier. If we were friendly, I might ask to see his hands. I am interested in the way his body interpreted his lineage. If he's a monster, then that means he has more than one mythic type in his blood. And it seems like one of his is a water creature. But I have no idea what exact mixture would make the form that he wore when he shifted. The form I saw in that metal statue.

"Did you go to college?" Bo asks his question without glancing up at me.

"I did. I got my undergrad in history, and I earned a master's in library science. Specifically in archival studies. I wanted to make sure I could properly care for old books."

"That's impressive."

I don't hear any sarcasm in his voice. No mockery. But he also still won't look at me.

Schooling must be a sensitive subject. My mind goes back to the dilapidated trailer.

Maybe Bo didn't have the money to attend college. I'm not sure what the scholarship situation is like at Ramla, but I would hope that they would have grants set aside for mythics in need. Although, he is from seventeen years ago, and I would say that Folk Haven still has outdated views on monsters.

Was there ever a time when monsters weren't allowed to attend the university?

That would be a good question to ask Levi or Moira.

Mary Jo—owner of Mary Jo's Bagels—calls out our order from the window of her food truck. When I make to stand, Bo waves for me to stay in my seat, and he quickly hops up to retrieve our food. When he returns, there's a twist to his brow that almost looks like confusion. I study our bagels, not seeing anything off about them.

"Is something wrong with the food?" I ask.

"No ..." He settles in front of me, eyes flicking back and forth between his meal and the truck. "It's only that there was no food truck in Folk Haven. Not that I remember. Not what feels like ... a day ago." His fingers fiddle with the paper in the basket that our food came in. "This is going to happen a lot, isn't it? I'm going to keep seeing things that weren't in the town that I knew." He heaves a massive sigh. "I wonder if this place will ever feel like the one I left."

"Was there any place in particular that you used to like to go to?"

Bo takes his time to think over my question, chewing on his bagel all the while. I follow suit, enjoying the sweetness of the cinnamon raisin melding with the savory cream cheese.

"I don't get out much," he admits sheepishly. "But I go to Martin's Alley to bowl sometimes. There's a hot-dog stand just outside it. Has a special on Tuesdays, two for one ..." He clears his throat. "And the movie theater. Like to go sometimes."

"I don't know about the first two. They might be gone, sorry. But if you're talking about the single-screen theater off Second Street, it's definitely still open."

If I hoped that one out of three would be enough to soothe the guy, then my hopes are dashed. Cobalt flickers in the corner of my eye.

Why can't I properly shield myself from him?

I don't go around bragging, but I'm a pretty powerful witch. Townsfolk still talk about the emotion-bubble obstacle I created for Galen's Gauntlet two years ago. That was some talented magic that I doubt another witch in this town could pull off. The bubbles that, when popped, forced competitors to deal with an onslaught of a certain feeling was my own invention and a contribution I made to earn some goodwill from the local coven.

All this to say, when putting in intentional effort, I should be able to fully block the monster's grid from my sight, like I do most days with everyone else.

But his aura keeps popping up.

Bo looks despondent as he methodically finishes off what I know to be an extremely delicious bagel.

I want to fix this, but I don't know how. I'm not the joy-bringer in my family. Anthony makes people laugh. Broderick asks the right questions. Ame is simply soothing to be around.

But I'm not my siblings.

"What can I do, Bo?" I abandon my bagel to reach across the table and place my hand on his forearm, wanting him to at least meet my eyes instead of staring dejectedly at the tabletop.

His gaze flicks up, sky-blue eyes meeting and holding mine.

"Please," I press, "tell me what you need."

10

Bo

That's what I want to say. That's all I need in this moment. To feel the beautiful witch's warm, soft skin against mine.

I'm not used to being touched. There aren't many people I've encountered during my lifetime who wanted to get close enough. I have vague memories of my mom hugging me. Kissing my forehead. Cupping my cheeks in her hands.

But then she was gone, and the touching stopped.

My father was not an affectionate man.

The kids my age were warned away from the monster. Then I grew, gaining inches, gaining heft. How tall I was, muscles increasing from my work at the mechanic shop, all just lent to my air of intimidation.

I didn't try to scare anyone. But the fear came naturally.

Georgiana touched me. That might have been why I fell for her so fast. Maybe I read too much into her touches because it was the first affection I'd received in years.

That must be why Mor's hand feels like heaven. Like a drug. I could become addicted to the weight of her fingers.

I should pull away.

But the ecstasy is already in my system, and I'm not strong enough to fight it.

I've never been a fighter.

"Bo?" She says my name, and a shiver drags down my spine.

"I ..." I clear my throat. "A job. I need a job."

A way to support myself so I don't have to rely on her waving her telephone around to spend her money on me.

"Of course. We can make that happen. Some of the places you knew might be gone, but there're plenty of new businesses." She retracts her hand to reclaim her bagel. "Levi owns a spa and hires monsters almost exclusively. And there're other options."

She takes a bite, then licks cream cheese off her middle finger.

I don't think that should be allowed in public.

Mor Shelly should only suck creamy white substances off her digits in the privacy of her own home. For the good of the public. So brains don't start melting.

Just like mine is.

I shake my head and go back to staring at the table. "You make it sound easy. Setting me up with a life even though I've been missing for over a decade."

I hear the sip of liquid and make the mistake of glancing up and catching sight of her plush lips wrapped around the straw of her sweet tea.

Why the hell can't I stop making everything she does erotic?

Mor swallows, then licks a stray drop off her lip, as if she knows how every move of hers affects me.

"Oddly enough," she says, oblivious to my inner thoughts, "my family has experience with this. Not that any of us went missing." She reaches into her back pocket and pulls out the glass rectangle that passes for a mobile phone today. "But I'll need to connect you to Jack and Ophelia. They were cursed. Lost chunks of their lives too."

She taps the technology a few times, then places it flat on the table in front of me. There's a crystal-clear picture on the screen of a group of people sitting on a dock. Three of the people are vaguely familiar, and I think they might have been there when Mor freed me. I wonder if the wolfman is also pictured, only in his human form. The three I recognize have red hair, the same rich shade as Mor's.

But she points to two others—a small blonde woman sitting on the lap of one of the redheads, then a dark-haired man with hooded eyes, who frowns at the camera while everyone else smiles.

"Ophelia and Jack. They're each partnered to one of my siblings."

"They were in the statue garden?"

They pissed off a dragon by planning to steal an item from his hoard? I actually want to ask, but Sev's binding is on me.

"No. A sorcerer spelled them into small animals—a rabbit and a cat, respectively—so he could keep them captive and drain their magic."

I grimace at the thought. At least I was only vaguely aware of my captivity.

"Neither was trapped as long as you, but still. It takes time to adjust." She retrieves her phone. "I'm here to help. I have a free room in the house. If you don't want to go back to Levi's."

Just the thought of reentering that towering building has me cringing.

Then an important fact pricks at my mind. "I'm a monster. Your house is in Of the Wing territory." I feel myself frown in further confusion. "And you're a witch."

"Yeah, I had to get special permission from The Council.

And they only agreed when my sister offered to work for them for a stretch of time."

"Why go through the trouble?"

Mor spine straightens, as if she's used to defending this point. "My book collection is special. I want it available but also kept safe. A house formerly home to a dragon's hoard has natural protections."

Which I know better than most.

Suddenly, sitting still feels too much like the prison I endured. I stand up quickly, causing Mor to lean back in surprise.

"Are there any other captives in the statue garden?" My anxiety has my voice coming out harsh.

Mor frowns. "No. You were the only one."

I shake my head, my brain and body burning with the twist of emotions I can't untangle.

"I'll figure things out on my own." I always have. Relying on someone else was trained out of me early on in life.

"You don't have to." Mor leans forward again. "There are plenty of mythics who can help ease your way."

I huff a sad laugh, lacking true humor.

Monsters have always had to fend for themselves.

"Trust me, they won't bother."

"What does that mean?" The beautiful witch studies me, and I'm sure that given enough time, she could pry out all my secrets, magical binding or no.

"Means this town found me easy to forget." I shove my hands in my pockets. "Because no one wanted me here in the first place."

"Bo. Do not say shit like that about yourself." Mor is too adorable when she scowls.

Makes walking away from her hard. But not impossible.

"Thank you, Mor Shelly. For what you did." I offer a deep nod and meet her eyes hoping she can see the sincerity in mine. "But don't worry about me. You've done more than anyone else ever has, and I'll always be grateful."

Then I turn and head toward the forest, no direction in mind.

Just away from the woman who has me wondering what it would be like to be wanted.

11

Mor

I THOUGHT for sure that I was alone in the library.

"Hello?" I call out.

No answer.

Ame and Jack should both be at work. Niko moved out a few weeks ago in order to live above the restaurant that he will be opening in town. And the last time the little tinkling bell above the door rang was twenty minutes ago, when the town's healing witch left with a new spell for soothing bug bites.

But I swear I hear movement. I dismiss the possibility that the rustling is Lucky, my sister's black cat familiar. Lucky always goes to the vet office with Ame. The feline helps the anxious animals calm down when my sister has her hands full. My brothers' familiars also don't tend to come by the library without them.

The house should be empty.

Then what the fuck am I hearing?

I carefully climb down from the stepladder I just scaled and hold out the Swiffer Duster I was using to clean the top shelf, as if the fluffy device could double as a weapon.

My nerves have been on edge all day, half my mind always on Bo. Wondering where he ended up. If he's left town. If he's hungry without any money. If he's cold and uncomfortable, holing up in that rotting trailer. Worry is an unwanted companion I can't get rid of. Maybe that's why I'm having an over-the-top reaction about this mysterious sound.

I try to move as quietly as possible from one room to the next. Tree wallpaper shifts to sage-colored paint as I shuffle into the sitting room. As I get closer, I hear more noises.

Scuffling. Rustling.

And was that a chitter?

"Hello?" I try the greeting again, doing my best to keep the snap of accusation from my voice.

I don't know why I am so suspicious. Maybe it's the stress of the last few days. Releasing a monster trapped in a statue on my land. And there's the fact that earlier this year, everyone who was asleep in this house was put under a spell to keep us that way while a rogue mythic attempted to steal a hidden item in the house.

For that encounter, I was very grateful for the leftover dragon hoard magic. I know it was traumatic for Bo to have been cursed and probably now sees the enchantment as inherently evil. But Hamish, the selkie who broke into the library, lashed out when he was discovered and almost killed my brother Anthony. When the house captured Hamish, we were able to escape whatever nefarious plan he'd had.

The witches handled his punishment. I just hope I never have to see the shifter again.

But now we're back to this mysterious noise. To someone in this library that I have not accounted for.

Someone who has not answered my gentle greetings.

The Swiffer quivers in my hand, and I remember, *Oh*

yeah, I am a witch. I haven't been studying any kind of self-defense or battle spells. Which seems like an oversight at this point.

I make a mental note to research the topic later. I'm sure Ame would like to learn them.

Jack would approve.

Letting my mental shields lower carefully, I search out any hint of an emotional grid in the house. I come up empty. But I'm tired and distracted, so a power boost might be all I need.

I finger the silver locket hanging around my neck. Inside, instead of a picture, there is tightly packed red powder. To anyone else, it may look like I have a small case of blush around my neck.

But this does a hell of a lot more than bring color to your cheeks. Witches have some natural abilities. Magic that we can utilize without assistance. I can pick up someone's emotional grid in a big sense. But to do anything impactful, we need potions and rituals and spells. Like those contained in all these books. And sometimes, we can do these beforehand, and not all potions are liquid.

This red powder is a family heirloom of sorts. A recipe passed down through multiple generations of Shellys. It is concocted to amplify our emotion magic.

I take a dab on my middle finger and quickly close my eyes to brush the powder across my lids.

Magical eye shadow.

When I blink my eyes open, I can now spy a subtle glow of my own skin. An emotional grid that I have trouble reading from the inside out. But now, I'm aware it's there. And I can see there is one other grid in this house.

It's a simplistic one. Something I might expect to see from a child.

Did someone leave their kid in my library?

Oh Gods, I am not good with children.

Still, I lower the Swiffer and soften my voice. "Hi there. Can you come out, please?"

I aim toward the next room, where the glow is now visible, even through the walls. I step around the corner and navigate down another row of shelves, only to realize it is not a child in my library. Nor is it an adult. And it's not even a terrifying villain.

No, the intruder in my library, who is currently sliding a book off the shelf, is a raccoon.

There's a *raccoon* in my library.

"Fucking Gods!" I scream.

The rodent whips its head toward me, the thing's mask-patterned face staring straight at mine, black eyes sparkling with mischief.

The creature lets out a loud string of chatters, and then it waddles away. Fluffy, big ass pointed in my direction, strutting off like it couldn't give a fuck.

Meanwhile, I give a hell of a lot of fucks.

"Oh my Gods," I whisper-scream. "What in all the hell dimensions?"

I don't know what to do about vermin in my house. Why is Ame not here right now? Animals are her thing.

This town doesn't even have an animal control; they just call the veterinary office.

That's what I need to do.

I will call Zara.

Thank the Gods I have animal people in the family who know what to do about the fact that there is a wild rodent in my home. In my business. Touching my books.

A forest creature *touched* my books.

"Where's that hoard protection magic now, huh?" I hiss the words into the air, as if the house might be listening.

There's no response as I frantically search for my phone in all my pockets while cautiously following after the raccoon. But

I also try to keep distance from it because I don't want the animal to end up being rabid and in a biting mood.

Not going to happen.

Only, when I turn at the end of the shelf, I don't see the raccoon. What I do see is an open window. With the screen popped out.

Can raccoons do that?

I don't know why I'm asking. Obviously, they can because it did.

I hurry over and slam the window shut. Then I press my shoulders back against the wall and try to catch my breath. Only when I am not gasping, as if I'd just swum the entire length of Lake Galen, do I make a call to the town vet.

Of course, my sister answers the phone.

"Thank you for calling Folk Tails. This is Ame speaking. How can I help you?"

"There was a raccoon in the library." I'm yelling, and I can't stop. "It broke in. How do I keep raccoons from breaking into my library?"

"Mor?"

"Yes, Ame, this is your sister. There are no other libraries in town. Do you think that Toccoa's library is calling you all to figure out how to handle raccoons?"

"You just surprised me is all," she says, her voice staying calm, unruffled by my outburst. "You're not normally a yeller."

She's right, and I drag in a deep breath through my nose to calm myself. "Sorry. Yes, it's me. Back to this raccoon problem."

"Raccoons are smart. You need to use locks. And latches."

"I do," I huff. "It opened a window. From the outside."

"Oh." Now her voice changes, but she sounds delighted rather than horrified. "Fascinating. I'll take a look when I get home."

Ame does not sound at all as anxious as I am about this. But

I bet that Jack will be on my side. When I present this as a failing in our security system, that is.

But then I immediately scratch that approach because Jack will probably go so far as to suggest that we install bars on the windows to keep all bad characters away from his precious mate.

Sometimes, werewolves can go a little overboard.

"Okay, yes. Please help me brainstorm how to raccoon-proof our house. I can't have them coming in here. They'll damage the books."

"Well, maybe you should look for a raccoon repellent spell. You're welcome. I just gave you a new research topic. It's your favorite thing to do."

Damn her. She's right. There is probably a particular repellent enchantment that would work perfectly at keeping all forest creatures away from my library. I have a lot of other projects that should come first, but this has reached priority level one.

Plus, it should thoroughly distract me from worrying about a certain monster.

"Fine. I'll research. Because you're making me."

I hang up to the sound of her soft chuckle. And then I go to reset the books that the raccoon decided to take off the shelf for me.

12

Bo

MY SAVINGS MIGHT HAVE ROTTED with time, but it turns out that my dad was smarter than me.

After bagels with the witch, I wandered around the altered town, and then I hiked back to the trailer for a third time and finally found something worth keeping.

Behind the bathroom mirror, which someone cracked, is a medicine cabinet. But behind the cabinet is a cavity, where I found one of my father's many cash stashes. He would ball up a few bills when he was drunk, tuck them away for safekeeping, then promptly forget where he had hidden them.

Then he'd holler at me for supposedly stealing from him.

The thing about his cash stashes? He'd always put them in a ziplock bag.

Sealed tight. Waterproof. No mold.

So, now I've got a few hundred dollars and an entirely new life to figure out.

The moment I decide to take my scant money to the bar, I know I've made a mistake.

This is exactly what Dad would do.

Unfortunately, that thought has a weird edge of comfort to it. Yes, my father spent most nights in Tipsy Howls—the werewolf-owned bar—where he could piss away the money he'd earned from repairing cars. But because he often imbibed too much to drive himself home, Kev, the bartender, would call me to come pick him up. That wolf always overserved Dad, no matter how many times I had politely asked him to cut him off after a certain point. Kev would just glare at me and tell me to stop being a waste of a son and drive my father home.

So, I did.

And now I'm back here to follow in his paw prints.

And maybe find out whatever happened to Arvin Folan.

Only it looks like Tipsy Howls got a makeover, including a new name—Local Brew. Sounds almost witchy to me, but I still pick up the scent of wolf when I push through the front door.

Tipsy Howls was a dive, with a grimy floor, bad lighting, and a welcoming face—only if you were a regular or member of the pack.

Local Brew has a scuffed but clean wood floor; low, warm lighting; and, from what I scent, a mixture of mythics. There's laughter that has no note of harshness, an atmosphere with no undercurrent of violence, and a crowd that doesn't pay me any notice as I make my way through.

Much different from what I remember.

There are open stools at the bar, and I settle on one, feeling the weight of shame and misery bow my shoulders.

"Welcome in," a deep voice says, the bartender having spotted me. A younger guy who's definitely not Kev. At least one thing has improved. "What can I get you?"

And here, we run into a speed bump on my road to getting drunk—I don't drink.

After watching the way my father wasted all his free time in alcohol's grasp, I figured there was no point.

But now I've decided there is a point—I don't care, so I will do what I want.

Only I don't know what to order.

Let's leave it to the expert.

"Your stiffest drink, sir." I pound a fist on the bar. My meaty hand sets the nearby drinks to rattling, liquid sloshing over the edge of a few.

People glare my way, and chagrin heats my cheeks.

"Sorry. So sorry." I grab a couple of napkins and help mop up the speckles of beer that escaped my fellow bar-goers' glasses because of my aggressive move. Once that's dealt with, I face the bartender again.

"Your stiffest drink, please," I mumble.

The bartender scoops up a glass and a bottle—all the while, his curious eyes stay on me, and a lopsided smile sits on his mouth. The expression tugs at a memory, as does the man's scent. But all I know for sure is that he's a werewolf.

"You look familiar." He slides a short glass of amber liquid my way.

The color of the alcohol is pretty. Kind of reminds me of the highlights in a certain redhead's hair.

I shake my head and focus on the wolf. "I was just thinking the same about you."

"Are you from Folk Haven?"

"Born and raised."

He tilts his head with curiosity. "You been away for a while?"

I huff a humorless laugh as I bring the glass to my mouth. "You could say that."

Then I take a sip.

And promptly spit it back out.

"Gods, that is disgusting!" I grab a napkin and try to wipe the taste off my tongue, but to no avail. "Did you pour me poison?"

The bartender blinks. Then the guy throws his head back and roars with laughter.

I don't see what's so funny about him trying to kill me in front of all his customers, but I'm distracted by the sound of his hilarity.

I would swear I've heard that laugh before. Maybe not as deep, but the cadence, along with the hiccup on the end, stands out in my mind.

"Griffy?" I ask, voice hushed.

The werewolf's laughter fades off with another two hiccups as he refocuses on me. He clears his throat. "What did you call me?"

"You're ..." Couldn't be. This is a full-grown wolf.

Seventeen years.

"Are you Griffy? Griffith Fangworn?"

His thick brown brows twist in confusion. "How do you know that nickname?"

"I made it." My tone is distracted as my eyes catalog his face.

Eyes and ears that seemed too large for a young boy now fit well with the way he's matured. The wolf let his dirty-blond hair grow long enough to touch his shoulders, which is a good thing because when he had it cut shorter, the strands would always stick out in weird directions and mean pack members would call him Scarecrow. What tells me I'm for sure looking at Griffy is the scar on his chin he got from an energetic bear shifter elbowing him in the face during a wrestling match. Werewolves don't inherit their speedy healing until puberty, when they have their first change, so the wound scarred.

How old was Griffy when the wolf first overtook him? I've missed seventeen years' worth of full moons.

The werewolf, who I last saw as a little boy, gapes at me, recognition hitting him. "Bo? No ... you. Gods, you haven't aged a day." He smacks his forehead. "A long-lived mythic. You're immortal?" He lowers his voice on that final word. As if asking about a secret.

Just like monsters, feelings on long-lived mythics are mixed.

It's not always safe to be around someone who never ages. They think differently when time isn't a factor in their life. Many have God-like complexes. Sometimes the centuries affect their minds in odd ways. Maybe it's the passage of time. Maybe it's watching everyone you know age and die. Whatever reason, every long-lived mythic I've encountered has had a subtle air of danger.

One is the reason I got frozen in a statue.

"I'm not." My voice is gruff. "I was cursed. A witch freed me last night."

"Hells." Griffith braces his elbows on the bar, staring at me. "I thought you'd just skipped town. That's what your dad said anyway." His face falls. "I missed you, but understood why you'd left. Always thought you deserved better than how they all treated you."

The back of my neck heats. "I got by." Clenching my hands together in my lap, I ask the question I've wondered since I came upon the trailer. "Do you know what happened to my dad?"

Griffith swallows so hard that I can hear it. "He left. A few years after you did. I mean, after you disappeared." His eyes turn soft with sorrow. "Heard not long back that he had challenged the wrong wolf. Fight went lethal, and he wasn't the winner."

There's a twist in my chest. Is it sorrow? I'm not sure. Can't tell if I have enough feelings for my father to miss him.

But it's good to know at least.

"Thanks for telling me." I pick up my drink, then get a whiff and set it back down with a grimace. "Can't believe you're old enough to work at a bar. And that you're serving whatever this toxic liquid is."

"Hey!" Griffith chuckles, taking the glass from me and using a rag to wipe up where I spit out the booze. "That's some decent whiskey right there. I'll not have you wasting another drop." The werewolf sips the drink himself, then pulls out a fancier glass. "You're not really a drinker, right? I'll make you something different. On the house. Pay you back for all the piggyback rides you gave me."

I smile at the thought.

Griffith was scrawny compared to other young werewolves, and I know some of the bigger boys bullied him. Whenever I came into town, I'd keep an eye out for him. I'd always wanted a little brother. A family.

The pack didn't want me, but Griffy was still too young to have formed a prejudice.

But he's older now.

"You ..." I clear my throat. "You don't mind?"

"Mind what?"

I scratch the corner of my jaw and try not to think too hard about the way Georgiana avoided my eyes. "One of my kind being in your bar?"

Griffith pauses with his big hands wrapped around a metal shaker he just poured an assortment of liquids into.

Then he sets it aside, steps forward, reaches across the bar, and hooks his hand around the back of my neck to drag me in until our foreheads press together. The wolf stares hard into my eyes, making it impossible for me to look away.

"You're welcome wherever I am, Bo." His hand tightens. "And I'm sorry for whatever happened to you, but I'm glad you're back. I look forward to getting to know my pack mate again."

"I'm not—"

"You are," he growls. "To me, you are." He presses a kiss to my forehead, then backs off.

Leaving me to deal with the first time I've ever felt welcome … anywhere.

"There're two packs in town now. If you're wanting to officially join, my bet is, both would be open to the idea." Griffith pours out whatever he's been concocting, and I smell the strong citrus scent of lemons and limes. "Margarita." He slides the glass to me, salt on the rim, and pops a tiny umbrella in it. "Not poison." He smirks. "You said you were freed from a curse. Did a Shelly witch break that for you?"

I jerk at the surname, then try to cover up how much the mention affected me by taking a sip.

Tart and oh-so delicious. Is there even any alcohol in it?

Doesn't matter. I take another eager swallow.

"That's good," I hum happily. "You might not be terrible at your job, Griffy."

"Thanks," he says dryly, smirking at my enjoyment.

"Why do you assume a Shelly witch?"

"They've freed two others. Both cursed by a sorcerer. They seem to have a specialty in breaking curses. Hell, they probably specialize in everything with that library Mor has."

The witch's name drags a shiver down my spine.

"What do you know about Mor Shelly?"

Every moment I'm not actively thinking about something else, my mind goes back to the memory of her licking cream cheese off her middle finger.

"Not a whole lot."

Griffith nods at a guy farther down the bar, who gestures toward an empty glass. While he gets busy pouring, I swallow more of my tasty drink and brainstorm how I can ask more questions about Mor without sounding obsessed. But as if sensing my fascination, Griffith keeps on the same topic when he returns to the chat with me.

"She seems nice enough, but doesn't leave that library of hers too often."

"Hmm." The habit sounds familiar. I rarely ventured far from the woods surrounding our trailer or Dad's mechanic shop.

I wonder why she keeps to herself.

For me, I was just doing my best to avoid others. Better chance that way that I wouldn't encounter someone who hated me.

Georgiana and I met by accident the first time. I mean, I had known who she was. The Stormwinds had nice cars, and they'd bring them by Folan Auto Shop for regular tuning.

I had been aware of her, but I'd never met her. Never spoken to her.

Then, one evening, as the sun was setting, I made my way out to the forest for a moment to myself. But then I heard laughter. That was an odd noise to hear around my home. I didn't laugh much, and my father never did.

Besides, it was a woman laughing.

I followed the noise and came upon a small cliff at the edge of our property. And there was Georgiana, wings spread wide, jumping off the edge. I stumbled forward in time to watch the breeze catch her wings. She glided around, laughing in delight, then returned to the cliff, only to do the maneuver again. As if she enjoyed the falling as much as the flying.

On her third round, she noticed me watching.

"What are you doing? Are you spying on me?"

She sounded angry, and I ducked my head and held my hands out in surrender, like I was used to doing, though I kept my fingers together to hide the webbing.

"Sorry. No. It's only that I live just near here."

"Oh." Some of the wariness left her voice. "You're that guy who works at the mechanic shop, right?"

She had brought her Mercedes in a couple of weeks ago for an oil change.

"I do. I work there."

"And you live here?" She waved at the forest behind me.

"Yeah. My dad and me."

"Hmm." Her wings flexed as she studied me. "That means you're a monster, right?"

"I am."

"According to my parents, I'm not supposed to associate with monsters." She snorted a laugh that didn't sound humorous. "I'm also not supposed to fly on nights that aren't the dark moon."

She waved behind her at the visible sickle moon between parted clouds.

At the dismissive tone in her voice, I found myself relaxing. "I won't tell anyone," I offered.

She smiled, and it was a gorgeous sight.

The siren opened her mouth to say something, but it was as if the world tilted and swayed under my feet. I reached out for the nearest tree to steady myself. And I tried to remember what just happened.

Georgiana said something. No, she sang something. The most beautiful song in the world ... only I couldn't remember it.

"Sorry," she said, not sounding too apologetic. "I never get to sing either, and I wanted to see if my voice would work on you. Looks like it does."

Ah. Of course. When sirens sang, the only people who could remember the experience were other sirens or someone a siren loved.

Could there ever be a day where I remember a siren song?

But that was a ridiculous thought. I should have just been glad she was not running away, screaming.

"Did you come to the Monster section so no one would see you flying?"

It was a good plan. There weren't many of us here, and humans didn't come this far.

"That, and I spotted this cliff when I was on my daddy's speed-

boat earlier." She pointed off to the side, where Lake Galen glittered in the moonlight. "I thought it would be a good launching point."

"Feel free to use this cliff whenever."

Technically, it was on my father's property, but I doubted he'd care about some random mythic jumping off of it. He barely thought past the hood of a car or doors of Tipsy Howls.

She quirked her head while studying me. "Do you fly? In whatever monster form you take?"

"No. I ... no. I don't look near as pretty as you do when I shift."

She smirked and gave a little half shrug. "Charmer. Probably better you keep that to yourself anyway."

I agreed, though there was an uncomfortable tug deep in my gut that wished I could have the comfort with changing that most other mythics have.

"I'll leave you to it. Sorry to interrupt."

I made to leave, but her voice halted my steps. "You can stay. If you want. I don't mind the company as long as you keep this little encounter to yourself."

"Of course. I won't tell anyone."

AND I DIDN'T. For years, I kept Georgiana's secret.

Sometimes, she'd come every week. Sometimes, months would go by without a visit, and I'd only see her from afar in town. She never acknowledged me there, but I told myself I didn't mind because on top of our cliff, she'd sit beside me and call me her friend and tell me how she chafed under the rules of her strict parents.

Then, one night, she kissed me, and I swore I grew my own set of wings from pure joy.

Georgiana stayed away for months after that, and I convinced myself I'd messed up the encounter.

Then she returned and acted like nothing had happened.

A week later, she kissed me again, only her breath smelled

like the bottles my father always clutched close. It was the first time I didn't want to kiss her back. She pressed me, tugging at my clothes and dragging my hand under her skirt. I didn't want to do what she was demanding, not when she was drunk. But I also didn't want to leave her alone in the woods.

The only thing I could think to do was hold her in a tight hug, roaming hands trapped between us. When she realized I wasn't planning to give her what she wanted, Georgiana turned from sloppy seductive to scathing. She cursed me, insulted me, and struggled to get loose.

I let her go and did my best to convince myself it was the alcohol talking. Not her.

She flew off before I could stop her.

Another handful of months, and I was sure she was done with the cliff. Done with me.

But then, on the first day of spring, there she was, in a pretty pink sundress, sitting on a picnic blanket, waiting for me.

"Hi, Bo," she said, smiling up at me.

And I instantly forgot every hurtful word she'd thrown my way. That wasn't the real Georgiana. This poised woman was, and I was just happy that she was back.

She kissed me again, and her mouth tasted like sweet tea.

We did more that night. Georgiana said she wanted me to be her first.

I wanted to be her everything, but I'd take whatever she was willing to give.

Riding that pleasure, I thought I was the happiest I could ever be. That there was no higher point in my life than to be what my siren needed.

"I know you want to go," she said as we lay beside each other, staring up at the stars, the sweat drying on our bare skin. I'd told her

how I was saving up money to leave Folk Haven. "But I want you to stay. Stay for me."

"I'll stay." Besides, when I had told her I wanted to leave Folk Haven, live somewhere else where no one knew I was a monster, that had been before. Before she claimed me. "I'll do anything for you, Georgie."

I turned my head then, hoping to see her gazing back at me. But her eyes stayed pointed up at the sky as a smile overtook her mouth.

"Good."

It wasn't long after that I went to the cliff and found her frantic.

"Oh gods, Bo. I'm in trouble. I need you to help me." Her eyes were glassy with tears, pupils blown wide with fear.

And just like before, I said, "Anything."

THIS IS MY OWN FAULT.

I offered her anything, and she took me at my word.

Now I'm still paying for it.

"I'm going to need another one of these." I wave my now-empty margarita glass in the air.

"Sure thing." Griffith chuckles.

And he keeps them coming.

13

———

Mor

"Hey, Mor. Are you busy?" Griffith—a bartender at Local Brew and the one I go to for high-quality spirits when a spell calls for a touch of booze—sounds like he's in the middle of a party wherever he's calling from.

I glance down at the almost-finished charcuterie board I fashioned for myself and the large glass of wine I filled past the point that a sommelier would find acceptable. The drink sits un-sipped, seconds away from my first big satisfying gulp.

Am I going to need wine to get through this conversation?

I can't fathom why the werewolf would be calling me.

Only ... last time I stopped by Local Brew I chatted with him longer than normal because I'd come across a text about a Gods Object. The book was vague, the ink mostly smudged, but what I'd gathered was that The Clawed One had made a tankard of some kind, filled with a mystical mead that did ... something. I'd hoped Griffith, a werewolf and beer brewer, might know more about the legend.

He didn't. What he did say was that we should go out sometime.

I'd left without giving him an answer.

Griffith isn't asking me out on a last-minute date, is he?

If the answer to the second is yes, then so is the answer to the first—yes, I will need wine.

Which again has me wondering, *What is up with me?*

Griffith is an objectively attractive guy with a friendly personality and a full-time job. Plus, as a werewolf, he's part of the same magical community I am.

He'd be a fine person to go out with and try to fall in love with. But when I think of him asking me out, I get a full-body cringe. Because, in my mind, I can already see me breaking things off and then all our run-ins turning awkward.

So, instead of making up an excuse or telling him the truth, I simply say, "What's up?"

"I, uh, have a situation here at the bar."

Well, that's not a date request. Color me interested. "Go on."

I could swear I hear singing behind Griffith's voice.

"You know Bo? The guy you freed? He's here. And I think you need to come pick him up."

I frown. "You don't want him in your bar?"

Griffith is a pure-blood werewolf, but I didn't think he held monster prejudice. Not when I know he's dated other mythics before.

"It's not that. I love Bo. I knew him when I was younger. Couldn't meet a better guy." The praise cuts off as some kind of wailing gets louder before trailing off. "The thing is, I might have accidentally overserved him."

"What?" I snap.

"He's a big guy! But the margaritas hit him hard, and now he's wasted. I'd take him home with me, but I've got two more hours here." The background noise lessens, and I get the sense that Griffith stepped into a back room or something. "He doesn't have anyone that I know of. And you Shellys seem to stick to the ones you save. But if there's another person I should call about him, you point me their way."

I open my mouth, ready to give him Levi's name. But then I remember the monster telling me about his pregnant wife. Moira is a badass selkie who can certainly handle herself, but that doesn't mean I want to put any extra stress on her or her husband's plate. Not when I'm the reason Bo is free to cause drunken mayhem.

And I certainly don't want to call the cops on him. I saw the way he cowed in the face of Samantha's badge.

"I'll come get him," I sigh.

"Thank the gods! His mopey singing is driving away my customers."

Not sure what to say to that, I simply tell Griffith I'll be there soon. With a mournful glance at my wine, I leave it on the kitchen table and stick my cheese slices into the fridge. As I grab my keys, lock up, and head out to my car, I shoot a quick text on the Shelly group family chat, letting my siblings and their partners know where I'm headed and why.

The overinforming habit started not long ago after the break-in at the library, and now the lot of us send regular updates for peace of mind.

My phone buzzes with *good luck*s and offers of help if I need them.

But I should be able to handle this monster myself.

Then I step into Local Brew and wince at the horrendous noise coming from the back corner, where there's a small stage. Sometimes, Local Brew will have live music, but I suspect whoever Griffith hires to stop by is slightly better than the rendition of "Roxanne" a monster is belting out.

"Mor! You're here." The bartender waves me down. "Thank the gods. I was considering using a tranquilizer just to shut him up."

As if in response to Griffith, there's a loud, drawn-out, *"Roxannnne!"*

"How many margaritas did you give him?" I'm having trouble taking in the quiet, insecure mythic now up onstage, shamelessly belting out a bad rendition of—ironically—The Police's song.

"Only three. I'm not sure he's ever imbibed before. Turns out, he's a sad drunk who likes to sing." Griffith shakes his head with a rueful smile.

I watch Bo clutch a mic while his other hand cradles an empty glass with a tiny beach umbrella skittering around the edge.

"Why'd you give him a microphone?"

Seems like a bad idea to offer anyone who isn't a paid performer a way to amplify their voice.

"I thought the machine was broken." Griffith waves toward a dented speaker. "But Bo sat over there for a while, tinkering with it, and next thing I know, he's onstage, thinking he's part of *Moulin Rouge.*"

"Rooooooooxxxxannnnnnne!"

Damn the Dark One's plans, is Georgiana his Roxanne in this scenario?

I need to get him down before he outs whatever kind of relationship he had with the Of the Wing council member.

"Okay. I'll get him. No more margaritas." I jab Griffith's chest with my finger for emphasis, then push my way through the crowd of spectators, who seem to be a combination of amused and horrified.

"Bo!" I call out when I get closer.

But his eyes stay closed as he sloppily sings out a verse about sharing with another boy.

My lips twist in a grimace, and I really wish I had shoved some cheese in my mouth before I left because, now, I'm hungry, along with baffled.

How am I going to get him off that stage?

"Bo!" I shout again, this time right in front of him.

He blinks glassy eyes down at me, and he lets out a huge, soul-weary sigh.

Then he says, "*ROOOOXXXANNNE!*"

Enough is enough. I scramble up onto the stage and grab his arm, trying to tug him down.

But he doesn't budge. The guy is pure muscle, and I'm only as strong as it takes to carry a stack of books.

"Come on, Bo." I try to reason with him. "It's not karaoke night."

What kind of sad, destructive force have I let loose on the innocent townspeople of Folk Haven?

"Sing it with me!" Bo hollers, ignoring my plea, then sloppily makes his way through the same verse he just sang.

"Bo, come *on*."

I try to take the microphone from him, but he simply holds it above my head and shouts, "*Roxanne*," into it.

The thing about me is, I like to be in control. Probably an issue left over from being raised by parents who literally drained my power on a regular basis. But I know that being bossy can easily earn me the label of 'bitch witch' so I do my best to keep my commands of others reasonable and delivered in a neutral tone.

But the times I can't suppress the bitch witch?

When I'm frustrated.

And hungry.

And tired.

Right now, I'm all three.

I cross my arms over my chest and hit the monster with my scathing—I'm disappointed in you glare—and let the bossy rampage begin.

"Bo Folan," I bark. "Stop singing right now and get off the stage. You do not have permission to be here." I step in close, crowding him as much as I am able. "I haven't had dinner. I haven't had wine. And a racoon broke into my house today. My 'give a fuck' well is depleted and you are officially *pissing me off*."

Bo stopped singing at the beginning of my tirade and now he frowns, the expression creasing deep lines into his cheeks. "Are you mad at me?"

"Yes!" That came out louder than I meant.

"Oh. I'm sorry. Don't be mad." He drops the mic, which lets out a reverberating thunk and a loud crackle of feedback throughout the bar. "We can go."

"Really?" I blink, surprise draining away my annoyance. "You'll come with me?"

"Yeah." Then Bo is the one tugging me offstage, his big feet stumbling on the steps. "Let's get drinks. I didn't think I liked alcohol. But Griffith made it taste good."

"Sounds like Griffith made some bad decisions tonight too," I grumble, glaring at the smirking bartender.

"More drinks," Bo demands, dropping cash on the bar top. "Mor wants wine."

Not happening. I scoop the bills up and stuff them back into his pocket. I don't know where he got that money, but I'm betting it's all he has.

"They aren't serving any more alcohol tonight," I inform him before Griffith can even think of mixing up another cocktail. "Come on, Bo. I want to go home. I'm hungry."

"You are? Me too. Let's find food together."

He's still got ahold of my hand. He drags me behind him—doing it relatively easily, I hate to add—and we burst out into the cool fall night. Leaves swirl around our ankles, and a sliver of the moon hovers high above us.

Bo stops suddenly, staring fixedly at the orb, his mouth slightly slack. The focus reminds me of how Jack sometimes stares at the moon. Of course, he never lets his mouth go loose like Bo's, as if asking for bugs to fly in. Still, I have to wonder if the type of mythics that make up Bo's monster might include a touch of wolf.

He shakes his head, then gives me an entirely too endearing grin. "Food?"

"Yeah, Bo." I nudge him toward the passenger side of my truck. "Let's find you some food."

14

Bo

THE LIGHT CREEPS underneath my eyelids and threatens to split my brain in two. I bite back a groan as I throw an arm over my face, trying to hide in the shadows. My body is experiencing a strange mixture of sensations. Many parts of me ache and hurt and cling to a queasiness I beg the gods to ease away. But I also notice how there is a luxuriously soft surface beneath me and an intoxicating scent teasing my nose.

The scent is earthy yet floral, like a rose garden.

If only I could enjoy it without also feeling a sticky film on my tongue and a turmoil in my stomach.

What hell did I go through last night to come out feeling like this?

And as if the question was all that was needed, memories begin coming back to me.

Local Brew.

The first sip of a delicious, fruity drink.

The many more sips of many more delicious, fruity drinks.

A fuzzy sensation of no longer needing to impress anyone.

The need to be loud and have every eye in the vicinity on me.

The need to be seen and acknowledged.

The need to sing.

The need to sing terribly.

Soft, insistent hands on my body. Strong arms around my waist.

A disappointed scowl on the prettiest face I'd ever seen.

No, not the prettiest. Georgiana is the prettiest.

But then why am I having trouble forming the face of the siren in my mind and I have a clear vision of a certain redheaded witch?

Trying to straighten my thoughts by bringing myself back to the present, reluctantly, I drag my arm away and blink my eyes open, wincing at the natural light spilling in above me. In truth, the room is not overly bright. There is simply a skylight above me that lets in the beginning of the morning sun. I tilt my head to the side and spy floral-wallpapered walls around me. A bedside table stacked high with books. A fainting couch that holds a curvaceous witch, who appears to be sleeping more soundly than I was.

Where am I?

And just like before, the moment I think the question, the answer comes to me.

I am in the dragon's house.

The magically imbued building that decided to torture me for seventeen years.

I jerk upward in bed, gagging at the sloshing in my stomach, but also releasing a gasp of relief when I realize that I have full control over every single one of my limbs. Even though I stepped over the threshold, I have not been turned into a metal sculpture once more. Not yet anyway.

Mor must've brought me here. But why?

And why is she asleep on a couch while I am in the most comfortable bed I have ever lain in?

As I drag my legs over to the edge, I eye her slumbering form, most of which I can see since her blanket is bunched by her feet. Mor is in a matching sleep set, the short shorts revealing the bottom curves of her ample ass. The exposed skin sets off a tingling in the back of my neck, and I have to swallow for a reason other than nausea.

Her red hair falls in a fiery cascade over her pale shoulders, and the little tank top, which matches her shorts, rides up to show a dip in her back that seems to want a large hand pressing against it.

That's a ridiculous thought, and I don't know where it came from.

She's not snoring, but I can hear her deep breathing. One more odd aspect of the situation is how relaxed she is, how vulnerable she's made herself, when she's in the room with a strange monster. She doesn't know me. She has no reason to trust me.

Maybe she's naive.

Or maybe she's so powerful that she doesn't bother to fear me.

But what I do know is, no matter how upset I am with this town, with this house, with this world, I do not want this witch to be afraid of me.

I especially don't want *her* to be upset with *me*.

As wrecked and as wretched as I feel this morning, a small glimmer of contentment settles in the deepest part of my gut when I realize that Mor not only brought me into her home last night, but also settled me in her bed and now sleeps soundly with me only feet away.

This witch is precious. And I have the strong urge to protect her.

Which is ridiculous because she has this hell of a house to protect her. What could she want with me?

Mor lets out a small sigh, and she rolls over on her makeshift bed. I bite a knuckle to hold back a groan when I spy the swell of her breasts and the sleek curve of her plush mouth.

Has there ever been a more erotic sight than this woman relaxed in sleep?

I was a statue for too long. I should be ashamed of these thoughts. Mor deserves better than to be gaped at while she's unconscious.

I tear my gaze away from her and make to stand from the bed. But once again—only in a small way this time—the house betrays me. As my feet press into the floorboards, they give out a loud creak. And I can't help thinking that this home wants to wake up the witch before I can escape.

Teeth gritted, I glance back at the fainting couch.

A set of green eyes stares back at me.

15

Mor

"You're walking very close to me."

And it's not just the heavy tread of Bo's footsteps that alerts me to his proximity. There's also the warmth of the monster. He's like a portable furnace, his presence hot against my back. He would be a pleasant companion to have around come January. Many people think that Georgia is too far south to get cold, but here, in the northern section of the state, near the mountains, there are plenty of days that drop below freezing.

"I don't want this house to curse me again," he mumbles. "And it seems to like you."

His words warm me more than his body heat. I like the idea that this house has sentience that approves of me.

"I'm your curse shield? Nice." Sarcasm infuses my comments as I glance over my shoulder.

Bo ducks his head and shuffles back a step. "I'm sorry. I shouldn't try to use you like that."

This monster continues to surprise me. Physically, Bo is built for intimidation. Towering form with broad shoulders and generous muscles on all of his limbs. But his posture reminds me of a crumpled ball of paper, all folded in on himself, as if all he wants is to take up less space.

Then there are his actions, which are like tiny sparks of rebellion, immediately smothered by apologies.

I don't think it's necessarily a bad thing that a big man takes notice of how he might bulldoze through the world, but I also don't like how he gives off the air of someone who has been mistreated and belittled until their self-worth is nonexistent.

"I was joking." Reaching out, I cup one of his massive biceps and draw him beside me. Now that we're on the second floor, there is plenty of room for us to walk together. "You can stay close if that makes you feel more comfortable."

He blinks down at me, eyes owlishly wide, and a blush colors his pale skin until I'm worried he may burst into flames.

The sight is a little bit adorable and a whole lot endearing.

"Come on." I give him another tug, and we head for the stairs, where I can already smell a hint of breakfast wafting up to us.

Bo was a stumbling, bumbling mess when I got him back home from the bar last night, but I managed to get him to eat almost half of a rotisserie chicken we had left in the fridge. I'm not sure what shape Bo would be in if I hadn't been able to get food in his stomach. Maybe still comatose.

In the kitchen, we find Ame pouring batter into a waffle maker while her mate fries bacon on the stovetop. I'm still standing close enough to Bo that I hear his stomach rumble.

Somehow, his face flushes a darker shade of red. I'm tempted to pull an ice pack from the fridge to help cool him down.

Instead, I ask, "Got enough food for two more?"

Jack doesn't respond, other than to hold up an unopened package of bacon, indicating he'll keep frying until there's enough for everyone.

"Yep," my sister chirps, pointing to the massive bowl of batter. "Wasn't sure who was here, so I erred on the side of caution."

Ame faces us, taking a moment to study Bo intently. Unlike me, Ame doesn't have the capacity to fully block off her mystical abilities to read others—though she claims Jack can sometimes act as a white-noise machine, blocking everyone else out. Right now, I wonder what desire she's hearing play through Bo's mind.

Whatever it is, she ends up turning to the werewolf at her side.

"Jack, you should be friends with Bo." She waves a spatula between them. "Spend time together."

Then she turns on her heel and strides out of the room.

Her mate stares after her. "Right now?"

There's no immediate answer, but a moment later, Ame reappears with her black cat familiar in her arms. The creature has gone fully boneless, hanging like a rag doll from my sister's grip. Ame strolls up to Bo and presses the cat against his chest until the monster takes hold of the feline.

He's gentle, cradling Lucky in his beefy arms, making his body into a spacious hammock for the spoiled cat.

Lucky immediately starts purring and making biscuits in Bo's sleeve.

"You like animals, don't you?" Ame asks.

Bo gives a silent nod.

"Me too. Maybe you can help Mor find her familiar. She's been wanting one for a while."

"Ame," I hiss at her, not about to let her start spouting off all my hidden desires.

Like how I want to find a person to fall in love with.

Or to at least have some good sex with.

There are some things a witch wants to keep to herself.

She only shrugs in that way little sisters do when they decide not to care if they're being annoying.

"Do you need help cooking?" Bo asks as his fingers scratch the cat's chin.

"We've got this. We'll call you back when things are ready." Ame blinks at me. "Mor, you should show Bo around. He can see how different this house is from how it used to be."

Ame probably made the tour suggestion because of whatever she'd picked up from the monster, and I don't see any harm as long as he doesn't panic and start demolishing the place.

"Sure. Follow me, Bo."

His heavy steps let me know he is behind me. I take him through the rooms, explaining how I organized the shelves and which parts of the collection are most popular. I show him the comfortable seating areas and pull an interesting title or two off their perches, just so he can see what treasures are available.

The more I talk, the more I warm up to the subject. This library is my passion project that I still can't believe I made come to life. I tell Bo about the renovations Ame and I made, hoping that pointing out differences will ease his mind.

Yes, this place is protected by residual dragon magic, but it isn't a secret hoard.

"As long as mythics come here with the genuine interest to read and learn, no one has had issues with the house," I say, trying to make my voice gentle so Bo doesn't interpret this as a scolding. "And I think Folk Haven is better for having all this information available. The coven certainly appreciates the access to a variety of spell books."

"You really love this place."

"I do. I always dreamed of having my own library." I let out a dry chuckle. "But I'm not sure I realized how much work it would be."

"Does your family work here too?" He tilts his head toward the kitchen.

"No. Jack and Ame live here, but Ame works at the veterinarian office in town, and Jack works at the university. Broderick is a professor there. My brother Anthony was helping for a bit, but he's got a job with a local seamstress. This is their busiest season because of the Halloween Ball. Everyone wants custom gowns."

Bo makes a humming noise in the back of his throat. He gazes around the shelves, and I allow myself a peek at his aura.

The colors are a fascinating mix.

Petal pink for curiosity.

Mustard brown for anxiety.

Chocolate for embarrassment.

Rose for longing.

While I can pick out the emotions a being is feeling, I never know exactly what the root of each is. Still, I take a chance based on what I see.

"Bo, would you like to work here?"

16

___

Bo

"You wouldn't want me as an employee." I blurt the response when Mor's question registers.

She stares up at me with a curious slant to her brow. "Why? Are you planning on destroying books? Being mean to patrons? Not showing up for shifts?"

"No." I hold up my hand that isn't cradling the black cat, as if that'll prove my lack of destructive urges. "Of course not. None of those things."

"Then explain."

Lay myself bare, more like. Mor doesn't understand that asking me to explain why I'm the worst employee for a library means revealing my vulnerabilities.

But if anyone deserves the truth, it's her. Especially because I physically can't tell her how I ended up in her statue garden. This I can at least discuss, no matter how much it makes my gut twist.

"I ... I can't read."

Her brows dip. "At all?"

"Some." I look anywhere but at the intelligent witch. "But slowly. And it gives me headaches."

"Headaches?"

I nod and brace myself for her to press. I get the sense that this curious witch wants to.

Instead, Mor redirects. "You wouldn't have to do a lot of reading. Just enough to sort and shelve the books. Mostly, you'd cover the front desk while I do other tasks and helped patrons with their research. Help straighten up the place. Maybe move heavy things. Dust. Point people in the right direction."

She's still offering?

"Your patrons wouldn't want me to be the one helping them."

I'm a monster.

But she knew that before telling me about the position.

"You can just tell me you wouldn't like working in a library, Bo. I won't be offended." Her smile is rueful. "Ame struggled to tell me, too, but I understand the work isn't for everyone."

"That's not it."

If it wasn't for the fact that this building cursed me, I'd find the place cozy. How Mor has arranged the place is so different from the dark house Dimitri Novac lived in. And the idea of having a profession where I can spend the day inside with a kind witch nearby instead of working in a cold garage, where customers get mad at how much they're charged, is so tempting.

"You don't need to make up a job for me."

"It's not made up, Bo. And selfishly, I'd like you close by. I'm going to help you navigate this world until you don't need me anymore. What do you say? Do you want the job?"

I frown. "I don't need your charity."

Mor sighs. "First off, could you not say *charity* like it's a bad thing? People need help sometimes, and they shouldn't feel shame, asking for it."

My neck heats at her words; I'm embarrassed that I never thought about it like that.

"Second, I really do need help. There's maintenance, cleaning, greeting patrons, repairing books. Yes, the searching for items requires reading, but I can handle that. I'll have more time to do that if you're covering all those extra tasks." She crosses her arms and stares up at me. "I'll give you a week to decide if you want the job. That's it, Bo. I can't wait any longer because I need help around here. If you're not it, then I'll start posting Help Wanted signs around town."

She's serious. The librarian actually wants me to work here even though my reading skills are elementary at best.

But those tasks she just listed off, I could do those.

Take care of the house she keeps all her precious treasures in. Even if it freaks me out.

"I'll take it."

Her red brows pop up, and then a slow smile blooms over her lovely face. I have to clear my throat a few times so I don't choke on my own breath.

"Fantastic. I'll get a hiring contract written up for you to sign."

Hell—

"And I'll read it to you, or you can ask someone else you trust to read it over before you sign it. Maybe Griffith? He said you all are friends. I won't be offended."

Griffith said that? I rub my suddenly warm chest.

"That's ... he is. My friend. But he doesn't need to read it. I trust you."

Mor blinks her big green eyes, and I can't read the emotion in them. I hope it's not pity.

"Thank you," she says eventually. "For trusting me." Then the witch reaches out and claims one of my hands, clasping it between hers. "It means a lot."

I shuffle my feet, sure my entire body has gone red with a blush.

"Do you have a place to stay?"

Is your bed an option?

I don't blurt that totally inappropriate question. It's just that it was the comfiest bed I'd ever slept in.

"I think Levi ... maybe ..." Gods, I split in the middle of the night on the only housing option I had. Who knows if the monster will give me a second chance?

"Well, I know this place makes you uncomfortable." She waves around the library. "But I have an RV in storage. Not doing anything but collecting dust. I can park it out front for you. There's an electric and sewage hookup and everything."

"Seriously?"

"Seriously. I'd be happy to know it's getting some use." She tilts her head and reroutes again. "Do you have friends in town? Other than Griffith?"

After a pause, I shake my head.

"How would you feel about hanging out with Jack and Ophelia? Ophelia is my brother Broderick's mate."

As I resume petting the purring cat, I gnaw on the inside of my cheek. "Why them?"

"They went through something similar to what you did. I thought it might be helpful for you to talk to people you could relate to."

Mor mentioned that before. How I wasn't the first one who needed help starting over after a curse.

"Yeah, I guess."

"Great. I'll set it up."

Why does it feel like the witch just planned a playdate for me?

Hell, she just arranged my entire life.

And ... I'm not mad about it.

17

Mor

"Here, I'll keep note of all the money I spend on you. Then when you get a few paychecks under your belt, you can pay me back." I hold up my phone to show Bo the Notes app. "Sound fair?"

His brows scrunch. "That's a notepad too?"

I glance at my iPhone, reminded once again of how long Bo has been gone.

"It can be a notepad. There are apps. Applications. It can be a lot of different things."

He nods even though his expression is still confused.

When I decided to spearhead this rehabilitation, I didn't consider how I would have to shepherd Bo through the advances the world had made in the past two decades. I'm not even a fan of the digital landscape, much preferring physical books and pen and paper.

Still, I can handle cell phones.

"Here, let me show you the basics."

I shuffle in close to his side, suppressing a shiver that wants to claim my body when I breathe in his earthy scent. Though I have mental shields firmly in place, I catch a flash of pink from his aura. Curiosity.

He must be curious about the phone.

For the next few minutes, I demonstrate how to use the touch screen, explaining what apps are, and which ones I use the most—music listening mainly. When I hand my phone over so he can try, the device looks tiny in his massive hands. Everything about Bo is big.

Even my five-nine stature appears diminutive next to his hulking form.

If he were a creep, I'd probably hate it. But it's almost as if Bo is constantly fighting to fit himself into a smaller area than he takes up. Shoulders hunched, chin dipped, eyes down.

He's going to get a hell of a sore neck if he keeps that posture up. I would know, after spending so much time bent over books.

Now I get monthly massages at Haven's Relaxation, and my body thanks me.

Maybe Bo would like to visit Levi's spa. Perhaps Bo could get a job there if he doesn't like library work. If the guy learned how to use his massive fingers to massage, there's not a kink or knot that could withhold against his thick digits.

After a moment, I realize I'm staring at his hands, wondering what they would feel like on my shoulders, pressing into stressed muscles.

I shake my head and clear my throat.

Bo offers me back my phone. "Seems useful," he murmurs. "But I'd worry all the time about breaking it."

Because of your massive hands? I almost ask but keep my fixation to myself.

"They're more durable now than they used to be. And you can get a case to protect it. I've dropped mine a bunch, and it's still working." I slip the phone into my back pocket and turn toward our next stop. "You'll probably need to get one eventually. Gets harder to survive in the world without a smartphone each year. But let's just focus on essentials for now."

He glances over my shoulder. "That's a bookstore."

"Exactly. Essentials."

There's a charming tinkle of a bell as I push into Never Judge a Cover—my favorite place in Folk Haven, outside of my own library.

Neri, the shop owner, comes around a bookshelf with her arms full of paperbacks.

"Hey, Mor! You saw my email?"

"Yep. Figured I'd just come by and check it out."

The siren took a trip to Atlanta and found what she suspects is a grimoire in a used bookstore.

The shop bell rings again, and I watch as Neri's attention lifts a few inches over my head. Turning, I find Bo standing behind me, his hands shoved deep into his pockets, his eyes flitting around the room, as if he's nervous to be here.

"Neri, this is Bo." Without thought, I press my hand into his lower back and guide him farther into the shop. "Bo, this is Neri Onassis. She's the owner."

His back is like iron under my hand, and I drop my touch away. His throat tenses with a swallow.

"Nice to meet you, ma'am," he mutters so low that I barely hear him.

"Nice to meet you too." The siren offers the monster a wide grin, and I'm grateful for her instinctual kindness. "First-time customers get fifty percent off of their first book."

"Oh ... I don't read much."

What he described earlier—about reading giving him headaches—I plan to dig into that more. But he's been through a lot in the last few days, and now is not the time for a sneaking interrogation.

The shop owner shrugs. "Never too late to start. Go on and

browse. Mor, I'll get your book from the back." Neri sets the stack she's carrying on the counter, then hustles toward the rear of the shop.

"This place is new too." Bo gazes around the space.

"What did it used to be?"

"A cobbler."

"Really? Like, for shoes?"

He nods.

"Not surprised they went out of business."

The tall shelves full of stories are calling to me, but I remind myself that I have plenty of books at home I still need to read, and this errand is not about my TBR. It's about a grimoire.

And getting Bo more comfortable in town.

"Neri is a siren," I tell Bo, letting him know mythic talk is safe in her vicinity. Then I have another spark of inspiration. "She's mated to Seamus MacNamara."

He jerks his gaze to me.

"MacNamaras are selkies," he says. "A founding family."

I thought that would catch his attention.

"Yep. A selkie and a siren. Then there's Calder MacNamara, who is mated to a dragon. And of course, you met Levi, who is mated to Moira MacNamara. They're about to have their first kid. One of the reasons I'm heading your welcome committee is, he's a bit distracted at the moment with the birth coming soon. So, yeah, looks like a founding family is about to have some monsters in the line."

He gapes at me, but I have an excuse to move away when Neri reappears with a slim volume bound in leather.

We spend the next few minutes poring over the pages. Immediately, I can tell this isn't an official grimoire, seeing as how Neri can read much of the text. Grimoires are written in witch's language, meaning they are illegible to non-witches. However, the detailed descriptions of how herbs can be used in spells seem legit. This may simply be a green witch's notebook.

"I'll take it," I say, planning to consult with a few members of the Folk Haven coven to work out the legitimacy.

"Perfect. Anything else?"

"I don't ..." My words trail off as I turn to spy Bo standing by the window, a tattered paperback in his hand, the sunlight spilling in, illuminating the words he's reading.

His hair spills over his forehead, and he worries his thick lower lip between his teeth as his eyes concentrate on the page. He holds the book low, farther away than someone normally might when reading.

Trying not to startle him, I casually make my way over to him.

"Found something you like?"

He jerks, then slams the book shut and shoves it back onto the shelve as a flush blooms across his cheeks. "N-no. Not really."

He wasn't great about getting the book back in its place, and a quick glance at the protruding spine reveals that he was engrossed in a historical romance. A large-print one.

"I liked that author. Vanessa Riley. She's local to Georgia. You should get it."

He shakes his head, still blushing.

"Come on. That's the dollar shelf. Which means the book is only fifty cents for you." I tug it free and hold it out to him. "There's nothing wrong with liking a good book."

He hesitates. Then he accepts the novel from my hand, our fingers brushing.

I try not to let goose bumps overtake my body.

I pay for my text, and then Bo fishes two quarters out of his pocket.

Neri waves us off with a, "Happy reading!"

Bo is quiet for the rest of our errands, letting me take the lead, which is honestly how I prefer things. I'm not a browser. I have a list with checkboxes I want to tick off because each task completed is a burst of satisfaction.

When the backseat of my truck is full of Bo's necessities, we head back to the library, and I'm glad to see the RV—Jack and Ame went to pick it up—parked off to the side as we pull up the drive, especially with how tense Bo gets at the sight of the house.

I reach across the console, placing my hand on his shoulder. He jerks his chin to the side to stare at me as I stop a distance from the library.

"I know this is just words, and only time will help you feel more comfortable, but I don't think the house is a danger to you anymore. And if it is—if it tries to trap you—I'm here. I'm looking out for you." I squeeze his shoulder, holding his wary eyes. "Promise me, right now, that you won't leave Folk Haven without telling me first."

He swallows hard. "Why?"

"Promise me, Bo."

"Yes, ma'am. I promise."

I give him a playful glare for the *ma'am*, and then I pat his shoulder. "There you have it. You won't disappear. Because if you're missing, I'll look for you."

As I retract my hand, I find it suddenly caught in a warm, rough hold.

"I ..." he starts, then blinks and looks at where we're touching. "Thank you," he eventually rumbles.

And I get the sense Bo has never had anyone watch his back before. No one to care about what happens to him.

Well, now he does.

18

Mor

I WASN'T sure how much of a help Bo would be. Not because of his reading ability. I was being honest about the plethora of tasks that didn't require literacy.

I think I just couldn't wrap my mind around someone else doing something for this library better than I could. At best, I figured Bo would watch the front desk, dust some things, and maybe run the occasional errand, like grabbing me coffee. Helpful, but not particularly life-changing.

But, oh, was I wrong. And I'm not one to easily admit that. When you have three younger siblings, admitting fault is like bleeding in a pool of sharks.

Consider me chum because Bo, on day one, officially became invaluable.

How so?

He decided the only way he could work in this house was to get to know every inch of it. Bo started at the top, working down, exploring all nooks and crannies. That included the bathrooms. And under my vanity, he identified a pipe with a crack that was already leaking water. On the verge of bursting.

Bo shut off the water to the house, replaced the pipe, and preemptively saved my entire life's work.

If that pipe had burst, water would have rained down on a room full of books. True, I've started spelling the texts against damage. But I doubt the enchantments are strong enough to ward off full submersion in water.

When Bo told me why he needed to temporarily shut off the water, the monster apologized. To me. For doing something that would protect my books.

Meanwhile, I was on the verge of hugging him.

But that's not what employers do, so I simply thanked him for his initiative.

And this week, he's stepped up in so many ways I never thought to. Fixing a whole range of small things around the house. Mowing the lawn. Washing the windows.

He even changed the oil in my truck when he saw the Check Engine light was on during his coffee run into town.

"Ma'am." His deep voice tugs me out of my contemplation. "I'm sorry—"

"Bo," I cut him off. "Stop calling me ma'am. And stop apologizing."

"Sorry, ma'am."

I narrow my eyes at him. "Was that a joke?"

A blush races up his neck. "Force of habit."

"Fine. I'll let you off with a warning. What's up?"

"I'm headed out to get you a coffee. Want me to grab you lunch too?"

Only when he mentions food do I realize I haven't eaten anything other than a bowl of cereal for breakfast. Sometimes, I get so distracted that I forget to feed myself.

"Yes, please." I stand up from my chair and bend my spine backward, letting out a groan when I hear a series of cracks.

Bo's face goes brick red.

Yeah, maybe I shouldn't make those noises around my employees.

I search for my bag, finding it hanging off the arm of a chair, and I dig out my wallet and pull out some cash to pass to Bo. He's diligent about bringing me back the receipt, even though I told him I believed him about how much a coffee cost.

I get the sense Bo is not used to being trusted.

That's probably something to do with being a monster in Folk Haven close to two decades ago.

Even now, I know there's a decent amount of mythics in town who shy away from monsters. Ones who judge inter-mythic relationships. I've seen the sneers behind my siblings' backs when they're holding hands with their mates.

I stare at those people, so they know I saw.

So they know I have their number.

But I also don't stir shit because, to many here, I'm still an outsider. And I want to be a part of Folk Haven. Want this town to be my home in a way that the house I grew up in never was.

Maybe Bo is looking for the same.

After I hand him the cash for my coffee and food as well as the keys to my truck, he turns to go. But he pauses when I place a staying hand on his arm.

"There's enough there for you to get food for yourself too. Why don't we have lunch together when you get back?"

Bo blinks at me. "I ... all right." He nods. Then nods again, though his focus seems inward.

Is an invite to eat together really so shocking?

"It's a plan." I give him a gentle push toward the door. "And when you get back, I challenge you to interrupt me without apologizing."

His smile is small and rueful.

Though I manage to sink back into my reading, I hear the

front door open an hour later. Still, I pretend to be entirely absorbed in my work. Just to test him.

"Food's here," Bo announces.

I grin. "Good job. Let's eat on the porch."

The autumn day is lovely, sunny with only the slightest chill. Georgia falls are wonderful. An easing between seasons rather than an abrupt shift, like up in Maine, where I spent my childhood. Here, I get to enjoy the change of leaves for longer.

Bo got us bagels, and the delicious scent of poppy seeds and cream cheese rising from the bag makes my mouth water. Living in small-town Georgia means food options are limited, but I think the residents of Folk Haven have a few more options than most. Mythics from all over have relocated here and brought a variety of offerings with them.

"One-week performance review," I say in an official tone.

Bo jerks his attention to me, his eyes wide, his cheeks puffed with the massive bite he just took.

"You're doing spectacular. I give myself all the credit because I hired you." I smirk, and his shoulders relax.

After he swallows, Bo offers me a quiet, "Thank you."

This mythic is fascinating to me.

Terrifying in his monster form.

Frantic and fierce when first freed.

Lost and loud when drunk on margaritas.

Quiet, hardworking, and overly respectful since the day I hired him.

Does Bo even know what version of himself is the natural one?

More than anything, I want him to feel comfortable.

"You've been navigating the modern world for a couple of weeks now. Any questions?"

I bite my bagel, humming in appreciation of the rich flavor.

Bo stares at the wooden boards between his boots, a look of indecision on his face.

"Ask me anything." I lean over to nudge his arm with my elbow. "I swear I won't make fun of you. This is a safe porch."

"Hmm. A safe porch, huh?"

"Yep. All questions are valid, and no secrets will pass beyond those steps." I point to the three that lead down to the yard. The freshly mowed yard, thanks to Bo.

"If you say so." He takes another bite, but this time, I can tell he's contemplating what to ask. "What is a zaddy?"

I jerk, out of surprise rather than offense. "A zaddy?"

"I heard Sonya say it," he explains, naming the siren who co-owns Coffee & Claws. "I think she was talking about Levi. But I thought you said he was a leviathan."

"It's ... well, it's slang." Good thing we don't have an HR department because this is definitely not normal boss-employee talk. Still, I did say all questions were valid. "Usually referring to a hot man who is maybe middle-aged. Like"—*wow, my face is hot now*—"a guy who dresses well and you want to call him Daddy in the bedroom."

"In the—"

"While having sex," I clarify, not sure how popular *Daddy* was as a sexy term seventeen years ago.

"So, when she said Levi had zaddy energy, she was saying ..."

"That he's a hot guy with good style who'd probably have an alpha personality if you slept with him."

Bo contemplates this as he consumes the rest of his bagel. Then he stares down at the flannel and worn jeans he's sporting.

"I do not have zaddy energy," he says on a sigh.

My heart squeezes. *Is he attracted to Sonya?*

"No," I admit because I'm not going to lie to the man. "But that's not a bad thing. There're other sexy energies to have."

"What ..." He shakes his head. "Sorry. I shouldn't ask you about this, should I? You're my boss."

"Yeah. HR will have my ass," I joke.

But silently, I answer.

Cinnamon roll.

When he's not coming out of a yearslong imprisonment, the guy is quiet and kind. Bo is a *sweet on the outside, sweet on the inside* cinnamon roll that someone will devour one day.

19

Bo

I'M STANDING on Main Street, staring at the sign that reads *Never Judge a Cover*, when I hear words I can't ignore.

"Thank you, Professor Novac."

That name.

His name.

The dragon whose hoard magic trapped me for seventeen years. Who stole almost two decades of my life.

You were going to steal from him, a small voice in my head tries to remind me.

But the consternation rises so fast in my chest that the words are drowned out. I turn in the direction of the speaker, searching for the gray-haired man with purple eyes. But all I see is a white woman with long black hair who sits at a table outside of Coffee & Claws. She has a laptop in front of her and glasses perched on her nose.

As if sensing my attention, she glances up. Through the lenses, I spy a set of purple eyes.

Novac.

I'm reminded that they said the dragon was dead. But that doesn't mean that he didn't have any offspring.

I stalk up to the woman, fists clenched at my sides.

"Are you related to Dimitri Novac?" I demand, looming over her.

She flinches. The reaction doesn't give me any satisfaction. All my life, I have been scaring people. You would think that I would be used to it by now. I rock back on my heels, then step back. Giving her space but still staying to hear the answer.

"He ..." She blinks up at me. "Yes. I'm his daughter, Delta. He passed away. Did you know him?" Her head tilts with the question as she continues to peer at me.

I frown. "His house cursed me."

Her eyes widen. "You're the ... Mor told me about you. I'm so sorry. I didn't know that happened to you."

I don't like her bringing up the red-haired witch. I don't like thinking of the kind woman in this moment when I am clutching my resentment like a safety blanket.

"Your father trapped me for seventeen years," I say with disbelief. "And you didn't *know* about it?"

Delta shakes her head. "If I had known, I would've told him to free you." She shifts in her seat, gaze dropping to her laptop and then rising to meet mine again. "But I'm also not sure that *he* knew how to reverse the enchantment."

"What is that supposed to mean?"

"It means that magic doesn't always work under our direction." She waves at her laptop like it's got something to do with her hoard protection spells. "I don't doubt that the magic trapped you. But I also don't know that my father knew how to fix what had been done."

"Well, a witch did," I grunt, glaring at the ground. "He could've asked for help. I could've been freed years ago."

But why would a mythic help a monster who had broken into his house?

It's a completely valid question that, for some reason, Dimitri's daughter decides not to ask me. She doesn't bring up how I ended up in my curse. Only reasons through how I stayed there.

"You're right." She nods. "He could have asked for help. He should have. But he didn't, and I don't know why."

"And now he's gone." Giving me no one to direct all this anger at. Not when I'm also spelled against harming Sev. All this rage and nowhere to place it. Will the fury live inside me and fester?

"Yes." Delta fiddles with the corner of her laptop. "He is."

One thing that definitely doesn't help my bad mood is knowing I've made this woman uncomfortable. I just stomped up to her and started interrogating her about her dead dad. Before I can think of another thing to say, a small whimper distracts me. That's when I notice for the first time that beside Delta's chair is a carrier, and inside of it is a small dog.

The little creature is not particularly attractive. It could be called cute in an odd way. Eyes too big, snout too small, fur a strange exploding tangle.

The dog's tiny body quivers in fear.

It's scared of me.

I'm frightening a helpless animal because I'm having a temper tantrum. Because I'm grumbling at a woman who did nothing to me. Delta merely shares blood with a man that I originally wronged.

This is all my fault.

And my old friend shame comes back and takes over.

"I'm sorry," I tell the daughter of the dragon, my voice gone low. "I shouldn't have said anything. None of what happened is your fault." My eyes rest on the dog, wishing I could soothe the creature.

As if sensing my want, Delta reaches into her pocket and comes out with a tiny dog biscuit.

"I'll forgive you if you give Gigabyte a treat."

"Oh." My thick fingers fumble to accept. "Okay." Taking a knee, I slowly extend my hand. The quivering creature freezes.

Then its nose twitches.

Then it lunges forward and gobbles up the peace offering.

"There." Delta hums. "We're good." Her purple eyes capture mine. "And if there's any way I can help you get settled here, let me know."

I nod silently, then stand, turn on my heel, and stride away from the living Novac. I pass by the bookstore with all its intimidating stories that I can't read. And I keep walking until I reach the end of Main Street, where I parked Mor's truck. As I drive out of town, trees rise on the sides of the road, and I let myself pretend that I am lost in the wilderness. Try to forget that I'm returning to the scene of my crime. To the house that punished me.

I'm going back to the woman who saved me. The witch who has offered me something that I can use to leave this place.

I will work in the library.

And then, when I have enough money in my pocket, I'll leave Folk Haven forever.

20

Bo

A FEW DAYS after my confrontation with Delta, I climb out of Mor's car, which she lent me once again, and wonder why Jack directed me to a barn near the edge of town for this get-together. This support group.

I don't know what this meeting is supposed to be exactly. Only that, apparently, I am not the only one who has missed out on years of my life.

Jack and Ophelia, mates of two of Mor's siblings, were both cursed by the same sorcerer to live as animals as they acted as his magic battery. In a way, despite their captivity times being much shorter than mine, I would hazard their experiences were more traumatic. I wasn't exactly aware of the world when I was trapped in a statue. The passage of time didn't compute for me. It was just a suspended state of discomfort and anger.

They were awake, if slightly disoriented, as far as Mor explained it.

And then there's the dragon.

Lee Blaythorn. I remember him actually, though he used to

go by Sulien. He was a few years older than me and popular. That's what happens when your parents are rich and you're a handsome, pure-blooded mythic. But he disappeared a few years before I had my run in with Dimitri. I didn't know why. No one in Folk Haven knew. But it turns out, when his parents discovered he had fallen in love with a harpy, they kidnapped him and took him to a dragon colony in Antarctica and forced him to shift.

It's well known that, when dragons take their beast form, they are unable to revert back to their human form for roughly forty years. Yet, somehow, twenty years later, Lee is back and looking very humanlike.

There's definitely more to that story, but I figure there's probably more to all of ours.

Is that what we're here to do today? Share our stories?

Well, joke is on them—because I can't.

I rub my throat, as if I could feel the binding Sev laid on me, while I walk past a couple more cars parked on a gravel pull-off. My feet take me to the barn, where I spy Jack standing beside a short blonde woman, a white man with a thick brown beard, and a Black man with broad shoulders.

When I get close, Jack steps forward and begins to point. Starting with me.

"Bo, you know Ophelia. And this is Lee." He points to the bearded man. "And that's Xavier." He finishes with the tall Black man.

Concise introductions done, he steps back next to Ophelia, who I met when she came to the library with Mor's brother the other day.

"All right now, you can use any of the machines that you want. But don't be bringing out that super strength on them. These are delicate pieces of machinery." The warning comes from Xavier as he pulls out a key and unlocks the door to the barn.

"Machines?" I ask, still not sure what exactly we hope to accomplish in this gathering.

"Our mates want us to talk about our feelings. What it's like to lose years." Lee is the one who offers this through his thick beard. His voice is scratchy and rough. A lot different from the pretty boy I remember from high school. "Figured we could do it while not staring at each other."

As he finishes explaining, Xavier opens the large door, and inside, I spy something beautiful.

Pinball machines.

Rows and rows of pinball machines.

"Welcome to my hoard."

The scene starts to make sense. If Xavier is friends with Lee, then there's a high chance he's a dragon. Most dragons pick some kind of item that they hoard.

But I've never heard of a dragon hoarding pinball machines.

Though it seems like a much better option to me than the massive amounts of scrap metal Dimitri had piled high in his home.

As I step over the threshold, I realize that this barn likely has the same magic seeped into its old wooden planks as the house Mor lives in. And if any of us were to attempt to steal one of these pinball machines, chances are, the protections would come to life and enact some type of punishment that would be just as bad as what I experienced.

Silently, I try to make my intentions clear to the dragon magic in this place.

The owner of this hoard has invited me here. I plan to be respectful to everything in this room. I will take nothing that is not already mine. Please don't hurt me.

"I ... I've never played pinball before." This gentle confession comes from Ophelia. She blinks around the room with big eyes, taking in all the colorful machines and missing the way that Xavier gapes at her.

Lee gives his friend an elbow to the ribs, and the guy clears the shock off his face before the small firebird turns her attention to him.

Xavier clears his throat and offers her a kind smile. "Well then, you're in for a treat. It's a pretty easy game to learn. But you're gonna have a lot of competition to get the high score." He waves her toward a game with a steamboat theme. "Let me show you how it's done. Then I'll leave you all to it."

Not too long later, the four of us set up at four machines that are side by side, and soon, I realize the genius of Lee's choice.

We don't have to look at each other. We don't even have to talk to each other. We all get to focus on something fun. Something that all of us either knows how to do, no matter how long we were away, or can figure out easily.

"Before the sorcerer, I grew up pretty sheltered," Ophelia offers as she starts her game over. "My dad didn't let me leave our homestead. That's why I've never played pinball before. I didn't know a lot of things about the modern world even though I had only been trapped for three years." Her voice is quiet but strong as she slips a quarter into the machine.

Xavier gave each of us a bag of his own money, grinning and saying that he wasn't going to charge us for the use of his hoard and this was easier than having to open up the change slot for every round that we played.

"How's it been?" I ask, counting her as the bravest among us since she shared first. "Trying to learn all the modern stuff? Mor showed me her phone, but I was worried that I'd crack the screen."

Ophelia tosses me a grin as she presses the buttons on the side of her machine. "Smartphones *are* confusing. But once you get the hang of using one, it's really fun. All the information that you can search online. I get lost on it sometimes, and Broderick has to gently take my phone from me just so I realize what is going on in the world around me. And don't worry so much about breaking the screen. I've dropped my phone while flying, and it still survived." She slips her hand into her back pocket and pulls one of the devices out to show me no cracks on the glass. "Google is also great when someone says something I don't understand."

Jack snorts beside her, but the sound doesn't come out as derisive. More like he thinks the slang is ridiculous.

"Town is different." This observation comes from Lee. "I know what it was like. When you were here before. What the people thought like back then." The dragon keeps his intense blue stare on the game in front of him, but I feel like he's digging into my brain and pulling out the questions that mean the most to me. "Not gonna tell you everyone's changed. But the close-minded ones, they have less power than they used to."

"Really?" I hear the doubt in my own voice.

"Your Shelly witches got that house in Wing territory. That was a big step."

All three of us stare at Lee.

"Big step toward what?" Ophelia asks, her voice quiet, as if whatever we're discussing might be illicit.

"Getting rid of the divides," he explains. "Blocking where we can live. Mythics are pushing back because it doesn't make sense."

He's saying what I never would out loud. Thoughts I had whenever I passed from the Claw section into the Monster one. Would my mermaid mother have stayed if we hadn't been shuffled off to the farthest corner of Lake Galen? Maybe there would've been less resentment from my werewolf father if he could've remained closer to the pack?

"Even if they get rid of the boundaries," I say, "that doesn't mean the groups will suddenly forget that I'm a monster."

"The groups?" The question comes from Ophelia.

I get the sense that she's the most curious of us. Possibly the most innocent too.

"The pack." I keep my eyes away from Jack and focused on the quarter that I'm slipping into my machine. "Doesn't matter that I'm half. Doesn't matter that the moon calls to me."

"I'm not with a pack."

I jerk my head up at that and stare over at Jack, his dark gaze meeting mine, his face revealing nothing.

"You're not?"

He's got two to choose from, according to Griffith. Why would he opt to be a lone wolf?

"No. My first alpha was the one who sold me to the sorcerer. Not looking to sign myself over to another." His voice is flat on the confession, but I get the sense fury roils just underneath. "Both packs here owe me."

Jack's attention returns to his machine as he starts to play another round, as if he isn't rocking my world with every single statement he makes.

"If you want to join one, I will make sure that you can." He flicks his eyes to me and then away again. "But if you just want someone to run with under the moon, then you have me."

I swallow. And then I have to do it again because my entire throat is blocked by emotion. I don't think this wolf understands how much he just offered me.

Even my father never ran with me on the night of a full moon. Since I was thirteen, I change on that night, just like every other wolf does. And on that night each month, when wolves join together, I run alone.

"Thank you. I ... I would like to run with you."

And when I glance Jack's way, I swear I see the start of a smile on the corner of his mouth.

21

Bo

CLEANING the library turns out to be a meditative task. I assumed I would hate it in here. That resentment would fester in my chest as I worked to care for the source of the power that had originally trapped me.

But ever since I encountered Delta, I'm having trouble blaming the house. The building had no vendetta against me. The protective magic didn't seek me out as I was innocently living my life.

I invaded this home and attempted to steal. The house simply protected the occupants the best that it could.

Though I find I still hold a grudge against Dimitri, even with him in the grave. Even if I deserved to be punished for my actions, I think many would argue that confinement to a statue state for seventeen years did not meet the severity of the crime.

He could have told someone. The Council or another witch might have freed me a decade earlier and then handed out a more reasonable punishment.

But the dragon is gone, and I have my agency back.

Focusing too much on what I lost will just poison the life I'm trying to rebuild.

Each day, the fury grows more muted, and I'm coming to realize I want to do better this time around. Be the leading role in my life now rather than a side character in someone else's.

I find a book abandoned on one of the reshelving carts. Picking up the leather tome, I hold it at arm's length and squint my eyes to read the title.

Fairies of Medieval Forests.

I know what section that belongs in.

Through the entryway, past the grimoire room and into the histories room, I seek out the shelf committed to fairy texts. The second shelf from the floor, there's a space where a book could have been removed. I squint to check the shelving number on the spine more than once and compare it to the books beside the gap. I do this check no less than three times, just to be sure I'm not misreading the numbers. By all accounts, that's where the book should go.

When I slip it home, I feel a sense of satisfaction. A small task, but worth the slight ache behind my eyes.

When I make to retrace my steps, the front door opens just as I'm passing through the entryway. I stand tall, pull up a smile, and fold my hands behind my back.

A slim man with slightly mussed hair and thick-rimmed glasses steps inside, a curious look in his eyes. His stare meets mine just as I nod in greeting.

"Welcome. How can I help you?" And I silently beg it's not a complicated question I'd need to bother Mor with. I want to show her I can work here without hand-holding.

"Hello. I'm Jaylen Breen. I have an appointment with Mor Shelly. This is her library, correct?" The man fiddles with the cuffs of his shirt and offers a hopeful smile.

He must have a major research query. In the time I've been here, I've seen Mor meet with a handful of patrons. Overheard them talking through their research. Watched her guide them through the stacks as they tugged multiple volumes off the shelves and paged through them together.

The visitors tend to be witches, and I take comfort in the fact that even if I had a PhD in literature studies, I still wouldn't be able to help them. If you're not a witch, you can't read witch's language.

Dr. Anna Lim, Jack's mom, is a human woman and linguistics professor at Ramla University. She's attempting to study witch's language from a mortal perspective, but from what I've heard, it's a slow-going task. She claims the books glamor themselves, and even when the symbols are revealed, they move.

"I'll take you to her." I throw a thumb over my shoulder, figuring the witch is where she normally is.

The study is in the back of the house, with a wide, multi-paneled window that faces toward Lake Galen. There's a large table, perfect for spreading books out, and tucked in the corner is a computer, set up for cataloging the books. I'm still baffled by the changes in the internet while I was gone.

Seventeen years ago, dial-up was the most common way to connect, and my dad never bothered to get internet installed in the trailer. I only ever saw people using it at businesses or on TV.

Mor sat beside me the other day, showing me how to use Google and email.

I tried to pay attention, but her shoulder kept brushing mine, and her hair smelled like warm roses. Plus, squinting at the screen gave me a headache, so I preferred to let my eyes unfocus and just listened to her speak.

Mor isn't at the computer now. Instead, she has a thick volume open, a notebook beside it that she's scribbling in, and her lush red hair is piled in a haphazard bun on top of her head.

I clear my throat. Then I do it a second time, louder, because she didn't seem to hear me the first.

Her head pops up, her messy bun wobbling with the abrupt movement.

"Bo. Sorry. Did you need me?"

Yes. All the time.

I blink that needy thought away and step to the side, gesturing Mr. Breen forward. "Your appointment is here."

"My appointment?" Her brows dip, and her full mouth purses.

I can practically see her rifling through an internal catalog of dates, trying to recall what topic this visitor asked for help with.

"Not appointment exactly." The man steps forward, hand outstretched and smile wide. "I'm Jaylen Breen. I work with Broderick at Ramla. We texted about getting lunch today."

Mor's brows rise as my stomach drops.

Getting lunch? As in going out on a date?

I reevaluate the man, studying him more thoroughly than when I thought he was only a patron.

The top of his head is level with my shoulder, and he has a similar distracted-professor look that Mor's brother maintains. As nice as her sibling is, I find his academic credentials intimidating. What would he think if he learned that I never made it past the seventh grade? Doubt he would be pushing me to set up lunch dates with his sister, not like the professor here, with his interested smile and tweed jacket.

"Oh. Jaylen. Of course. I can't believe I forgot."

Mor's face takes on a pink hue, and I wonder if she's embarrassed by her gaffe or flushing that pretty color because the man in front of her is someone she's interested in.

Of course she is. He's probably smart and funny, and he knows how to use the internet.

"No worries. I understand what it's like to fall down a

research rabbit hole." He waves at her books. "But I also know that's hungry business. You up for taking a break to get a quick bite? I have a few hours before I need to be back on campus for my next class."

A class that he teaches. A class I wouldn't even be qualified to attend.

"Food. Yes. That's a good idea." Mor pushes to her feet, only to bend backward enough to set off a series of cracks in her spine while also pressing her full breasts against the clinging fabric of her sweater.

Then her eyes meet mine.

"Hey, Bo, would you be okay with watching the library for an hour? If anyone shows up, looking for me, you can give them my card or tell them to wait until I'm back."

I scratch the back of my neck, then fist my hand and tuck both of them into my pockets before Breen gets a look at my webbed fingers. "Sure."

Mor hits me with a big, broad smile, and I stutter through my next breath.

"You're the best. I can bring you something back for lunch."

"Don't trouble yourself," I mumble.

"No trouble." She circles the table and tugs out one of my hands, and then, like the webbing spread between my fingers bothers her none, she drops the skeleton key for the front door into my palm and tucks my fingers back around it. The metal is warm from being in the pocket of her jeans. "Remind me that I need to make you a copy of that."

All I can manage is a nod, then remain standing as still as the statue I used to be as Mor falls into step beside the intelligent man escorting her out for food.

I've never been so jealous of another living creature in my life.

22

Mor

THE PROBLEM with going on a lunch date in a small town is that everyone at the café we choose knows me. The barista—who makes a new latte concoction for me without asking because she knows I rarely ever drink the same thing twice—flits her eyes between Jaylen and me. A little smile playing around her lips widens when he holds out cash for my order before I can remember what pocket I stuck my credit card into.

"You two take a seat, and I'll bring your drinks out," the siren sings. Okay, she doesn't actually sing the words. If she did, we'd both forget what came out of her mouth less than a minute later.

One of the mythic's interesting traits. Also why sailors used to crash their boats on rocky shores. They wanted to get closer, hear the music again, because they couldn't recall the exact sound of it, only that it was the loveliest tune they had ever heard.

"Thanks so much, Lily." Jaylen reads the moniker off her name tag as he stuffs his change in the *don't tip cows, tip me* jar.

Nice to waitstaff. Generous tipper.

Those are both green flags.

And still, when we settle at a two-person table by the window and exchange small talk about books we like and his work and mine, I search for a spark that's not there.

It's not that I'm seeking out a fated mate. There's no definitive lore stating that witches have or should expect a destined lover. So, no, I'm not looking for some sign from the gods.

I'm simply hoping for a touch of attraction. On my part.

But no. Nothing.

I can look at Jaylen and say he's good-looking. That he's successful, that he's generous.

But there's no part of me that can picture us in a bed together. Not even kissing.

This is why I hate dating. It's not that I don't want a partner. It's that I do, and no one, not ever, has felt right. Plenty of the people I've gone out with should have been tempting to me. For their mind, or looks, or personality. I'm not a virgin, having slept with a few in the hopes that would get the spark burning. But at the most, all I've ever ended up wanting was friendship.

Jaylen is the same. I could envision doing trivia nights with him. Inviting him over for happy hour on the dock. Maybe going to a bookstore together. Nothing sensual though.

I'm not broken, I remind my despondent self. *Just different.*

I'll love someone someday. I'm sure of it.

"Your library is impressive," Jaylen says, his words catching my attention enough to fish me out of my despondency. "When I first heard about it, I thought you'd have only a few shelves of books. But that back there was the real thing. How did you even find so many grimoires?"

When Broderick first set this up, he told me Jaylen is from a family of witches, though the guy has a low level of power and more interest in the political science he teaches at Ramla. I agree with my brother's assessment, noting only mild interest, flaring pink on his emotion grid.

"My sister Ame and I road-tripped around the country for a few years. We stopped at every used bookstore we could find." I lean forward in my seat, wrapping my hands around the almond peppermint latte the barista dropped off not long ago. "Did you know grimoires disguise themselves sometimes? A lot of the time actually."

"What do you mean, disguise themselves?"

"If you think about it, since witch's language is legible only to witches, to anyone else, grimoires would appear to be books of gibberish. And books of gibberish get thrown away."

"Sure." Jaylen sips his drink and smiles encouragingly.

"Like many magical things"—such as enchanted houses—"they can take on a touch of self-awareness. And even personalities. And a self-aware object does not want to be thrown away." My eyes track to the window as I think back on all the books I've collected during my travels. "So, what little awareness and magic they had resulted in them glamouring themselves. Just enough to appear to be a normal book, typed in a legible language."

"Did they reveal themselves to you? Is that how you have them all?"

"No. I'm not sure the books had that much understanding of the world. But they do give off a slight magical signature if you know how to look for it. Ame and I trained ourselves to spot the disturbance in the air."

"Fascinating."

I certainly think so, and I'm happy another agrees.

"Do you ever worry about a bad character misusing the library?"

"You mean, like, damaging a book?"

He chuckles, though I find book damages no laughing

matter. "I meant the spells. You have a lot of powerful knowledge in one place."

"Oh." I pause to think about his question as our lunches get set down in front of us. It's not that this is the first time I'm considering it. But I know not all share my stance. "I tend to be of the belief that tools—for the most part—are not inherently good or bad. People misusing them decide. And we shouldn't get rid of tools just because a bad character might get ahold of them. But also, the library has built-in wards to keep out anyone truly nasty who wants to harm people."

Jaylen hums in agreement. "I like the way your mind works."

That's a top-notch compliment. Much better than if he'd remarked on my hair or complexion or outfit. I'm proud of my mind.

But that doesn't mean I want to date Jaylen.

He smiles at me over the small table, the skin around his eyes crinkling and his broad mouth stretching wide to show off a set of healthy teeth.

Why do I feel nothing in response?

Why do I always feel nothing?

Is there something wrong with me?

I see my siblings with their partners, and I know I want that kind of supportive love. But I also long for the passion. The need they have for their mates.

A passionate need I've never experienced and I'm beginning to doubt I ever will.

Hell, at this point, I would settle for the barest flicker of attraction. Something to prove I'm not destined to die alone.

But maybe that is my destiny. Three happy siblings and one lonely spinster who never learned how to love.

23

Mor

WHEN I RETURN from my date, I enter the house through the back door to drop the food off in the kitchen before seeking out my employee. I find Bo at the front counter, tongue pinched between his teeth as he repairs a book spine. I'm quiet as I approach, not wanting to startle him and mess up his project. When I'm only a handful of feet away, I pause, and then I stop.

He carefully spreads the glue and presses the pages into place, holding them steady as the glue dries. His chest expands on a particularly deep inhale, and a moment later, his head pops up, eyes locking with mine.

"Mor." He straightens. "You're back."

"I am. With food. You like the roast beef sandwich from Coffee & Claws, right?" I hold up the to-go bag.

Bo's nostrils flare, and my curious mind wonders once more what type of mythics make up his monster. Most Of the Claw mythics have heightened scent. With his size, he could easily be part bear shifter.

"That's my favorite. Thank you."

"Thank you for looking after the library on your own. I know being in this building still has to be uncomfortable for you."

Especially when, every night, he goes out to sleep in the RV rather than moving into one of the open bedrooms upstairs.

Bo's eyes track around the entryway, as if expecting the house to move.

Everything remains still.

"I can take over." I circle the counter and offer him the food. "Take a lunch break."

"I can eat later. If you need to finish what you were working on when that guy showed up."

"Nope. I'm good. Go eat, I insist."

Bo hesitates for another moment, then gives a nod, collects his food, and heads toward the back of the house. He may have found some type of truce with the library, but I've noticed the monster always eats his midday meal out on the dock.

I wonder though if that has less to do with this building and more to do with wanting a slice of freedom in his day after being trapped for so long. If I took the time to focus on and sift through his emotions, I might have a better idea, but I pull back on that urge.

Bo deserves privacy.

Still, as I settle on the stool behind the desk and take a closer look at his project, I think back on Jaylen's words. About villains using the library for nefarious deeds. Knowing Bo like I do, he's low on my list for potential baddies.

But I'm almost certain he *did* do something bad. He entered this house without permission and tried to steal from Dimitri's hoard. Why else would the ward magic have attacked him?

I have a good guess as to what Bo was searching for. Likely the same item that Hamish wanted to get his hands on when he ensorcelled our household to sleep while he crept through the halls. Just like the house had turned Bo to metal, it also fought back against Hamish.

The way the walls came apart to capture the selkie was intimidating, but compared to the complete imprisonment of Bo, kind of mild. My best guess is, since the dragon no longer lives in the house, the protection magic is still here but diminished.

At least for now. Who knows what housing all these magical texts in one place will do?

My mind circles back to Bo and what he was likely trying to take.

The golden apple.

The god object.

One of the reasons I didn't hesitate to hire him is that the apple isn't here anymore. Once Lucky alerted us to its presence, we took the mystical object from its hiding place in the wall, and I have it stored in a high-security lockbox at Wolf Trust Bank.

But Bo doesn't know that.

And he's made no move to find it again.

Is it because he's properly chastised from his first punishment?

Or was he never truly interested in obtaining it?

The mystery pesters me for the rest of the afternoon, as I help a coven sister find spells for dream walking and as I brush past Bo throughout the day. He also seems tense. I wonder if it's because he senses how my mind is stuck on him. How I'm working up to a kind of interrogation.

When I flip the front-door sign to *Closed*, I've made my decision.

"Bo, can we talk?"

He blinks at me from behind the counter, eyes owlishly large. "Did I mess something up? I'm sorry. I'll fix it."

My heart squeezes at his immediate assumption that he's in the wrong.

"No. You're fine."

And because I don't want him overly anxious during what I suspect is going to be a tough conversation, I wave for him to follow me back through the house. As always, I hear his heavy footsteps and take a strange comfort in their clomping.

When we're in the cool fall evening, the sun dipping behind the trees, I lean on the porch railing and face Bo, bracing my hands by my hips in hopes that my open posture will set him at ease.

"I get the feeling this is going to be a very one-sided conversation, but I'm hoping you might be able to lend some weight to a theory I have," I start off.

"Yes, ma'am."

I purse my lips, but don't chide him. "What were you trying to take the night you were turned into a metal statue?"

Bo's eyes go wide again, his mouth popping open, but no words emerge. After a breath, his jaw snaps shut, his neck flexes with a swallow, and he drops his eyes, along with his shoulders. The whole posture screams of shame.

"Bo, please look at me."

He drags his gaze upward, and I swear I can see a silent apology.

"Do you *want* to tell me what happened that night?"

"I ..." He clears his throat. "I do."

"But you can't," I guess.

He doesn't respond. In a way, that is all I need. I nod, and I reach for the locket of spell powder around my neck. I pop it open and rub a small pinch over the palms of my hands.

Bo watches the process with hesitant fascination.

I extend my red-powdered hands to him. "If you let me touch you, I can get a clear read on your emotions. You won't need to say anything. Just feel how you feel as I ask my questions." I keep space between us. "But I won't force you. It's your choice."

"You can read emotions?"

I nod. "But I've trained to shield myself. So most of the time I'm not. I don't like to invade people's privacy."

How will he react? I can easily see Bo turning his back on me. Quitting his job because he doesn't want to be around someone with a power like mine.

The thought brings a pang of sadness to my chest.

Bo blinks once, then steps forward and sets his hands in mine, wrapping his webbed fingers around my palms.

The trust is an act of bravery, and I remind myself not to abuse it as Bo's emotional grid flares to life in more vivid detail than I could ever hope to achieve on my own without potion powder and touch. The twisting rainbow of threads reach toward me, and I fight the urge to shield myself, instead choosing to focus on each of them. To feel what Bo feels so I don't misinterpret anything by only relying on color.

Time to ask my questions and see what emotions respond.

I breathe slow and evenly, tempted to smile when I realize Bo's inhales are matching the pace I set.

"Were you enchanted not to discuss that night?" I ask.

Surprise fills me, flashing lime green.

Relief. Lilac.

"You were," I respond for him.

Bo smiles hesitantly, along with a turquoise flare of eagerness.

"Were you told to hurt anyone?"

Emerald of shock.

Charcoal gray of disgust, which twists my stomach.

"No on that," I say, and Bo lets out a deep breath. "Were you here looking for an item?"

Daffodil yellow of hope.

"A golden apple?"

Gold of triumph.

Burnt orange of guilt.

My guess was correct, but he feels bad about it. Like he didn't want to steal the golden apple, but felt as though he needed to.

"Were you sent here by Sev?"

Bo stumbles back a step, dropping my hands and breaking the connection.

But not before a flaring tangle of colors reached me with shadows of the emotions they represented.

Saffron of fury.

Cobalt of devastation.

Ochre of betrayal.

Cream of hopelessness.

And the searing white of fear.

I nod, keeping my composure as I remind myself that bombardment wasn't mine.

Bo stands stiffly before me.

"I thought that might be the case. He came here for a meeting once, but wouldn't come in the house. And I've heard rumors that he collects things. It would make sense that he sent someone else into danger on his behalf."

"We ... we shouldn't have done that. You shouldn't—" He coughs, eyes watering. After swallowing multiple times, he manages to say, "I want you to be safe."

I study Bo, experiencing my own mixture of anger and frustration. But not with him.

"I'm sorry you're still bespelled." I wipe the powder off on my pants so Bo doesn't have to worry about me still reading him. "And if he ever tries to make you do something you don't want to do again, please come to me. You aren't alone."

"I'm not fired?" He whispers the words, as if speaking them too loudly might make me change my mind.

"No, Bo. I know what it's like to be manipulated by someone

with stronger magic. I won't hold it against you." I step close but keep my hands to myself. "The apple isn't here anymore, in case he presses you."

Then, because I realize Bo probably needs a moment to himself, I give him one more parting comment before heading inside to wash my hands. "No matter what happened in the past, I'm glad you're here, Bo. I like having you around."

In the corner of my eye, I swear I see the black of need.

But I must be mistaken.

24

Mor

"I'm off. Thanks for your hard work today, Assistant Librarian." I give Bo a salute as I slip my purse over my shoulder.

His snow-pale cheeks redden. "You don't have to call me that."

"I know I don't. But I'm a librarian. You're my assistant. Therefore, you are an assistant librarian." Holding his eyes is easy when they're such a pretty blue. "I'm being accurate. Feel free to use it on a résumé for future jobs."

Bo slips his hand up to the back of his neck, massaging the thick column. The first few times I watched him make the move, I thought his neck might be paining him. Now I theorize it's a move he makes when he's embarrassed.

"Do you not want to be an assistant librarian?"

He stares downward, still tugging on his neck. "I-I guess I do."

I'm still baffled how such a big, powerful, conventionally attractive man could be so insecure. What kind of life did he have in that trailer? What world did he live in seventeen years ago that curved his shoulders with so much invisible weight?

Now, it's not like I wish Bo were a cocky asshole. We've got enough straight white cis mystics who think they are the gods' gift to the world.

But the more I get to know Bo, the more of his kind core I spy under his stony exterior. Every workday, he shows up and is helpful, humble, and curious.

Three of the most attractive qualities in a person. I find I like knowing he's nearby. That he's watching over my library when I get distracted by some half-legible passage about god objects in an ancient grimoire.

I trust Bo.

Which means he's more than earned the title of assistant librarian.

"We should get name tags," I declare, embracing the sudden urge to emblazon the job title on a little metal pin that he can wear for everyone to see. Where he can't doubt the truth. "One for me and one for you. It'll make it easier on patrons." That last bit is bullshit. Most everyone who comes here is a local or a professor at Ramla. They already know my name, and Bo's is easy enough to remember.

But who cares? Name tags are happening.

"Uh ... okay?"

"I'll order them next week."

Bo drops his hand and nods. Then he steps out from behind the front desk and follows me toward the front door. Even though he was a few steps behind me, somehow, he manages to grab the knob before I do and holds the door open for me, showing some of that Southern gentleman charm I didn't think I cared for until Bo started doing it.

"In addition to name tags," I say, not sure this is the best segue, but I keep going, "you also have access to health insurance. As a full-time employee."

"Oh. Okay."

Now for the tough part. The theory I hope to broach without making Bo retreat.

"That includes vision."

"Hmm." The hum sounds like he's humoring me. Because he doesn't know why I'm bringing this up.

I sigh, then dive into the deep end. "Bo, I think you get headaches when you read because of your eyesight. Not because of your intelligence. You should schedule an appointment. It's fully covered under your insurance."

I hand him a business card for Galen's Gaze, Folk Haven's optometry.

"Oh." He swallows hard and accepts the card. Then he squints at the tiny text.

Proving my point.

I grasp his wrist and guide him to flip the card over, where I wrote the phone number in bold, large print.

"Thank you," he mumbles, cheeks reddening. When I release his hand, he tucks the card into his back pocket.

"Any fun plans for tonight?" I change the subject as I lock up the house. "I can give you a ride to town if you need one."

"Maybe. I ..."

When I turn, I find Bo frowning down at the toes of his boots. The scuffed footwear he found at a secondhand store is probably better for yard work than working inside at a library all day. But when he asked about needing more professional attire, I pointed out that, most days, I'm in leggings and sweatshirts. As long as Bo is comfortable in his clothes, that's all I want for him.

After years of discomfort, he deserves it.

"You what?" I prompt him when he hesitates to finish his sentence.

"Never mind. I can walk."

"Walk to town?" I jingle my car keys in the air. "I just told you I'd take you. I don't mind."

"You probably have plans to get to," he mumbles.

"My only plans are with the cereal aisle in the grocery store. I'm low on Chex Mix."

He perks up. "You're getting food? That's what I need too."

Doesn't surprise me. He's a big guy, and the RV has limited pantry space.

"Perfect." I wave him to follow me to my car. "We'll go shopping together. Drive all the food back right after so nothing spoils."

Bo grunts in agreement, but before I realize my normal shields have relaxed, I catch the lemon yellow of eagerness, paired with rosy longing.

This guy must be pretty hungry.

Our drive from the library to the supermarket is quiet, only broken by the radio station playing Top 40 hits. I turn the volume up a few notches. "Music. That's something you might want to catch up on," I offer, figuring a few three-minute songs are easier to digest than the entire internet. "This is Taylor Swift."

Bo's brows pop up. "I know her. She's got that song about teardrops on her guitar."

"Wow." I give a dry chuckle. "That takes me back."

"It does?"

"Yeah. That was her first big hit. But she's had tons more. And her career ... actually, she's a pretty good place to start to get an idea of the evolutions in pop culture." I toss Bo a quick grin. "What do you say? Want to hear about the last seventeen years of T. Swift history?"

From the corner of my eye, I swear I see a twitch toward a smile on his mouth.

"Please. Educate me."

So, that's how we spend the rest of the car ride and all the time in the produce section of the supermarket that sits techni-cally just outside of town limits. I walk Bo through awards show drama, and toxic label contracts, and musical genre shifts, and A-list dating, and everything else Taylor-related he would've heard about if not for spending years as a statue.

He laughs at the funny parts and growls in outrage when I describe the injustices.

"I'll play you a few of my favorites tomorrow. Before anyone gets to the library."

"But only if they're Taylor's Version," Bo insists, and I smile in response.

He pushes the cart behind me as I add foodstuffs to a growing pile.

We turn down the cereal aisle, and I seek out the Chex Mix. Some people like to snack on chips, but I like to munch on a bowl of cinnamon breakfast food. Once I toss two of the extra-large boxes in the cart, I turn to find Bo holding a box of Lucky Charms, frowning at the front.

"What's up? Is it damaged?"

Bo blinks, then places it back where he found it. "No. I just …" His eyes sweep the cereal aisle. "I recognize the brands, but it's like they all decided to redo their boxes in one night. Familiar but different. It's eerie."

His hands return to the cart handle, knuckles white. Before, Bo seemed interested in my Taylor Swift saga. Eager to learn about what changes occurred. But now he's back to looking lost.

I wish I could ease the strangeness of this time for him.

"What's your favorite food?" I ask.

Bo's brows crinkle. "My favorite food?"

"Yep. Favorite food that's sold in a grocery store."

"I guess … barbecue potato chips."

"Perfect. Let's go." I march down the aisle and scan for the one I want, knowing Bo will follow. When we reach the chip selection, I point to the Lays Barbeque chips. "These. Or another kind?"

"Those." He nods. "Yeah, those."

I grab one of the bags off the shelf. "Is the logo different?"

He glances at it, then at the tiles beneath our feet with their dull shine. "Yeah."

"Close your eyes."

Bo's brows crinkle again, but he does as told. There, in the middle of the supermarket, I tear open the bag and pull out a single chip.

With a gentle knuckle, I tap the bottom of his chin. "Open."

His lips part. I place the chip on his wide tongue.

"Chew. Swallow. Tell me how the taste is."

Bo follows my instructions, surprisingly obedient. "Good," he rumbles. "Just like I remember."

I grin and still am when he blinks his eyes open and stares at me, confusion a fog in his eyes and in his aura.

"A lot will look different," I explain. "But under the surface, past the distractions, I think you'll find a lot of the good things are still the same."

Bo blinks, and then he lets a hesitant smile claim his mouth before plucking another chip from the open bag and crunching down on it. I situate the chips in the kiddie seat of the cart so Bo can keep snacking as we shop.

"Any reason chips are your favorite food?" I ask offhandedly, my main focus on checking a dozen eggs for any cracks.

"Never thought about it," Bo says. Then, after a pause, he goes on. "I think it's because of my dad."

That gets my attention, but I try not to show how piqued my interest is as I carefully set the eggs next to his chips.

"They were his favorite too?" I hazard the guess.

Bo shrugs. "Maybe. But I remember when my dad had some extra cash, he'd take me out for subs, and sometimes, he'd tell me I could get a bag of chips. Only if he was in a really good mood though. Guess I associate chips with my dad being happy. Which was a rare thing."

Is he part of the reason that Bo is hesitant? Did he teach his son manners, or did he teach him to be afraid?

"What about your mom?" I stare at the rows of butter, but I can't see them when I just want Bo to keep talking. "Did she ever treat you to some food?" *Did she give you love on the days when your father wasn't happy?*

"Don't remember anything. She left when I was four. A mermaid who said this lake was too small for her. Not sure where she went."

"You didn't keep in touch?" I think I know the answer before I even ask the question, but my heart aches to find some ray of happiness in Bo's past life.

"No."

An uncomfortable silence settles between us, and Bo doesn't reach for any more chips.

So, of course I blurt out the first thought that comes to mind. "If it helps you feel less alone, I just want to say, my parents are both horrible. Like, truly terrible beings. I'm not sure they are capable of loving anyone other than themselves and each other."

Bo's brow furrows. "But ... they have four kids."

"No," I mutter. "They had four experiments."

25

Bo

My feet stumble as I trip over that word.

Experiments.

"What does that mean?" I ask the question slowly, not sure I want the answer while also needing to know.

There's an urge in my chest to learn every detail about Mor Shelly. To tuck the facts away like little treasures.

All the more precious if the pieces of knowledge come from her pain because her sharing them means I have some of her trust along with them.

That's something I've realized about Georgiana. She trusted that I would do anything, be anything for her. But she didn't give truly deep parts of herself to me. Only some of her truth, but not all.

Not like Mor is doing right now, in this grocery store as she stares at yogurts.

"My parents are both witches. Strong ones. They are fascinated by spells." Her throat bobs with a hard swallow. "If they hadn't been born with magic, I know they would have become sorcerers, stealing it from any mythic they could find."

"How do you know that?" I rasp the question, not asking because I doubt her, but because there's a sickening note behind the surety in her voice.

Mor flicks her eyes to me, then away. "Because they had plenty of power, but they still used a leeching spell on me." She straightens her shoulders, then reaches for a four-pack of strawberry-flavored Greek yogurt. "I was twelve when I got my powers. It took me two years to figure out how to build shields. After that, they couldn't take anything, but only because it seemed like I had nothing left to give. I trained my powers to present as dormant. They thought they had drained me."

I'm going to be sick.

My mother left me.

My father ignored me.

But neither of them *used* me.

"Mor—"

"I was stupid."

"No—"

"Yes, I was. Stupid and selfish. Because I convinced myself I was the only one at risk. That Broderick and Anthony and A-Ame"—her voice cracks on her sister's name—"were safe. That they would only leech from me."

"They did it to all of you?"

She nods. "Male witches take longer to age into their powers. But Ame, she was just a little girl, and they ... have you noticed how her skin looks sunburned?"

I nod, recalling the redness on the youngest Shelly's arms. I figured it was because she liked to be outside and forgot to apply sunscreen.

"That's this." Mor fingers the locket around her neck. The little piece of jewelry holds the red powder she coated her hands in before reading my emotions. "A special concoction for us Shelly witches. Helps to strengthen and focus our powers."

"How ..." I'm not even sure what I'm asking.

How does that red powder connect to reddened skin?

"They were bathing her in it. Scrubbing it into her skin. Trying to cause her powers to manifest before puberty." Mor lets out a chuckle with no humor. "An experiment. And it worked. She was exhibiting magic really early."

"That's sick."

Mor nods and tucks the locket into the collar of her shirt. "When I found out, I told them the same. Screamed it. My mother ... she just waved her hand like I was a fly. Told me to stop being dramatic." Mor tucks a wayward red curl behind her ear. "My siblings, me—I don't think we registered in their minds as individual beings. To my parents, we were simply extensions of themselves. To be used how they wanted."

"What happened? Between you and them?"

"When I found out what was happening with Ame, I swore a blood oath that I would sabotage all my parents' spells if they experimented on her or the twins again. It was the only threat I knew they'd care about. So, they stopped, and when I was sixteen, I emancipated myself, and I took her and my brothers away."

"They let you go?"

"I'm not sure they noticed. They didn't fight me about it. They aren't the fighting kind. They're like fucked-up magical scientists."

"Have you seen them since you left?"

Mor shrugs. "A few times. Not because I wanted to. But Ame and I had to go back to the town they lived in because a friend was storing my overflow of books while we traveled to find more. They didn't attack us or threaten us. They seemed almost amused. Like we were a set of Pinocchios, wandering around the world, telling everyone we were real boys."

"They sound like sociopaths."

Mor nods and silently leads the way to the checkout. As we load our groceries onto the belt and the clerk scans everything, I can't help studying the witch.

She might not have been trapped in a statue form for years, but it sounds like she knows exactly how it feels to be helpless and unable to escape.

Maybe that's why she's so quick to assist me.

I'm both grateful to her and agitated at the thought that Mor might only want to be around me because we have similar trauma.

Could the pretty witch ever choose to get close to me for no other reason than she enjoys my company?

A mortified blush floods the back of my neck at my neediness, only growing deeper when I realize Mor is handing over her credit card to pay for all the food, including mine.

"No, wait." I shove my hand into my back pocket and tug out some of the few crumpled bills to my name. I thrust them toward the grocery worker, who accepts the payment with wide eyes.

"You don't have to, Bo," Mor says. "I can cover these."

"I want to pay my own way," I mutter, my voice gruff and face hot with embarrassment.

"Fair enough."

She still hands over her card because the money I had wasn't sufficient to cover everything in our cart. Food prices have also crept up while I was frozen.

At least I'm getting a paycheck from the library now.

Mor and I stay quiet to her car, silently unloading our bags into the trunk, and I roll the cart all the way back to the front of the store, wanting to give her a moment away from me before the car ride back to the library.

When I climb into the passenger seat, she doesn't immediately pull out of the lot, instead turning to face me.

"I'm sorry, Bo. I kind of unloaded on you back there. That's not something I normally do."

I blink at her, surprised by her apology. "You don't?"

Her lips twist in a grimace. "No. I only meant to tell you my parents suck, but then"—she flares her fingers in front of her mouth—"the rest came spilling out. You're just ... really easy to talk to. But that doesn't mean I should make you my therapist."

"I'm glad you told me. I want to know things about you."

"You do?"

"Yes. I want to know everything." *Whoa. Slow down.*

Mor tilts her head, studying me, and oddly enough, I'm reminded of the raccoon I keep running into on my nightly walks. The furry creature tilts its head at the exact same angle, only the raccoon is cute while Mor is gorgeous.

"You know, I think I feel the same way." Her smile is small and a touch confused. "About you. I think I want to know everything about you."

I clear my throat and tug on the back of my neck, the skin hot under my palm. "There's not much."

And why would she care? The beautiful, smart witch has much more interesting topics to fill her time, I'm sure.

Mor shrugs. "Short stories are still stories." She starts the car. "Will you tell me more? About yourself?"

"What do you want to know?"

"Whatever you'd like to share."

I ponder that as she pulls onto the two-lane road that'll take us back through Folk Haven and toward Lake Galen.

"How about the first vacuum cleaner I fixed?"

She huffs out a breath that sounds like a curious laugh. "A vacuum cleaner?"

I offer her a hesitant smile. "Yeah. I, uh, I've always liked vacuum cleaners."

Mor's smile widens to a grin, and I'm relieved to read only delight and no mockery in the expression.

And a shiver brushes down my spine at her next husky words.

"Tell me."

26

Mor

THE STRANGEST THING happens on the drive back from the grocery store—and not just the fact that I find myself fascinated by Bo's description of a vacuum cleaner.

No, what really throws me off is how I become suddenly fascinated with Bo himself. I mean, up until this grocery run, I found the monster interesting. His past, his tangled grid of feelings, his plans to approach a world he hasn't lived in for almost two decades.

But that was a general curiosity that I'm sure plenty of people who know about his circumstances would feel.

Now though, my interest has widened to include more things.

Like his forearms and how they tense when he gestures.

Like his deep voice and how the pitch leaves goose bumps rising along my skin in waves.

Like his thick thighs and how they shift in his jeans as he turns toward me in his seat.

Like his broad body and how much space he takes up.

And how I like it. I like all of it.

I've never been so mesmerized by someone's physicality before.

Aware, sure. I notice how people look in a general sense.

But suddenly, with Bo, I want to *explore* his body. Want to touch and caress parts of him I can see and parts of him that I can't.

So odd.

The urge remains when we arrive at the library and as he helps me carry most of the groceries into the kitchen of my house. When he sets a bag down on the table, my eyes find the way his fingers flex around the cloth handle. In fact, I can't remove my focus.

That is, until Bo shoves his hands deep into his pockets.

A flash of rich brown calls my attention, and before I can block out my magical insight, I'm already interpreting the emotion.

Mortification.

Bo is embarrassed about something, and the knowledge sets off an ache deep in my chest.

"I'll go," he mumbles when, only a moment ago, he was happily explaining his fascination with the advances from Dyson.

"What's wrong?" I ask, worried about this change in him. "I liked hearing about the vacuums."

There have been times I've accidentally rambled on about books for too long, not realizing I was boring my audience. I don't want Bo to think I regretted asking him about his interests.

"Oh. I ... I'm glad."

But the chocolate shade remains, and from the way his pockets bulge, I can tell Bo has fisted his hands beneath the material.

This combination of events sparks a realization.

His hands. Hands with fingers that don't look exactly human. Not with the webbing that stretches between them. The flexible pieces of skin that hint there may be something just a bit different about Bo Folan.

Maybe I should keep this theory to myself. But his suppressed distress has my bossy nature coming out. I want to demand that he realize there is nothing wrong with him.

But things are never that easy. Still, maybe I can help in a small way.

"Bo?"

His eyes flick to mine, then down to the floor tiles between his boots. "Yeah?"

"I want to see your hands."

He flinches, and I know I'm right.

"You don't … why?" The words are hesitant, then harsh, his vulnerability showing.

"Because I'm nosy," I say with a shrug. "And because I think you want to hide them from me."

His pink flush spreads up to his forehead. I find the color endearing. Reminds me of the rosy hue of longing that I might find in an aura.

"They're monstrous," Bo mutters, as if the simple words will make me accept what he believes to be a fact.

But that is merely an opinion, one I'm starting to think other people in Bo's life formed for him. Pressed upon him when he was vulnerable enough to believe whatever someone who was supposed to care about him said.

"They're different," I volley back. "And interesting." I step forward and lay my hands lightly on his elbows before tracing my touch down to his wrists. "And they're a part of you." My voice is quieter now as I circle my grip around his wrists. "And I like you."

"You do?" he rasps.

I nod and give a small, questioning tug, trying to use my bossy bitch witch nature for good. "Show me, Bo."

"Yes, ma'am."

At his slightly defiant words, I hide a smile.

The large monster—who, by all accounts, shouldn't have reason to fear anything or anyone—takes a bracing breath before extending his hands to me.

Treating this as the gesture of trust it is, I don't hesitate to cradle his palms in mine, just like when he let me sift through his emotions the other day. Only this time, I'm not studying the colorful aura surrounding the man. I'm entirely focused on the physical.

"Spread them, please," I murmur, not wanting to force his fingers apart. That seems like too much of a violation.

If I'm going to examine this part of Bo, he needs to actively give it to me.

Another heavy breath on his end, and then he does.

As Bo splits his fingers, the thin webbing stretches with them, creating small bridges just below each first knuckle. The skin is so thin that I can see the shadow of my fingers through it as I trace the underside.

This piece of him is warm and flexible. I can't help stroking along the edges, bending my face closer so I can study every detail.

I have the oddest urge to press my lips against the triangle between his thumb and forefinger. Instead, I run the pad of my thumb over the webbing, wondering if I'll be able to find a pulse.

Bo lets out a noise—part grunt, part gasp—and he fists his hand.

"I'm sorry." I glance up at him. "Did I hurt you?"

His pupils are blown wide, mouth slightly parted.

"No. Not hurt." He clears his throat, and his neck, which

already holds the touch of a flush, deepens to a red that reminds me of wanting. "No one has ever ..."

He doesn't have to finish that statement for me to understand. To read the words lingering beneath the surface.

It's on the tip of my tongue to ask about Georgiana. Something obviously went on between them. But maybe it wasn't physical.

Or maybe it was, and she still avoided his hands.

That second possibility has me seething on two fronts.

The first for Bo, who deserves to be cherished for all of himself.

But also because the thought of her touching Bo brings me an irrational storm of jealousy.

That siren had better keep her talons to herself. The fierce words stay behind my clenched teeth because I have no right to say them.

And I don't even know why I want to say them.

Bo's brows furrow, and I scramble to change the subject.

"I wonder if we would have met," I land on.

"Hmm?" Bo continues to stare at where I trace his webbing.

"If you'd never gotten turned into a statue," I explain. "If you were forty instead of twenty-three, I wonder if we would have met."

"We ..." He trails off, expression turning introspective. Then he frowns. "We would have."

"I don't think so. You deserved better than what Folk Haven was back then. You would've found somewhere better."

Bo's mouth goes slack, and I'm surprised by his shock. Is it really so outlandish of a thing to ponder? Georgiana was the one who said he'd had plans to leave Folk Haven. If he had, we likely wouldn't have ever come to know each other.

The thought makes me sad. I like knowing Bo.

But who knows if he feels the same way about me?

And yet I don't regret our honest confessions.

I've never talked to anyone about my parents. I'm only close with my siblings, and they have plenty of their own trauma. No need for me to pile mine on their shoulders as well.

But Bo didn't fold under the darkness of my past.

And maybe that's why I give in to the urge to thank him in a way I know I shouldn't.

Without meeting Bo's eyes, I dip my chin and place a quick kiss on his knuckles.

"Thank you for showing me," I mutter.

Then I retreat from the kitchen, not ready to see what reaction my actions had on the monster.

Bo

Jack keeps his word.

On the evening of the first full moon since my freedom, he knocks on the door of the RV. I just finished my dinner of microwave ramen noodles and was trying to ignore the tingling in my bones that precedes the call of the moon.

When I open my door to find the wolf waiting, barefoot and only wearing a pair of athletic shorts, I still have trouble believing he's here to keep his promise.

"Sun sets in twenty. You coming?" His words ride a growl, but I suspect that's more from the urge to change than because he's angry.

"Yes, sir."

Jack scowls. "Gods, don't call me sir. I'm not an alpha, and I don't want to be."

I turn over his words and what I know about Jack as I tug off my shirt and pants before following him outside.

He's a lone wolf in a town with two packs, and from his tone, the guy has no respect for alphas.

I'd hazard I'm not the only one who's had negative experiences with a pack.

Tonight, it'll just be the two of us then, and that's fine by me.

"You heading out?"

I jerk my chin to the side at the question and find Ame exiting the library, cradling her black cat. Suddenly, I'm wishing I'd kept my pants on until we made it to the tree line. The witch has seen me in less, but that doesn't mean I should be strolling around their property in boxers.

And as if the gods want to compound my embarrassment, Mor follows her sister, blinking slowly as she catches sight of me. Luckily, the dying light should hide most of my blush.

"Yeah. Bo is coming with me. We'll be back before sunrise." Jack plucks Lucky from his mate's arms and sets the cat on the ground despite its meow of protest. Then he tugs Ame into an embrace and kisses her deep.

I avert my eyes, not because I think the two care about privacy, but because I can't help the pang of envy deep in my gut as I observe their affection.

What would it be like to love and be loved in return the way those two do?

Could I ever hope to find that kind of happiness, or am I doomed to walk my life alone?

"Bo."

At the sound of my name, I climb from my dark thoughts and find Mor's eyes are still on me.

"Jack will watch your back, and I don't think anyone will bother you, but if they do, come back here." She stands on the top step of the porch, her arms crossed, red hair loose around her shoulders in a fiery riot. "This is my territory. You're safe here."

I gape at her, this witch who keeps giving to me.

She's claiming she'll protect me. Me. A grotesque monster

who strikes fear into the hearts of those who look upon my mythic form.

And Mor offers me safe haven.

"Thank you," I finally choke out.

She nods, then turns on her heel to go back inside, Ame soon following after.

When I face Jack again, he's breathing heavy, and I would swear he's gotten taller.

"Come," he rumbles, then lopes toward the woods as the last glow of sun disappears and the moon takes over the sky.

When I catch up to Jack, he's stripped off his shorts and taken on the form of a large gray wolf.

Praying to both The Clawed One and The Finned One that Jack remains open-minded, I shuck off my boxers and let the moon drag my beast to the forefront. I don't know if the glowing orb has a softer call to me than a full-blooded wolf, but I still always know her phases and drown in her song.

Jack doesn't flinch away from me or growl in challenge as I lumber to my feet. Four webbed paws dig into the freshly fallen leaves.

The wolf snorts, then dives into the forest with a howl.

A welcoming sound.

Come, he seems to say. *Run with me.*

My heart clenches, and I shake my massive head to rid myself of the sentimental feeling. I don't want emotions slowing me down on this night.

I just want to run as I've never gotten to before.

And we do. Jack leads me northwest, into the mountains, farther from civilization. We hunt small critters and race one another. We leap over streams and find cliff edges to gaze up at the moon and howl our appreciation. The sound I emit isn't as smooth as Jack's, but he still sings with me.

Is this what it's like to have family? To have a brother?

Another scent reaches my nose.

Wolf.

Jack tenses and turns toward the trees.

The werewolf steps out, moves more curious than aggressive. The beast's focus is on me. It scents the air, then sits and lets out a yip.

Like a question.

I shuffle forward, breathing in deeper until my moon-drunk mind identifies the newcomer.

Griffy.

I let out a bark that sounds more seal than wolf, but the bartender replies with his own and wags his tail.

Jack huffs, picking up on the lack of tension, and he trots back into the woods.

Griffy comes with us, joining our full moon run.

I hear other howls throughout the course of the night. Members of the official packs. Likely they sense us here.

I wonder if Jack's presence keeps them away.

Then a massive gray wolf steps from between the trees in front of our group, and I rethink my theory.

This werewolf isn't one I know—at least not by scent. But I can tell they're powerful.

An alpha?

The mythic's eyes are trained on me, and it gives the beginnings of a growl. Probably in response to my not-quite-a-wolf appearance.

Then something strange happens to Jack. Shadows shift and meld to him, and when they dissipate, a wolfman looms over all of us.

The night I was freed from the statue, I thought I'd imagined the nightmare creature.

But here he is, Jack in a third form.

"Friend," he snarls, saliva dripping from a snout I don't think was meant to speak words. "Mine."

Did he just claim me?

It seems so because after a heavy sigh, the powerful gray wolf sinks back into the shadows.

Griffy trots by me, letting out a farewell bark before heading in the same direction as the gray wolf.

With another swirl of shadows, Jack resumes full wolf form and takes the lead, directing us back toward the library as the moon makes its descent. We skirt around the statue garden and find our clothes hanging from the branches where we left them.

Or at least, Jack's shorts are where he left them. My boxers have a raccoon sitting on them.

I grumble at the rodent.

It chitters back.

I nudge it with my paw.

The thing takes its time waddling away.

Back in my human form, dressed in boxers now probably infested with fleas, I face Jack, who already has his sights set on the house where his mate sleeps.

"Thank you," I rasp.

Jack nods. "It's a standing invitation."

There's a sudden pressure behind my eyes that I blink away. "You sure? That gray one didn't seem happy about it."

Jack scoffs. "Baron can shove it."

"Is he an alpha?"

"Of the Folk Haven wolf pack." Jack confirms my suspicions.

"He's not a good guy?" The last Folk Haven alpha wasn't cruel, but he made it clear I wasn't welcome.

Jack sighs, the deep exhale hinting at a long story he doesn't feel like telling. "He's a decent alpha as far as I can tell."

"But you don't like him?"

Jack shrugs. "It's complicated." His eyes flick to me, then back to the house, and he starts walking. "He's my dad."

"Oh." That's not what I was expecting him to say.

But if anyone knows about complicated father-son relationships, it's me. I let him go with no more questions, pointing my feet toward the RV.

And I let my mind revel in the experience of finally running free on the night of the full moon with something resembling a pack.

28

Bo

IT'S NOT until I'm in the waiting room of the office that I realize I'm not sure exactly what eye doctors do.

I mean, check your eyes, obviously.

But what does that involve? Shining a light in them? Will the doctor touch my eye?

I shiver at the thought and blink rapidly as my eyes water in protest at the idea.

I've worked myself halfway into a panic when a woman wearing scrubs and a kind smile opens the door next to reception and calls out my name.

"Here," I grunt, pushing to my feet and bowing my shoulders when I notice her gaze widening at my stature.

At least she doesn't flinch away from me.

"I'll take you on back then."

She guides me into a dimly lit office and proceeds to have me read letters on a wall chart while I cover each of my eyes. That's easy enough, no matter how small they're printed, but when she hands me a laminated sheet to read off of, I feel my cheeks heating while I struggle, and that familiar ache starts in my skull.

"That's quite all right," she coos, accepting the sheet back when it's clear I can't get through it. "The doctor will be in shortly, and he'll take a closer look."

While I wait in the chair, I do my best to ignore the odd machine covered in round gears and study the motivational poster on the wall that says, *When life gets blurry, adjust your focus.* Then my eyes catch on a framed photo, and my stomach bottoms out.

There, sitting next to a plastic model of an eye, is a beautiful wedding photo of a man with his arms wrapped around Georgiana.

Oh shit—

The door opens, and a slightly older man from the image steps in with a nod and a smile.

"Hello, Bo. I'm Dr. Stormwind."

My eye doctor is Georgiana's husband.

Every muscle in my body tenses as I wait for him to say something cutting or dismissive. Wait for a warning to stay away from his wife or maybe even a threat.

But he just nudges a rolling stool closer to me, perches himself on the seat, and flips through the sheets on his clipboard.

"So, you made this appointment because you've been having headaches when you read?" he asks, oblivious to my mounting nerves. "Would you say this is a newer development?"

I have to clear my throat twice before I can get the words out. "Um ... uh ... no. I don't think so. I, uh ... I've never been a good reader." I wince at the admission, suddenly certain he'll use the information to emotionally gut me.

But he only hums in the back of his throat before setting

down his clipboard. "Well, let's see if we can help you with that."

Dr. Stormwind spends the next ten minutes giving my eyes a more thorough examination—which does involve some light shining, but not as terrible as I expected—and by the end, I'm convinced he has absolutely no idea who I am other than a new patient.

Georgiana must not have told him about me. At least not using my name.

There's a melancholy in my chest at the thought, and as Dr. Stormwind makes notes on his chart, I examine the feeling.

Am I jealous? Resentful?

No, I realize.

I'm just sad. For a stretch of time, Georgiana meant the world to me. But I didn't even mean enough to her for her to mention me to her husband.

Or maybe she didn't want to share her secret mistakes with the doctor she'd married.

Whatever the reason, I find I don't have any ill will toward this man. If anything, I wish him luck, dealing with a partner who might never share all of herself.

"What we've got here is a common enough problem," Dr. Stormwind announces. "You're farsighted. You can see things far away perfectly well, but up close, your eyes can't properly focus. You trying to force them to is likely causing strain and headaches. We'll get you set up with some glasses, and I bet you'll be reading fine in no time. No more squinting. No more pain."

He offers me an encouraging smile, and I realize I'm returning one of my own.

"Really? Just like that?"

"Yes, sir. They can help you pick out frames up front and get a set ordered with your new prescription." He holds up his clip-board as if any of the numbers written on it will make sense to me. "I'll see you back in a year to check if anything has changed. You should be good to go."

"I ... thank you." My throat is suddenly thick.

How would my life have been different if I'd found out about this years ago? Would I have stayed in school?

I just needed a little help. Just needed someone to see I was struggling and realize why that might be.

Turns out, I just needed a clever witch.

29

Mor

BO IS WEARING GLASSES, and it is doing odd things to my body. For example, it's completely possible that I might burst into flames.

This should not be the reaction someone has to a set of metal frames and two glass lenses perched on a man's nose, but here I am. Suddenly combustible.

When Bo got back from the eye doctor a few days ago, he mentioned the man gave him a prescription. But I hadn't realized that little trip to the doctor would result in *this*.

"Glasses," I croak. Turns out, I've lost the ability to form a sentence made up of more than one desperate word.

Bo raises his eyes from the book he was reading at the front desk, and now he's looking at me over the rims of the spectacles. He brings a large hand up and slides them off, and I shiver at the simple move.

Then he smiles, and I'm done. I think I need the day off.

"You were right. I picked these up yesterday, and ... gods, everything is clearer." He raises the book he's cradling in his palm. "I'm not even interested in the history of forest nymphs. But I couldn't stop from reading the first chapter. Just because I can." He closes the book and sets it down on the counter. "Thank you. For pushing me to go."

I nod and clear my throat, trying to think of something I can say other than asking him to slip the glasses back on, but slowly this time.

"I'm glad," I manage. "That they work."

He nods, his smile turning earnest. "Now I can really help you here. I swear I'll be the best employee."

Employee.

I repeat the word a few times in my head. A reminder that Bo works for me and I should not be mentally undressing him. Undressing every inch—except for the glasses, of course.

Well, this seems to be a terrible turn of events.

I suppose the silver lining is that I now have the reassurance I am able to be attracted to someone.

It just sucks that it took thirty years for me to find that out and that the first person I'm attracted to is so much younger than me, just getting out of a very traumatic situation, and is also my employee.

Bo checks the spine of the book he was reading and carefully arranges it on the rolling shelving cart we keep at the front desk. He shoots me a grin.

"Well, I think I might be getting the hang of this." These words come in the delicious Southern drawl that pairs with Bo's gentle nature.

Now, me, as a northerner having moved to this Southern town, I have heard plenty of people in Folk Haven speak with a Southern accent. A nice Georgia drawl.

But no one has perfected the tone like Bo.

I have the urge to listen to him speak for an endless stretch, like a tape stuck in a boom box that cannot be unplugged. Because I don't want him to stop talking.

I don't want him to stop being proud of the fact that he is navigating this library with ever-growing ease. That he's no longer hiding the webbing between his fingers as he reaches for books and places them back on the shelves in the proper order. He no longer frowns and squints at words, but smiles instead.

Bo is a beautiful torture to be around.

And then there are times when he says my name and I think that I might die. I might actually die.

Just self-combust.

I am tempted to tell him to use my full name—Morgana—because how the hell am I supposed to listen to his sexy Southern drawl say *Mor*?

More.

More.

Oh my Gods, I picked the worst nickname in the world.

He's only saying my name, but I want him to be giving me direction. I want him to tell me what he wants from me. Because I'll give it to him. I'll give him more. I'll give him all of me if he just keeps talking and keeps being sweet and keeps being the kindest goddamn mythic that I have ever met in my life.

This was a mistake.

To know what longing and lust and attraction feels like was a mistake.

I've become jumpy. For such a big man, he's pretty quiet when he moves. And it seems like every time I walk around a bookshelf—*boom*—there he is. Beautiful bomb right in my face.

And then he smiles at me.

And then he says my name.

And then I die again.

My only solution to this unplanned attraction is to work harder. Is to work so hard that I forget the world around me. It used to be an easy thing to do. I would lose track of time until Ame set down a coffee beside my book; I would only come out of my focused mindset long enough to take a few sips, and then I'd get right back to it. That's what I need. I need to forget that the world exists.

I need to forget that Bo's sexy Southern voice exists.

That's why I hired him, isn't it? So I don't have to focus on all the minutia of running a library. That I only need to be called in when someone has a more in-depth research question. And until that happens, I can focus on my own research. Which is interesting. Which should fully distract me.

I just came across a new chapter in a book, talking about a subject that I'm interested in—god objects. This chapter could explain to me what exactly is up with that golden apple that I have tucked away in a deposit box at Wolf Trust Bank.

But am I poring over every single word in this new chapter?

No, I'm not. I'm staring at the doorway, waiting for Bo to walk through it and ask me a question. Waiting for him to walk through that doorway and say *Mor*.

"Mor?"

A shiver travels down my spine and back up into my skull, melting my brain.

"Yes, Bo?"

The monster blinks slowly as he stares at me, as if he briefly forgot whatever question he planned to ask when he entered this room. But then he clears his throat and makes words with his beautiful voice.

"I was just wondering , after we close the library, would you mind if I took a swim off the dock?"

"Of course not. Our dock is your dock."

Oh no. Oh Gods, no. He is going to be wet. He is going to be in only a bathing suit.

I have found a way to die. A new way to die.

"Thank you. But I was wondering if it would be an issue if I swam in my other form." He shifts his feet and ducks his head, as if bracing for a blow. "It's supposed to be a cloudy night, so I'm hoping that it might be all right."

I push my attraction to the back of my mind long enough to really study the man. The monster.

He's used to being judged for his other form.

He thinks I'll deny him the right to be himself.

I step forward on instinct, scooping up one of Bo's webbed hands. Then I don't know what to do with his hand other than give it a firm, reassuring squeeze.

"It is always all right, Bo. You are always all right. Better than all right. You are ..." Oh gods, where am I going with this?

His sky-blue eyes are staring at me now, and he has those damn sexy glasses on again, and I've never felt so flustered in my life.

"Good," I blurt.

"I'm good?" His question comes out soft, as if he's testing the word.

I nod too erratically. "So good."

And because I've lost hold of myself, I'm almost blinded by the burst of yellow that fills his aura.

The sunshine shade of pure happiness.

30

Bo

THE CLOUDS OBSCURING the moon have a weight to them, as if they might break open and spill their insides at any moment.

I would welcome a storm. More cover for my swim.

Mor didn't seem concerned though when I asked her about using the dock. If there were any danger, I'm sure she would have warned me. At least to keep her library safe from backlash.

The moment I have the thought, I'm guilty for the callous view. Mor cares, and that's been rare in my life. My doubtful thoughts about her motivations stem more from my history than from anything she's done to me.

I stand alone at the end of the dock, dressed in only a pair of jeans, and tell myself not to look behind me. Not to stare at the cozy glow emitted from the windows of the house that used to so terrify me.

Now, after spending days wandering through the rooms, learning every scent, memorizing the floorboards that creak and the door hinges that squeak, I feel like I've met the house.

That I've apologized for my invasion and the building knows I'm seeking to right my wrongs.

And now I regret turning down an offer of a room under that roof. The RV is nice enough, but everything about it is temporary. Too similar to the flimsy mobile home that my father and I lived in.

The Victorian is like a tree, with thick roots dug into the ground.

Not long ago, I thought I wanted to be mobile. To leave Folk Haven the moment I made enough money.

Now though, I want an invite inside.

An offer to stay.

I want a certain witch to look at me and see more than an employee. More than a monster needing charity.

I let out a sigh and keep my gaze forward, fixed on the choppy waters of Lake Galen. As chill droplets patter against my shoulders, I unzip my fly and push my pants down my legs. Then I take a moment to fold them and set them back from the edge. Not that the move will keep them dry if the rain keeps up.

Bracing for the chill, I leap into the lake. Cold water swallows me, and I mutter curses that only come out as bubbles.

But the next moment, I tug on my beast form, and every sensation alters. The once-frigid water is now pleasantly cool as it passes through my fur and over my scales. The urge to return to the surface for a breath disappears as my lung capacity expands. The webbing between my digits, which is useless on land, now helps to effortlessly propel me through the water.

I glide under the surface, hidden from all who might judge my appearance. Able to pretend for a time that I am fully free and that there is no shame to my beast.

What would Mor think if she saw me like this?

She has, I remind myself. *This is the first way she ever saw me. Frozen in stone as my most terrifying self.*

And she helped me. She saved me.

Is that the reason I feel this constant draw to her? That my mind is always on the library, wondering what small things I can do to make her life easier? To make her smile.

No. I don't think it is all from being grateful, though I am.

I just ... like Mor.

I like her so much.

I like how she's passionate and loyal. How she takes care of people in a brisk, no-nonsense manner. How she can get so lost in a book that the world around her loses meaning.

How she was determined to build something and did.

How she's fair, never treating me like I'm other.

How she smells like roses and has hair like fire.

But I doubt she'll ever feel the same.

So, I tuck away the pain of never getting to hold her—one sting in a lifetime of emotional wounds—and I swim until the sky booms with thunder and flashes with lightning.

31

Mor

RAIN POUNDS against the windows in a constant barrage that I normally find soothing. Nothing better than staying inside when there's a rainstorm, curled in a chair to read or wrapped up in soft blankets as I drift off to sleep.

But this evening, the rattle of droplets on the roof can't soothe away the restless energy fed by thoughts of Bo Folan.

I push back the covers and roll off the plush mattress, abandoning my attempt at sleep to descend from my bedroom and try to work through the grid of my own emotions. But the colors overlaying my skin have always been difficult to discern.

All I know is, the air is cool, but my skin is flushed. Memories of his forearms flexing while shelving a book continue to play through my mind, and I occasionally wonder what it would be like if Bo wrapped those arms around me. If he held me close and never let go.

"What is wrong with me?" I mutter, pressing hard fingers against my forehead, as if I might be able to massage away the new rise of urges.

"I don't know. What is wrong with you?"

The question has me starting in surprise, and I realize that my sister isn't twined with her werewolf lover a floor above me, but instead is perched on my research table just next to the kitchen. Ame cradles a steaming mug in her hands, and though she stares at me, the rest of her body faces the back window. In the muted light of the moon, a torrential downpour rages just past the glass.

"What are you doing up?"

Ame always goes to bed at a reasonable time. Mainly because, at eight p.m., Jack usually announces, "It's bedtime," then carries her upstairs. Like he's had enough of functioning in the world and he's finally reached a socially acceptable time of day to sequester Ame in his den to enjoy all to himself.

I might protest the move if my sister didn't grin wide every single time. If she's happy, then I'm happy.

"Anna had shoulder surgery today." She names Jack's mom, a human woman who moved to Folk Haven not long after Jack settled here with us. "Everything went fine, but he felt better, staying over with her, just in case."

Ame sips her tea, and a warm beverage on this cold, wet evening sounds perfect to me.

As I refill the teapot, I ask, "You didn't want to go too? I'm surprised Jack was willing to part with you for a whole night."

My sister goes back to staring out the window. "I think Anna would like to have him to herself for a little bit. Have her son's undivided attention." She shrugs. "Jack can be a little too focused on me if I'm in the room."

"I'm betting it's the same even when you're not in the room." I spoon loose chamomile tea into my infuser. "He's obsessed with you."

Ame frowns.

A worry pricks at my nerves. "Does that bother you? Do you ... not feel the same?"

My sister is self-contained and developed top-notch emotional shields years ago, so it's hard to tell what she's feeling sometimes. I imagine having the loving intensity of Jack focused on her all day and night could be wearing, especially if she's realizing she doesn't have the same level of devotion to him.

"I feel the same. Jack is mine." There's a warning note in her voice, but when I glance up from pouring the hot water into my mug, I realize the tone wasn't directed at me. More like my sister was putting the vibe out into the world.

A warning to the universe.

"But, yes," she continues, "how much he loves me bothers me."

"Explain." I probably should be less demanding, but she's used to it.

With my own tea warming my palms, I join her in the research room, choosing to settle in an armchair by the window that faces the room. I don't need to see the rain. I just want to hear it, gentle background noise to our conversation.

"If something ever happens to me—not that I think it will, only it *could* because bad things happen all the time—it will devastate him. No ..." Her brows scrunch in thought. "Destroy. Decimate. Obliterate. I think that's it. My death would obliterate Jack."

Trepidation creeps down my spine. If something were to happen to Ame, Jack's not the only one who would be obliterated.

"You're worried about dying?" I manage to keep my voice neutral.

"Not usually. But it happens to all of us. Even the long-lived mythics go at some point. And when I do, Jack won't survive it." She frowns at her mug. "Most days, I love how Jack loves me. With every bit of himself. But I don't like thinking that loving me could be fatal to him."

That's heavy. But also correct as far as I can tell.

Jack has a job. He has family and friends. He has interests that aren't my sister.

But Ame is the blood in his veins. More important than that even—since you can replace blood, but you can't replace my sister.

"Ame."

At the sound of her name, she finally glances my way, her vulnerable eyes seeming too large for her face.

"I will do everything in my power to make sure you live a long, healthy life. And your wolf will have no reason to even consider a future without you."

She blinks, then offers me a small smile. "Thank you."

I nod just as a flash of lightning lights up the room and a boom of thunder shakes the glass.

I hope Bo is sleeping soundly in the RV.

Thoughts of the monster remind me of why I couldn't sleep, and a question pops out of my mouth before I consider if I even want to have this discussion.

"Did you think Jack was attractive when you first met him?"

Ame tilts her head to the side. "When I first met him, he was a cat. So, no."

I huff a laugh. "I meant as a man." My voice turns a touch serious. "The first time you saw his human form, were you attracted to him?"

Ame doesn't need long to consider the question, nodding almost immediately. "I never planned to act on the attraction. Even after he kissed me. But, yes, I thought Jack was handsome right away. Intimidatingly so."

"Have you ever ..." I don't know how to phrase it other than, "Not been attracted to someone, then suddenly, you are?"

Maybe it's strange I'm bringing this question to Ame when she's younger than me. Normally, I'm in the mentorship role. But before Jack, Ame had a relatively full dating life, often having flings with men and women we met on our trips. I never understood how she could encounter a person and be kissing them later that night. I didn't judge her for it; I just didn't get it.

This time, Ame does take a moment to consider my question. "I think I've always known right away whether or not I find someone attractive. Those feelings can grow if I spend more time with them. Or change into love, like with Jack. But I can't remember a time when there wasn't at least that initial spark."

"Hmm." I make the noise in the back of my throat, hoping I don't sound disappointed.

"Is that something you're feeling?" Ame asks. "Attraction you didn't feel before?"

"I don't know." I sip my tea and try to untangle my own mind. "Shouldn't I know right away?"

"Not necessarily." She uncrosses her legs and swings them over the edge of the table. "Attraction isn't always a physical thing."

Bo's muscular body and flexing forearms come to mind.

"This is definitely physical."

"Oh. Okay. Maybe ... have you ever considered you might be demi?"

"Demi?"

"Demisexual. People who only form physical attraction after they've established a deep emotional connection to a person. Kind of like ... you can't find someone sexy unless you trust them first. I think." The upward quirk of her mouth is rueful. "Honestly, I only have an idea of it."

"That's ... I'm not sure I ..." Words fail me as I examine what Ame just described. Is that truly a possibility?

"Mor?" Ame's voice pulls me out of an internal whirlwind, and I meet her searching eyes. "If that word helps you, then great. But while I know how much you love organizing things" —she waves around to encompass the library—"keep in mind, you don't need to label yourself. If you like someone, you can just like them. If you find someone attractive, you can just find them attractive."

"Stop lecturing me," I grumble.

Ame grins, and it wrinkles her freckled nose.

Whatever we might have said to each other next is interrupted by a soft yet distinct noise.

A scratching at the back door.

Ame and I share a look, and I press up from my chair to explore. Cracking the door lets in a chilly breeze, the cacophonous pound of precipitation, and a soggy raccoon.

The creature waddles into the kitchen like it owns the place and merely forgot its key.

"Hey!" I yelp.

"Oh." Ame's voice is soft with wonder. "You found your familiar."

"I ... what?"

Then it occurs to me that Ame works in a veterinarian's office and is much more used to reading the emotional auras of animals than I am.

"I'll grab some towels," my sister announces instead of explaining further, disappearing in the direction of the laundry room.

As if understanding what Ame just said, the creature sits back on its haunches and waits, little arms rubbing droplets from its face.

"My familiar?" I whisper, half to myself, half to the raccoon.

Two liquid black eyes meet mine, and something settles in place in my chest.

I lower to a crouch myself, extending my hand. The raccoon reaches out and curls its little clawed digits around my pointer finger. Almost like we're shaking hands.

"Hello."

The raccoon chirps.

Then Ame returns with towels, and we carefully pat the forest creature dry, braced the whole time for it to stage a protest. But the raccoon merely sits still, then wanders over to one of the many cat beds placed around the library for Lucky. It curls up on the plush cushion and falls asleep.

"Aren't they supposed to be nocturnal?" I whisper to Ame.

She shrugs. "Familiars make their own rules. But I can ask Lucky to keep an eye on your new friend."

So, with my familiar asleep in my research room, under the watchful eyes of a black cat, I retreat up to my bedroom. But I'm still not sleepy, so I prop my laptop in my lap and proceed to google *demisexual*.

At some point, I must have dozed off because my screen is black when I wake up to a thunderous crash overhead.

32

Bo

THE BOOM of thunder wakes me up, but it's the rending crack of a tree that sends me stumbling out of bed and into the torrential downpour. In the flashes of lightning, I catalog the damage, spying a massive branch that's torn free of a tree and smashed into the roof of the library.

The roof of Mor's bedroom.

Without thought, I'm shifting, taking on the horrific form of my monster as I charge toward the house. Navigating inside would be too slow, so I leap for the lowest point on the roof and climb upward. The storm rages on around me, not satisfied with the damage it's done.

Please let her be okay.

As my claws scrabble across slick shingles, I realize that this panic in my chest is from fear of something happening to the fiery witch. That she's come to matter to me in small ways, even if I matter very little to her.

And the idea that she could be hurt even now ...

No. I refuse to entertain it.

Having reached the skylight, I try to shove my head past the protruding twigs and destroyed roof to get a sense of how much damage is inside. How much has been done to Mor Shelly.

"Gods-damn it!" a lovely voice snarls.

And there she is, by a closed door, trying to pull debris away from the exit.

I let out a snarly cough to get her attention.

Mor turns to look up at me. She freezes, mouth going slack.

Gods, what must she think with my horrendous face peering down at her while she's trapped? And I'm not one of the mythics who can speak while in my nonhuman form. I gather the power to shift back, even if it will leave me butt-ass naked on her roof in the middle of a storm. But before I can morph my face to look human again, she lets out an audible exhale.

"Bo! Hells, you scared me for a second. All I saw were your eyes."

She pushes damp hair off her forehead, and I spy speckles of blood on her skin.

She's injured.

The knowledge makes me want to tear the storm clouds from the sky and ripped them to pieces for daring to harm the strong, kind witch.

"Can you help me get out? The door is blocked." She waves at the splintered rubble keeping her in the room, talking to me like my monstrous visage is commonplace. Nothing to be remarked upon or concerned about.

The reaction makes me feel ... things.

But she's talking again, so I don't have time to decipher exactly what those things are.

"There are plastic tarps in the basement. Maybe if I can cover the floor of the room, it'll keep water from getting downstairs." She stares around at the rain collecting near her feet.

I scrabble off the roof, leaping to the ground in one smooth move, then shift back to my human form before pushing inside the house, regretting how I have to break the knob to do so. I mentally put it on my list as an item to repair. Mor loves her little skeleton key, and she'll be sad if the lock is ruined.

Taking the stairs three at a time, I climb up to the third level, only to find Jack and Ame working on freeing my witch as she shouts directions to them. That task covered, I pick a new destination, hustling to the basement and easily finding the plastic tarps on the shelf above the laundry machine. A toolbox sits in the corner, and I grab that too.

Meanwhile, I'm grateful I haven't caught anyone's attention while I'm running around nude.

Outside once more, I retake my monster form and scale to the roof again, tools in tow, held by my tail. When I peer into the bedroom, Mor is gone, and the place is empty, which means I don't have to worry about falling debris when I wrench the branch out of the roof and fling it far away from the home.

Then I'm human and naked again, needing opposable thumbs.

In my birthday suit, I proceed to stretch the plastic tarps over the hole in the roof and nail them into place, trying to secure the protection as good as possible. The rain chills my skin, and the rumble of thunder mixes with the pound of blood in my ears.

Eventually, I'm as satisfied as I can be that the house is mostly waterproof again.

The rain is still coming down in heavy sheets, so I make the shift once more, feeling the drag of so much magic usage against my muscles. Normally, I don't alter my shape so rapidly and so many times over a short period. I hope I don't get stuck in my monster skin as I wait to regain strength.

Maneuvering carefully, I descend from the roof, only to find Mor, Ame, and Jack waiting for me on the front porch. Expressions are some variations of surprise and shock.

"Did you just patch the roof?" Mor asks, her voice breathless.

But I'm too focused on the blood trickling from a split on the bridge of her nose to bother nodding.

Instead, I force my weary muscles to change once again until I'm standing as a human man, sweat mixing with rain, trying not to pant at the pain.

"You're hurt," I growl. "How badly?"

Mor's beautiful face flushes a deep red in the glow of the porch light. "You're naked."

"Here." Jack, who I didn't realize had stepped away, strides out the front door and tosses a blanket my way.

I wrap the covering around myself as I trot up the stairs toward Mor, cataloging all the injuries I can spy on her.

Cut on her nose.

Gash on her left cheekbone.

Bruise forming on her collarbone.

Scratches on her left arm.

"Those need to be disinfected." I herd her inside, and thankfully, the witch lets me. "Ame, do you have a first aid kit?"

"On it." The smaller witch jogs through a side room as I direct Mor toward the kitchen and plop her down at the table.

"Did you really cover the hole in the roof? All by yourself?"

I grunt and shrug. Then I realize she'll probably want more clarity than that. "Yes, I did. It should hold till the morning."

Ame appears at my side with a plastic white case that sports a Red Cross on it.

"I can take care of my own cuts," Mor insists.

And she can argue all she wants while I make sure the abrasions are clean and cared for.

Besides, a grumpy, wet Mor is kind of cute.

I'd appreciate her in this state more if I wasn't panicking over how close she came to truly getting injured.

That branch could have gone fully through the roof and landed on her.

Crushed her.

Impaled her.

And I wouldn't have been able to stop it from happening.

I tear open the disinfectant wipe a little too aggressively and remind myself to rein it in. Thankfully, despite her earlier protestations, Mor is willing to let me play doctor. She sits still as I clean her wounds and cover them with Band-Aids.

The Band-Aids have bats on them.

"I don't think you need stitches," I mutter. "But you should get checked out by a doctor."

I toss the bloodied wipes on the table and turn back to her, only to find myself enveloped in a warm, soft, decadent hug.

Mor has plastered her top half against mine, her arms encircling my neck, our faces pressed cheek to cheek.

"Thank you," she whispers.

"Uh, sure. Of course."

"For saving the books."

I gape, watching over Mor's shoulder as Ame smiles and Jack rolls his eyes.

A laugh of relief and astonishment bursts from my chest, and I allow myself to hug the ridiculous witch back.

Nothing I did tonight was for the books. It was all for her.

Because she's what matters.

To me. Mor matters to me.

I close my eyes and enjoy the embrace as I try to keep doubtful thoughts at bay.

Is this me repeating the past? Falling for the first woman who shows me a hint of kindness?

Will Mor drop me just like Georgiana did once she gets whatever it is she wants?

33

Mor

It's a few days after the destructive thunderstorm, and I'm pleasantly tipsy.

When my siblings and I were officially invited to join the Folk Haven coven, I expected meetings to take place late in the evening, maybe under a full moon.

Turns out, they happen over Sunday brunch. Witches like pomegranate mimosas.

I'm sporting not a full buzz, but a little bubbly feeling when I return from the monthly get-together. The outing was much needed after the stress of cataloguing the repairs my home needs. Luckily, my room was the only one to take true damage, mainly because of Bo's quick reaction.

But sleeping in a spare room as opposed to my tower for the last few nights has me sad, especially whenever I think about how long it'll take me to arrange for contractors to come out to my library.

Instead of going inside, I meander down to the dock, sit

cross-legged on the edge, and stare out at the glimmering water.

"The window is done."

I jerk in surprise at the unexpected voice, turning to find Bo standing on the shore with his hands tucked in his pockets.

"You mean it's covered?" I ask, shielding my eyes against the sun. "Like, you nailed some plywood over it?" That's somehow more depressing than the idea of plastic stretching over the hole.

"No. It's a skylight again. Wanna come see?"

"I ... do."

Being in my bedroom with Bo is not going to help me subdue the growing attraction I have toward him, but I can at least keep a handle on my actions. No matter how close we get to my bed, I will not launch myself at him.

I have self-control.

At least I think I do.

Truth is, I've never been tested before.

Bo waves for me to lead the way through the house, even though he's the one who has something to show me. He claimed that it's fixed? How did he get a window here so fast? The skylight is not a normal shape, and Folk Haven is kind of off the beaten path.

Curious, I climb the steep steps to my tower room. The furniture did not sustain any damage, only had to be cleaned and dried. Now everything is arranged as it once was, no sign of any construction having gone on.

My eyes track upward, and I gasp.

There is a window, but that seems like too tame of a word to describe the beautiful piece in place of what was once just clear glass.

The largest sections are still simple transparent glass, which I appreciate because I would have missed the stars. But curling around the edge is a thorny vine that ends in a delicately blooming rose.

My favorite flower.

My favorite scent.

Did he know?

"I'm sorry," Bo mutters. "I should've asked first."

In theory, yes, he should have. But in practice, the piece is wondrous, and I have no notes.

"How?" I gasp the question.

"Well, you know, Ophelia is good with glass. She makes it with her fire and sand. And she partnered with this werewolf, Manny, who welds these metal art pieces. Learned how from Novac, turns out. Plus, Manny is mated to a witch named Blossom, and she loves your library." Bo clears his throat. "Anyway, I sketched out what I thought you might like, and they were kind enough to help. Worked all day yesterday, and I installed it while you were out. Wanted you to come home to a fixed house."

"That design"—I point up at the rose—"you came up with that?"

He scratches the back of his neck and stares between his boots. "It's simple. But I thought ... just thought maybe you'd like looking at it."

This man. This insecure, wonderful, amazing monster does not realize how lovely he is, which only makes him even more appealing.

"That is the most beautiful window I've ever seen in my life, and I am honored to have it in my home."

"Oh. Um ... good then." Every inch of his skin I can see has started to take on a rosy tint. "And I asked Ame to read this for me." He holds up a grimoire. " 'Cause of your records, it looked like this might be one with protection spells. She found one that makes structures sturdier." He flips open to a page marked with a ribbon. "I thought maybe you'd want to try casting it on the roof. And the walls. And the whole house really. Just in case."

Oh no. Gods, if this monster keeps going, I'm going to fall in love with him.

That is, if I haven't already.

And as he rambles on about protection spells, I realize how —even in this small town—the world is still dangerous. Any day could be my last. That tree branch could have done me in, and I never would have experienced what it was like to kiss someone who I actually like.

If the Dark One gather's me into her cosmic embrace tomorrow, I will have to leave this world never having known the joy of romantic love.

Bo is younger than me.

He is my employee.

He's still figuring out his place in the world.

And if any or all of those reasons have him choosing not to be with me then that's his decision to make.

But right now, my choice is clear.

I can't let another moment go by without telling him the truth.

34

Mor

"Bo Folan, I am attracted to you."

I'm not a coy person. Nor am I secretive.

I'm forthright, and I would rather deal with Bo's clear rejection than the hazy possibility of him not feeling the same.

I'm an information seeker, and even if the answer is not what I would like, I still want to know it so I never have to doubt.

Bo's emotional grid flashes Technicolor as his face goes slack. I do my best to press my magical insight away, not wanting to intrude on his private thoughts without his consent.

"Physically," I clarify. "Though the attraction arose from an emotional place first. Basically, I trust you, and that has now allowed me to desire you." I gather my hair in a bun, then let it fall back down when I realize I don't have a hairband on me. "At least I think that's how it works. I'm kind of feeling this out for myself at the moment too. But however it came about, I am now —officially—attracted to you."

His eyes are focused on my hair, which I'm now twining

around my fingers because I need to do something with my hands.

"What?" He mutters the question, voice so low that I get the sense he's more asking himself.

Still, I'm now committed to being up front.

"I am telling you this because it's only gotten more intense. I would like to do something about my attraction."

He frowns. "What?"

"I want to act on it. With you. If that sounds appealing." Gods, this is sounding more like a job interview than when I first hired him. Which brings me to an important point. "To be clear, you can absolutely tell me no. This will have no bearing on your employment at the library. And I will do my best to direct my feelings elsewhere."

He gapes at me. "What?"

Frustration pricks at me. "I get that this might be slightly surprising, but could you please attempt a response other than *what*? It's overused at this point."

Bo blinks at me, swallows hard, then asks, "Are you making fun of me?"

Now it's my turn to gape. "What?"

Oh no, it's a *what* disease, and I've caught it.

"My ... my obvious crush on you," he says. "And you ... you're so much smarter than me. And so fucking gorgeous that I swear my eyes will start bleeding when I see you."

Oh. Well ... that's possibly the nicest thing anyone has ever said about me while simultaneously being a little too graphic.

"This is not a joke," I assure Bo, encouraged by his comments. "I've never figured out how to flirt. Never saw a reason to try. So, I'm just going to say, I'd like to do sex things with you if you'd also like to do sex things with me."

Damn The Dark One's plans. *Sex things?* Could I not have found at least a slightly more seductive way of phrasing it?

Problem is, Bo is staring at me. Hard. And the undivided

attention from the first man I've found physically attractive in ... well, ever, is making my brain a little mushy.

"I ..." He trails off, clears his throat, then says, "I would like to do sex things with you too."

Doubt is thick in his voice.

"You don't sound sure about that." I do my best to keep disappointment hidden, not wanting to guilt him into an encounter.

He shakes his head slowly, and my hope dips further.

"I'm sure I want to. I'm not sure this is reality though."

"Oh." I feel better now. And very horny. "It is. I assure you."

With a quick step forward, I poke his side, and he gasps when I hit what must be a ticklish spot.

"Now, here is what I propose." I point to his pants. "You take those off." I point to the chair. "You sit there." I point to my mouth. "I suck your dick until you come or tell me to stop."

He's gaping again, and I have the unfamiliar urge to nibble on his bottom lip.

"What?"

We're back to the *what*s.

"Here's the thing. I've had sex before, but it was a kind of go-through-the-motions thing. At some point, my body got on board simply because of stimulation. So, I want to just take some time stimulating you and see how I react to that. Physically. Does that make sense?"

"Not really. But I'm an idiot so ..." He shrugs.

Ice encases my libido.

"Bo," I say carefully, fury shivering through my body, "I know people have called you that in the past. People you cared about." I step in close and place my hands on the sides of his face, making sure he doesn't duck his head and avoid my eyes. "But you will *never* say that about yourself again. You do not insult my friend."

He swallows hard, his Adam's apple bobbing. "O-okay."

"It's okay if you don't understand something. There's no shame in learning."

He nods, his stare vulnerable, and the ice of my anger—directed at the world who misused this man—fades to the back of my mind as the heat of wanting him returns.

"And how do you feel about the scenario I outlined? Me using my mouth on you."

"Good," he grunts. "Very good."

Eager joy lights up yellow at the edges of my sight, little fireworks of my own emotions.

"Do you want to take your clothes off? Or do you want me to?"

"Whatever you want," he gasps.

I trace the edges of his stubble with my thumbs. "Whatever *we* want."

"You. If you'd enjoy it."

I smile. "I think I would." My hands drop to the top button of his flannel and pause. "If you ever want me to stop, just say so, and I will."

"Same. With me."

"Agreed." And I start slipping buttons free, eager to discover more of his body.

True, I saw every last inch of his that first night. But I didn't care about his form back then. He was a stranger I didn't quite trust. There was no attraction. No curiosity past wanting to know who had been trapped.

Tonight, it's like I'm discovering him again, and I'm panting for it.

The flannel is soft under my fingers, his skin smooth but for the slight brush of burnished blond chest hair. Now that Bo has agreed to this, I plan to give in to any physical urge I have, wanting to take full advantage of this attraction.

As his chest is revealed, I lean forward, nuzzling my nose

into the little hairs, then sliding sideways to lick the flat disk of his nipple.

Bo's breath catches, and his heavy hands settle on my hips. But he doesn't push me away or tell me to stop, so I keep going.

When the shirt is undone, I guide it off his shoulders so it pools on the floor. A puddle of fabric on the wood floor.

This monster, who took care of the house that hurt him. Now I want to return the favor, even though this truly feels like a gift to myself.

The old leather of his belt slides free, as smooth as melted butter. My fingers struggle some with the button of his fly, and without my realizing it, the frustration manifests in me biting his pec. I release my hold.

"Sorry."

"Don't. Don't apologize for any of this." Bo's voice is a needy rasp.

When I glance up, his expression is so stark that I can't help but see the red of desire and canary yellow of eagerness weaving thick blankets in his emotional grid. I blink the magic away, only wanting to look at him.

The button slips free, and I carefully unzip his fly and push his jeans and boxers down his legs, fingers coasting over the firm globes of his ass.

Bo's breathing accelerates as his erection juts forth, brushing the cotton of my sweater.

"Sit down," I tell him, palms flat on his chest, directing him toward the chaise lounge.

As always, Bo does what he's told.

He sits back, hands fisted on his thighs, chest expanding with deep breaths as he gazes up at me. His cock is thick, the tip of him an almost-angry red with the increased blood flow.

My mouth waters at the thought of sucking on him. Never in my life have I gotten turned on by the idea of giving a man head. I wasn't repulsed by the idea. Just uninterested.

Now though, I am full of erotic fascination. Sensual curiosity. I want to research every inch of this monster with my tongue.

And that's why, after I settle on my knees between his spread thighs, I don't immediately direct my attention to his lap.

Instead, I reach out and take hold of his left forearm, pulling one of his white-knuckled fists to me.

"Mor ..."

I pause. "Do you want me to stop?"

"N-no."

Carefully, I guide his fingers straight, then spread them until the webbing between each digit is stretched tight.

And I lick the warm, delicate skin, laving affection and fascination on this vulnerable area.

Bo gasps, his hips rocking with each pass of my tongue.

"Gods," he mutters. "You're gonna kill me. With just your sweet mouth on my hands. Hell ..."

His head drops back, and as I give the same affection to his right hand, I enjoy the salty taste of him while watching the muscles strain in his neck and down his torso.

All the while, my panties grow damp, and my excitement at knowing that I'm physically turned on by Bo only makes me hotter.

Throughout my webbed-finger sucking, his dick twitches and jerks, pre-cum beading on the slit and starting to drip down the mushroom-shaped head.

I want to know what that part of him tastes like too. I set his now-relaxed hands back on his thighs and lean forward. A thick vein runs from the base to the tip, and I trace that easy-to-follow guide with my tongue until I reach his juice. Then I encircle the flared head with my lips and suck.

"Ah!" Bo barks out the guttural exclamation and reaches

back to grab hold of the ornate wooden frame of the chaise. As if he's afraid his body might float off the couch.

No need for him to worry though because I strap him in with my body. I drape my arms over his thighs and slip my hands between his ass and the cushions, loving the feel of his clenching glutes against my palms.

Once his member is in my mouth, I see no reason to ever let him leave. He's all warm and savory. Fun to lick and suck. I experiment with how much of Bo I can fit in my mouth—which is not too much, unfortunately. A deep-throater I am not. But he seems plenty pleased with the inches I manage from the words he babbles out.

"Gods. Holy fucking gods. Your-your mouth ... I'll die. I'll die if you stop, Mor. Gods, I want more. I want you Mor. Always. Always, Mor."

Then he continues to chant, either my name or a direction for me to give him more.

Either way, I'm happy to oblige, sucking harder, humming my happiness at how much I'm enjoying this activity, then letting out little moans when I press my thighs together and envision him sinking this same dick inside me.

Goddess, I can't wait.

And knowing that I want to have sex, that I'm eager for it, has me grinning wide when I let Bo slip out of my mouth.

He stares down at me over his sweat-slicked chest that rises and falls rapidly, his eyes wide with bewilderment, like he still can't believe this is happening.

"Do you want to come in my mouth? Because I also want to ride you. No pressure, but I've never orgasmed with another person before, but I think you could get me there, Bo."

35

Bo

"I THINK *you could get me there, Bo."*

This beautiful witch speaks like I'm something special. Someone special.

As if I can do for her what no one else can.

Mor gazes up at me with such trust, such wanting, that I'm not able to manage a response at first.

Yes! my mind roars loudly, but the bellow doesn't reach my throat.

I'm too bowled over by the possibility that this smart, sexy, powerful woman could want me.

I'm not used to being wanted.

Mor seems to sense this, giving me the time I need to absorb her words, even as her breaths are heavy pants and her pupils are blown wide.

"Me?" I mutter eventually. "You're sure?"

"You." She nods once, driving home the point.

"Then I'm yours." *Destroy me if you wish.* At her hand, I don't think I'd mind.

Mor grasps my hand and tugs me toward the bed. I didn't want the window reveal to be ruined by plastic sheeting everywhere, so I made sure to clear out all signs of this having been a work zone and remade the mattress with clean linens.

"Sit down," she directs me.

I hurriedly follow my orders, though I'm half distracted by Mor's movements.

She pulls her sweater over her head, revealing the mouth-watering mounds of her breasts. Fuck, I want to cradle them, find her nipples and tease them.

As if hearing my thoughts, she strips her bra next, revealing a set of areolas as rosy as the witch smells.

Her black leggings go next, leaving lace stretched over a meaty ass I long to dig my fingers into and knead.

"Lie back on the bed, Bo," she directs me, pointing at the pillows I've longed to sink into ever since that first night where my drunken self didn't fully appreciate the honor of sleeping in her bed.

The mattress springs squeak when I drop onto the bed, and I drag myself back until I'm braced against the headboard. With the best view of her crawling toward me, tits swaying.

"Mor." Her name is a choked growl. All need.

And lucky me, I get to watch a flush overcome the skin of her neck and chest.

She kneels beside me, captures my hand as I reach for her, and instead guides my hand to my already-hardening cock. She encourages my strokes, and I revel in the direction from her soft hand.

"I have a contraceptive tattoo." Mor's voice is lower than normal, husky in a way that makes the back of my spine tingle and tighten. "Do you mind not using a condom?"

"Mind?" I grunt as her grip tightens. "No. Gods, I just want to feel you."

She tilts her chin up, moving her gaze from my erection to meet my eyes. "I want to feel you too, Bo."

Wreck me. She will wreck me.

But that doesn't stop me from bracing her hips as she slings a leg over mine. With one hand on my shoulder and the other reaching between us to grasp my cock, Mor lowers until my tip kisses her folds. A wretched groan tears through me at this simple touch. This careful approach she has to fucking me.

Nothing like the quick exchanges Georgiana and I had in the woods, where I could feel her need to move fast before she second-guessed her choice.

No, Mor is precise. She's thoughtful.

She's using my hard cock to stroke her clit, little gasps accompanying the movement.

"Gods," she moans. "Bless The Dark One. This feels so good. How do you feel so good, Bo?"

"I don't know." And the truth of those words lends them a desperate edge. I don't know why Mor wants me. Why I'm the one her body responds to. If I did know, I'd make sure to lean into it.

But all I can do is let her use me how she likes and hopefully learn how to keep her close.

"I'm going to put you in," she tells me, and I nod too many times in response.

The first inch threatens to undo me. The rest leave me sure I've died and ended up in a pleasure realm.

"Gods, I can feel how good it is for you," she pants while bracing a palm in the middle of my chest. "You're glowing with it."

My emotional grid, she must mean. At first, I was wary of her power, but soon realized that anything I feel, I'm happy to share with her. I hope she can see my aura now. Hope she knows this moment is transformative for me.

Then the witch sways her hips, and I bark with the spike of pleasure that shoots through my limbs.

"Gods. Mor. Again. Please."

"Touch me," she commands as she keeps up her rhythm.

Her breasts are heavy weights in my palms, and I love the velvety texture of her skin, contrasted with the tight points of her nipples. I stroke my thumbs over them.

Then I lean in to suck one. Mor gasps, plunging her fingers into my hair and holding me to her.

Her taste is earthy, tinged with sweat, and I feast on the sensations of being buried deep inside her while also dragging her into my mouth, all the while listening to her whisper my name.

"My clit, baby. Touch my clit."

The words are whimpers. But one of them spears me.

The endearment. A sweet little word.

She called me baby.

I let her nipple pop free to meet her needy gaze.

"Say it again," I growl, so overwhelmed by lust and longing that I sound angry.

But Mor understands.

"Baby." Her fingers comb through my hair. "Stroke my clit. Make me come."

Yes. Fuck yes. I'll be the one to give her this. The only one who has.

My touch tracks down over her soft belly, dives through her crimson curls, and slips under the little hood that hides her pleasure center.

"I'll give you anything," I promise her, wishing there were more to me to offer.

But if she wants my soul, hell, it's hers.

"You, baby." Her eyes go half lidded with my strokes, and she leans in to kiss me deep. When our lips part, she sighs, "I want you."

Then a sob spills from her throat, and I can feel Mor's body flutter, then grip mine hard with her orgasm.

She keens, and I growl in triumph, gripping her hips again to guide her up and down my length, fucking her as she rides the ecstasy. Milking myself until I reach the crest.

"Gods!" I shout, my balls emptying into the witch, the space between us slick with both our pleasure. "Gods," I gasp again as I collapse back, Mor a puddle of spent woman on my chest.

We lie there for a time, our breathing eventually slowing into a matching rhythm. Sunlight filters through the skylight, casting rose petals across Mor's back.

I want to see her like this every day.

I want to fix the things that break around her.

I want her to call me baby.

Worry creeps in.

What if this is like the last time? What if this was just a fuck for her?

"Bo?" Mor's voice pulls my focus down to hers. She has her chin resting on my chest, eyes on my face.

My softening cock still inside her channel.

"You're mustards."

"I'm ... what?"

Her lips tilt in a rueful smirk. "Your aura. There's a bit of mustard brown." Her lips flatten. "You're anxious. Did I do something wrong?"

"No. No." I emphasize the word when I catch a flash of doubt in her eyes. "Mor, I ... I'm worried this is all you'll want. That you and me ... that there won't be a you and me."

She blinks, then rises up on her elbows and studies me, still making no move to disconnect our bodies.

And with her glorious tits on display, my cock is trying its best to harden a second time.

"How would you feel about being my boyfriend, Bo?"

Hope. Joy. Want. Need.

They crash through me in what must be a storm of colors I belatedly realize Mor can see.

And her response is to grin, lean in close, and brush her lips across mine.

"You like that ... baby?"

This time, I groan and give an involuntary thrust of my hips, half-hard cock wanting to go another round.

Mor places gentle kisses along my cheeks and nose and jaw, ending at my ear.

"What you want, Bo? I want it too."

Bo

I've started to get used to seeing Georgiana. We both live in this small town, and unlike before my curse, I'm venturing out more. In the past, I kept to the Monster section of Lake Galen as much as I could manage, only coming into town for work and necessities. Now though, I make sure to stop by Coffee & Claws most weekdays to get Mor a surprise coffee.

Not a surprise that I'm getting her one, but the flavor combo is.

And I grocery shop with Mor. And I stop into Never Judge a Cover to find a new story to enjoy now that reading isn't painful. And I stop in at Local Brew some evenings, where Griffith makes me virgin drinks so I don't try starting my own karaoke night again.

So, on these excursions, yes, I occasionally see the siren. Sometimes, she's with a friend. Sometimes, she's with her husband.

Dr. Stormwind. He looks distinguished with his neatly styled salt-and-pepper hair, perfectly ironed slacks and button-up shirts, topped off with a thick metal watch that I bet is a Rolex.

Could a man be any more different from me?

Educated. Wealthy. Not a monster.

If Georgiana married a man like that, then had she ever truly considered a future with me?

But when I glimpse the siren with her doctor, no self-loathing arises. Because, I realize, Georgiana's life choices no longer matter to me.

Not like when Mor went out with that good-looking professor not too long ago.

That day, my jealousy was so strong that it made me ill. But that guy meant nothing to Mor.

And I mean something to her. I'm the one with her hand in mine when we come into town, the witch unapologetic about her claim on me.

And I'm the one with her savory taste on my tongue each night in the highest room of her enchanted library.

Today though, I'm alone on my coffee errand. And so is Georgiana when she turns away from the front counter and meets my eyes. Hers go wide with shock.

"B-Bo," she stammers, her voice not matching her composed look in a pink sundress and heels.

For some reason, the color choice annoys me. She's all summer a few weeks before Halloween. Doesn't she know it's time for burnt oranges and dark greens?

Rich, rusty reds, like the curls I want to tangle my fingers in. "Hello, Georgiana."

It's easy not to use her nickname. She isn't Georgie anymore. I'm not sure she ever was. That woman seems more like a mask she wore to fool a lonely boy into trusting her.

But I don't resent her. As terrible as my captivity was, Mor made an astounding observation.

If I hadn't been trapped, I likely would have left Folk Haven.

Georgiana wouldn't have gone with me, but at the time, that would have given me all the more reason to go. Discovering that the woman I cared for never felt the same.

And I would have stayed away.

And I never would have met my lusty witch, who thinks my glasses are hot and calls me *baby* with affection and lets me care for her in the way I've wanted all my life.

I don't know if I can say thank you to my never-true friend. But I also don't hate her the way I did just a month ago, when I learned how she had given up on me without even trying.

I choose to nod and offer her a tight smile before stepping up to the counter.

Sonya, co-owner of Coffee & Claws, is working the register today, and she offers me a wide grin. "Ah! Here for Mor's caffeine fix? Let's see, what fun can we have today?"

"Something fall-flavored," I tell her. "Pumpkin spice maybe. But with something extra."

Sonya snaps her fingers. "Spicy pumpkin spice. I'll add a dash of cayenne to it."

Spicy pumpkin spice. I've never heard of a more perfect flavor.

"She'll love that. With oat milk, please. And let's go hot."

The siren claps in delight and adds my dark roast coffee to the order without me having to ask. I also point to a couple of apple turnovers, knowing they'll add a sweet, cinnamon punch to the coffee break I'm about to take with my delicious woman.

And I only realize I've completely forgotten about Georgiana when I'm walking out of Coffee & Claws and a demanding hand wraps around my forearm. The pink-dressed siren drags me into a nearby alley, and I let her more from shock than because she's strong enough to move me.

"What's wrong?" I ask, figuring some dangerous catastrophe must be about to befall us because that's the only reason Georgiana Stormwind would willingly break the cold shoulder she's been giving me.

"Bo, I ..." She dithers, glancing behind my shoulder, then up into my face with a feverish gleam in her eyes.

"What—"

She cuts my question off by diving forward and plastering her mouth to mine.

And once again, I'm too shocked to come up with an immediate reaction. Also, my hands are full of coffee and pastries, so I don't have any limbs free for pushing.

After a beat of befuddlement, I whip my head to the side and suck in a breath, trying to clear her artificial strawberry scent from my nose and my mouth.

How rude would it be for me to spit?

"What the hell?" I gasp instead.

"I'm sorry, Bo." Georgiana licks her lips, and I think she's apologizing for molesting me, until she continues, "I've missed you, and I needed to do that."

Still reeling, I gaze around us, as if the environment will help this make sense. But, no, we're just in a shadowy alley that smells like dirt and dust. Georgiana tucked us away in the shadows to take what she wanted from me. Just like she always has.

"You dragged me into this alley to kiss me in secret." I glare down at her. "Like something shameful."

"No! It's just that ... I just wanted to talk to you. In private." She stands taller and reaches out to place her hands on my chest. "I still want you, Bo."

I step back, dodging her touch.

"Still want me?" I shake my head, flummoxed by this whole turn of events.

"Yes." Her voice is breathless, pupils wide as she reaches for me again, and the wall at my back halts my retreat. "We were young and wild together. I miss that. I miss you." She drags her touch downward, as if cataloging my muscles through my flannel. "I want to be with you."

My brain clicks back online, and I slide to the side toward the alley's entrance.

"Do you?" I ask, my voice hard. "Because that all just sounded like you want to fuck me." I frown hard, hurting, like rusty nails are in my stomach. Not because I was hoping for Georgiana to want me again, but because it's painful, being reminded how little I mean to someone I used to see as my world. "Are you ever going to stop trying to use me? Just because I cared for you once doesn't mean I'm going to be your twenty-something side piece because you're bored, married to your human doctor."

Georgiana flinches back, eyes wide, manicured nails glinting pearly white as she presses her fingers against her lips.

"I was always your dirty secret. Now you're looking to repeat the past." The anger drains out of me as fast as it rose. I was never great at staying mad. My next words only carry exhaustion. "Maybe you do actually want me. But *I* don't want *you*."

My eyes drop to the hot latte in my hand, where I see Sonya's sloping handwriting.

Bo & Mor.

"Bo, please—"

"Bo?" a voice asks from the mouth of the alleyway, and I turn to find Ame in a set of scrubs. "Is Georgiana bothering you?" the witch asks, not caring for tact in the slightest.

Gods, I love the Shelly family.

The siren, whose voice sounded vulnerable and hopeful just a moment ago, tucks those emotions behind a haughty mask. Or maybe it's the other way around. I guess I'll never be sure.

"Talking is not bothering, dear," she huffs, then struts her way out of the alley, as if she didn't just try to proposition me.

Ame steps aside to let the siren pass, and then the witch

waits for me to join her on the sidewalk in the bright autumn sunshine.

"You have great timing," I tell her.

"I heard a big *I want to fuck Bo Folan* desire and thought it was Mor." Ame stares up at me, expression unreadable.

"I hope that's what Mor wants," I mumble, staring at the sidewalk between my boots. "I'm not going to ask you to keep what just happened from her. But I'd like to be the one to tell her, if that's all right by you."

Ame stares at me. "You're very bad at shielding your emotions. Did you know that?"

"I ... no."

"You are. Mor will know right away that she's the only one you want. If you're going home right now to tell her what happened, feel free to FaceTime me if you want someone to corroborate your story."

"FaceTime?"

"Video call." She holds up her phone. "But I don't think you'll need it. I believe you. Mor will believe you." Ame takes a step back, and then she runs her eyes from the top of my head down to my boots, then settles back on my face. "Would you like a hug? Jack likes when I hug him, but he's also obsessed with me, so I don't actually know if I'm any good at it."

This witch. She's kind of hilarious.

And when I consider her question, I find the answer almost immediately.

"I would like a hug." I spread my arms, hands still clutching coffees, but that doesn't stop me from wrapping them around Ame as she encircles my waist in a firm hold. "You're good at this," I tell her because she is.

This is a high-quality hug.

Ame gives an extra squeeze, then steps away. "My lunch break is running out. I'll keep an eye out for your call."

But she was right.

When I return to the library, I sit Mor down and tell her about more than what just happened. I give her all of my history with Georgiana. Up until the point that Sev's magical gag cuts me off. But she understands enough.

Mor listens to what happened, and the first thing out of her mouth is, "I don't care if she's on the Mythic Council. I'm going to tit-punch that bitch the next time I see her."

"You ... what?"

Mor stands up, fists clenched, brow furrowed in anger. "She thinks she can turn her back on you, then just decide she wants a nice young boy toy to fuck when she gets bored in her marriage? That she can just play with your emotions like that? No way in any fucking hell dimension. Her tit, my fist—they will have a meeting!" Mor waves said fist in the air.

And I snort. Then chuckle.

Then full-on belly laugh.

"You know what's going to be hilarious?" She thrusts a finger at my chest, which is still vibrating with chuckles. "How wonky her boobs will look when I punch one so hard that it points in the wrong direction. That bitch. THAT BITCH!"

"Mor, Gods, please stop," I beg through tears of laughter. "I already adore you too much. I can't hear you talk about tit-punching a woman to defend my honor."

I snag her around the waist and haul her into my lap. She's vibrating with fury, and her raccoon chitters in encouragement from the top of a nearby bookshelf.

"Are you jealous?" I ask, suddenly curious.

"What?" she sputters, letting out a few indignant huffs, then crosses her arms and pouts. "I'm too mature to be jealous. I am above jealousy." Then she turns, grabs my face, and kisses me like we've sunk to the bottom of Lake Galen and I'm her only source of oxygen.

I groan, the sound deep and needy. "Yes," I pant between kisses. "Only want you."

She bites my bottom lip, and my hips thrust in response.

"We haven't been together long," Mor says quietly, frowning around the words and glaring at my mouth, as if she can see some remnant of Georgiana's kiss.

I tighten my arms and shove a hand down the back of her leggings to get a nice, meaty handful of her bare ass.

"Then leave your mark on me, witch. Because I don't want anyone doubting who I belong to ever again."

Her response is frenzied, and we barely manage to flip the sign to *Closed* before she drags off my shirt.

For hours, Mor drives me wild by sucking hickey after hickey into my skin, growling in frustration when they each heal in a matter of minutes.

She rides me so hard that I swear the house will be too scandalized to ever open its shades again, but still, that's not enough for my witch.

When we finally lie sweaty and exhausted, tangled in the sheets that we might have partially shredded, Mor tugs a blue ribbon out of a book where she was using it as a bookmark. Using fingers that shake with weakness, she ties the ribbon around my wrist, knotting it tight.

"There," she wheezes. "You're marked. You're mine."

Grinning so wide that I swear it will break my face, I let out a howl.

37

Mor

AFTER RECEIVING a vague text from Owen MacNamara—a local selkie who visits my library pretty regularly—I pull on my shoes and head down to the dock. Ame and Jack are on their way down, too, but they pause to feed Lucky her evening meal.

I'm not surprised to find Bo with his pant legs rolled up, feet in the water. He's made a habit of settling on the edge of the floating platform and staring out at the lake as the water laps around his legs.

He jerks his head up at the sound of my approach, and then a beautiful grin overtakes his face.

"Ma'am," he says when I'm within earshot.

I glare.

He chuckles.

The sound is so happy that I can't fight off the small smile that claims my face.

"If you keep calling me ma'am, I'm going to start calling you old man," I warn as I take a seat beside him. The water is cool, claiming the fall chill more thoroughly than the air has at this point.

"Hmm. I guess, technically, I'm forty. You're the baby compared to me." He smirks as I pretend to scowl at his young face.

"Shut up before I shove you in," I grumble, setting off another round of his laughter. I regret losing the sound of it when the steadily growing roar of an engine drowns it out.

The humor on Bo's face fades to a confused frown as we watch a pontoon boat approach our dock.

Owen slows the boat down a ways out, approaching at a slow clip that allows me to jump up and toss him a rope. He shuts off the engine and uses the rope to draw the pontoon close enough that I can step aboard. Ame and Jack arrive on the dock and also climb aboard the boat.

"What's happening?" Bo is on his feet now, eyes flicking between me and the selkie.

"Secret meeting," I tell him.

"It's not secret if you tell people about it," Owen chides, but with no true annoyance in his voice.

"Oh." Bo still seems disconcerted, but he steps back from the boat, immediately accepting that any secret meeting occurring would not involve him.

And I think that's a load of bullshit.

I pop open the tiny door leading onto the pontoon—a door Bo could easily step over—and wave the monster on board. "Come on. Secret meeting time."

"I'm invited?" Bo asks.

"He's invited?" Owen says at the same time.

"You said this has to do with town safety," I point out. "Bo is ..." I trail off as I try to explain a connection I made in my mind but have yet to put words to.

He dips his chin and shoves his hands into his pockets. "It's okay, Mor. Y'all go on."

"No," I snap. "Bo is the least likely to hurt someone. Anyone." I turn on Owen. "This town was shitty to him seventeen years ago, and he's still here. Just being an all-around decent guy. So he deserves to be there. And I trust him." Holding Bo's wide eyes, I say the words I know to be true deep in my soul. "I trust Bo with my books. I trust him with my home. I trust him with my family." Then I shake my head, letting out a small laugh. "No, he *is* family."

"Hear, hear!" Ame chirps.

"Agreed," Jack grunts.

Every inch of Bo's skin that I can see blushes a deep shade of red. The poor guy is about to overheat.

Owen clears his throat. "Delta Novac. You have a problem with her?" he asks, and I realize I might have made an oversight.

The dragon who trapped Bo is dead and gone, but his daughter is still here. And she's mated to Owen's brother. Basically part of one of the founding families.

"We talked," Bo rasps. "I got mad, I admit. But I apologized. Gave Gigabyte a treat."

Owen grins, quick to forgive and forget. "Well, all right then! Hop on board, buddy. We've got places to be."

Bo doesn't hesitate. He strides onto the boat, then claims my hand, slides his fingers between mine as much as his webbing allows, and draws me down to sit beside him.

He holds on to me as Owen tosses the rope back onto the dock and points the pontoon toward open water, cruising at a speed slightly too fast for us to be able to chat over the rush of wind.

But I can see what the exchange we just had did to Bo.

Daffodil hope, mixed with lilac relief and a dash of sunshine joy.

I never thought being a Shelly was too big of a deal, but it seems like I've rewired Bo's entire emotional grid. Every so often, he'll bring my hand up to his mouth and press a kiss against the back before resettling our clasped palms in his lap. When I shiver at the cold wind, mixed with spray from lake water, Bo drapes his free arm around my shoulders and draws me into the shielding warmth of his body.

And I think I want this boat ride to go on for forever.

But of course, it can't. Owen turns us down an inlet and then navigates into a long, narrow cove. The banks spike up high on either side of us, which means the water is probably still pretty deep.

We go around one more turn, and up ahead, I spot a small floating dock. A few Jet Skis are tied to it, leaving just enough room for Owen's pontoon. The selkie skillfully maneuvers his vessel into an open spot, and using his own rope this time, he disembarks and ties the boat to the dock.

"We're meeting up at the house," Owen explains, pointing to a set of switchback steps that cut up the steep bank.

"This ... this is Monster territory," Bo murmurs, staring around, probably trying to orient himself after the boat ride.

I always find it hard to connect where roads lead versus where sailing on the lake ends us.

"Right you are," Owen agrees a moment before we hear the repetitive noise of large, flapping wings.

A blue being descends, landing in a crouch on the dock so smoothly that the wooden surface barely rocks.

When the new arrival stands, I stare at a blue creature with a feminine figure, bald head, and scales instead of skin. Their eyes—a murky purple mass—land on the monster at my side.

"Bo Folan?"

38

Bo

"SATINE?" I whisper the name, not quite believing what I'm seeing.

The Satine I remember was a young girl, though still covered in blue scales with bat-like wings popping out of holes in the back of her altered shirts.

She was not this proud figure, flying freely with a carefree grin on her slim lips.

"I didn't realize *you* were the monster the Shellys freed! I'm sorry. I would've come to visit you if I'd known." She lunges forward and wraps me in a strong hug. "Hells, you look exactly the same."

"You don't," I blurt.

She backs up, laughing a joyful noise I wasn't sure I'd ever hear from the shy monster, hidden away from most of the world because of her appearance. My webbed digits are nothing compared to what Satine is working with. She'll never pass for human.

"That's what seventeen years does. You grow up." She tilts her head toward the witch at my side. "Hi. I've seen you around, but we've never met. I'm Satine."

She thrusts out her blue hand, and Mor immediately accepts the shake.

"Morgana Shelly. But you can call me Mor. I run the Mythic Library."

"I know." She sighs. "I've been dying to go."

"Come anytime you want. It's mythics only."

That earns Mor another grin, and then Satine reaches out and grabs my arm.

"I'm so glad you're free. And that you're back. I missed you when I thought you'd left."

I blink in surprise. Satine missed me? Griffith claimed the same, but I still have trouble believing it.

Although that's probably my own insecurities. Maybe I put too much weight on how the adults of Folk Haven thought of me. Seems the younger generation didn't care so much.

"Glad to be back," I mumble.

"Come on. Most everyone is here." Satine guides us toward the steps, walking this time rather than flying, though I'm sure it would be quicker.

As we ascend, Satine tells Mor about the handful of times I babysat so her parents could have a date night. Satine claims I was a pushover when it came to bedtimes, which ... fair.

Mor's hand tightens in mine as she chuckles through the stories.

At the top of the steps, a house I remember sits among the trees.

"Satine's property has high-quality wards," Owen explains. "And she was kind enough to offer her home as a meeting place."

On the front lawn, we come upon a large group, only some

of who I know. Griffy is here, and he strides over to give me a one-armed hug. A few others smell of wolf. One tall, broad man with a commanding air carries the scent of the gray wolf Jack and I encountered.

Is that his father?

From the way he stares at the wolf at my side, I'd guess yes.

Levi is here, and he offers a nod and a smile that feels like my abandonment of his hospitality might be forgiven. He clasps hands with an obviously pregnant woman with curly hair who looks like she could be related to Owen.

Selena—the witch council member who comes by the library regularly—smirks at Mor, her eyes dropping to our clasped hands.

Will our relationship cause problems for her?

Mor doesn't seem worried about it with the way she keeps a firm hold on me.

The witch shifts to the side, and a familiar siren steps forward.

Georgiana.

Her eyes widen when they meet mine. But there's nothing really to say, and I have a warm hand grasped in mine that's keeping me grounded.

Also, I may have to use my hold to restrain Mor from a tit-punch. This doesn't seem like the proper venue for an act of aggression against a Mythic Council member.

"I made a few changes since you were last here," Satine says conversationally, unaware of the awkward situation potentially unfolding.

"Last here? When was he last here?" A big redheaded brute comes hurrying up to us, his eyes jumping between Satine and me.

"This is Bo. I used to know him when I was younger," Satine explains to the anxious man. "An old friend."

"Ah. Friend. Okay." He leans close to Satine. "You still like me more than him, right?"

Satine snorts, then wraps her arms around the redhead's neck. "I *love* you more than anyone else in the world, you silly bear." Then she kisses him quick and throws me a smile over her shoulder. "This is Mahon. Bear shifter, my mate." She lowers her voice into the projected hush of a stage whisper. "He's a little bit obsessed with me."

"Sorry about that. Always good to meet a friend of Satine's." Mahon keeps one arm around his mate's waist and extends the other to me for a handshake.

I return the gesture enthusiastically, chest full of an indescribable amount of joy—knowing the shy girl, who once asked me if her blue scales were ugly, is now happily in love and radiating confidence.

"Good to meet you too, Mahon. Really good. Do you know Mor?" I tug my witch closer.

Mahon pouts. "You never have me deliver you coffee anymore, Mor Shelly!"

My witch rolls her eyes. "You'd always spill half of it, carrying it on that ridiculous scooter."

The bear shifter lets out a dramatic gasp. "Do not blasphemy my beautiful Vespa."

Mor pretends like he didn't say anything. "And Bo is my coffee delivery guy now. He works at the library. My right-hand man."

I blush, and smile, and overall enjoy this simple moment of making connections.

Then Owen lopes up to the top step of the porch and claps his hands twice to get the gathering's attention.

"Thank you, everyone, for coming here at my request." His voice easily projects over the group of mythics. "I'm sure many of you are wondering what this is all about." Gone is the silly selkie driving a pontoon boat.

This man commands the audience.

"Do you know what this is about?" I whisper to Mor.

"I have an idea," she murmurs back.

But speculation isn't necessary because Owen provides the answer.

"We're here to form a protection force for Folk Haven."

39

Mor

THERE'S a moment of shocked silence, then a rolling wave of voices after Owen's announcement.

He lets people chatter. Lets the idea simmer.

If everyone in this yard is on board, this potential protection team has a variety of heavy hitters.

Levi Abadi, monster council representative, descends from the leviathan—yeah, that's right, *the* leviathan. Plus, he's got witch blood.

The entire Mythic Council lineup is pretty impressive.

In addition to Levi, there's Juan Greymark, the second most powerful werewolf in the original Folk Haven wolf pack. Jack would knock him down a peg if he ever committed to joining. But he's still a lone wolf, and maybe that's why he's attending this get-together too. Ame is at his side because most everyone knows her magic is fucking scary if she ever wants it to be.

I spot at least three more wolves. Jack's dad, Baron Moonson, leader of the Folk Haven pack. Griffith, bartender at Local

Brew and a kind of ambassador between the Folk Haven pack and the newly minted, as of two years ago, Lake Galen pack. Their alpha is also here, Veronica, a petite white woman with long blonde hair and an edge of violence in her eyes.

Selena—witch council member and head of the local coven —sits on a low tree limb as she observes the group.

Moira—selkie, Of the Fin council member, and Levi's mate —cradles her rounded belly and sits in a lawn chair with the monster just over her shoulder. I don't know that selkies are particularly intimidating mythics, but Moira's from one of the town's founding families, and therefore, she wields a great deal of political and social influence. Plus, Samantha—chief of police and mermaid—stands near her.

Lastly from The Council, there's Georgiana, also a holder of great influence and a voice that could render anyone in this yard into a forgetful, reeling mess. And tonight, she seems on edge. Her eyes flicking to Bo and then away and then back again.

I don't like that.

However, I'm not about to brawl with the siren at this meeting, as much as I'd like to follow through on that promise of a tit punch. Bo turned her down, and unless she tries to use her council seat to manipulate or intimidate him, then there's no reason for me to step in.

Though, if Georgiana tries to grope Bo again, I can't say what I'll do exactly.

But I've got a library full of options and a protective streak urging me to utilize some of the nastier spells I've come across.

There's a scattering of other mythics, including Mayor Nightson, though the griffin seems fine with standing back for the moment and hearing Owen out. I think her preference for listening to her constituents is one of the reasons she keeps getting reelected.

"To be clear"—Owen's voice reclaims the crowd—"what I propose is not a secondary police force." Owen nods toward Samantha. "We wouldn't be patrolling our neighbors. No authority to simply attack anyone we suspect is a threat." Owen spreads his arms. "Think more along the lines of emergency responders. Prepared to go into action if the town calls on us."

"This seems dramatic," Juan says. "What looming threat do you expect to face?"

"Sorcerers, for one."

The entire gathering tenses at the mention of humans who are not only aware that mythics exist, but have found ways to siphon their magic for their own uses.

Everyone is blatantly *not* looking at Jack. The wolf knows better than anyone in this town how twisted those wielders can be.

"Sorcerers are rare," Georgiana says, voice prim. "More likely to burn themselves up with stolen magic than actually be able to wield it. And even if one were to approach Folk Haven, that's what the wards are for."

"Selena," Owen calls on the coven leader, "how are the town wards holding up?"

I already know the answer to this. She's been by the library multiple times, searching for a solution.

"They are weakening," she admits, and a chill washes over the group.

A few don't look surprised. The mayor. Samantha. But others gape. Not everyone knew then. Did Georgiana?

"Verona and Marney were strong protection witches, but after they passed a year back, we haven't been able to fully re-create what they accomplished."

I never got to meet the mated witch couple who kept casting a safety net over this town until they were in their nineties. In the final years of their lives, they stayed holed up in their woodland cottage on the edge of the Folk Haven boundary.

"We appreciate the coven's work," Owen says, and I'm pleasantly surprised at how much like a leader he sounds. I've only known him as a goofy guy who runs the local recycling company. But he's from the same founding family as Moira, and he obviously cares deeply about this town. "But weak wards leave us vulnerable, and we're a feast if sorcerers ever discover what exactly Folk Haven is. And hunters are equally as risky."

He names the group that doesn't bother to siphon the magic, but instead get paid by trapping mythics and delivering them to sorcerers.

In the town where my siblings and I were raised, we never had to worry much about either group. Multiple warding witches lived in the area. I'm tempted to offer that we could send word, requesting their help. But large wards need to be renewed continuously and are stronger if the caster is nearby. Plus, there are people in my hometown I don't want visiting Folk Haven.

Bad players in a different way.

"Then there are the threats we've yet to comprehend," Owen continues. "All I'm saying is, I would rather be anticipatory as opposed to reactionary. If we put plans in place that we never need to use, then great. But if we do nothing and something terrible happens, I could never forgive myself." His hands drop. "I'm not powerful. I know that. What selkies are is cautious, and that's because we always live with the fear of half of us being stolen away." He refers to the pelts his kind use to shift into their other forms. If stolen, selkies are slaves to whoever has their second skin. "Now though, I choose to look at that instinctual fear as a good thing. It is a warning that as much as we hope our world is kind, often, it isn't. To live safely, let us prepare defenses against the evil in the world."

The mayor steps forward. "That was well said, Owen." She turns to the group, hands clasped in front of her. "Most of us recall the story of how Lake Galen was created. Folk Haven itself is proof that there is evil we need to watch for, and I believe that Owen's proposal makes sense. In addition, our town needs to stop erecting divides and instead find more ways to work cohesively."

"Sounds like you're looking to build a town of monsters," Juan grumbles.

Levi glares at the werewolf beta. But he's not the only one. Most of the gathering throws scathing looks the wolf's way. Does he not realize that in addition to the monsters present, there are a decent amount of mythics mated to others not of their kind? Hell, the pregnant selkie has a monster in her belly.

Read the room.

"I am trying to build a town that is a haven for mythics. *All* mythics." Mayor Nightson faces the group. "Now—without insults—please, let's discuss what this emergency team might look like."

Owen takes the stage again. "First and foremost, it'll have to be a group that works well together. If something bad is going down, there can't be arguments and sniping about who is in charge."

"So, basically, everyone has to listen to you?" Veronica, alpha of the Lake Galen pack, asks, a note of judgment in her voice. Tensions are high there, with pressure for her to meld her pack with the Folk Haven one and give over control to Baron Moonson—Jack's father.

Owen doesn't let her tone rattle him. "No. Not me. I suggest The Council choose a leader. I'm here as a consultant. Offering up my recommendation for mythics who should be included on the team." He steps into the middle of the group. "Ones who are cunning." He waves toward Selena. "Fast." Griffith. "Stealthy." Satine. "And of course, muscle." His grin starts out directed toward Mahon, the bear shifter, but then he shifts to face Bo.

That's right. If they want true muscle, then they'll need my monster.

40

Bo

OWEN SAILS the four of us back to the library, the return trip quiet, but not just because the wind stops conversation. We all appear to be sitting with the idea of a protection team for the town.

A month ago, I might not have cared. But now?

Now I have people I want to protect.

Mor cuddles into my side, and I angle my body to block most of the wind.

We left without any official decisions having been made, other than Owen being required to write up a detailed proposal of what this team would look like, to be presented at the next Mythic Council meeting. I got the sense he hoped for more forward movement, less bureaucracy, but he agreed.

When we approach the library's dock, Owen slows the boat to a crawl, skillfully docking it, while Jack and I help with the ropes. The witches head up to the house, Jack on their heels, and I'm about to push Owen off when he stops me.

"I'm going to get The Council to sign off on this, Bo. And

when I do, I hope I can count you in. Mor's right; you'd be an asset in a fight."

Owen doesn't know that I've spent my entire life trying to do as little damage as possible. That joining some battle team would be going against every lesson I've lived by.

Make myself small.

Make myself unnoticeable.

Don't give anyone a reason to fear me.

"I'm not a violent guy." I offer him a hopeless shrug, feeling like I'm failing him when he's reaching out a hand of friendship.

The selkie tilts his head, studying me. "Are you a pacifist?" Owen asks in a surprisingly gentle voice. "If so, no need to say another word. I'm not trying to make you do something against your beliefs."

A tension eases from my shoulders at the knowledge that he's not about to bully me. I've dealt with enough of those for a lifetime.

"It's not that. I just ..." I scratch the back of my neck. "I don't want people to be scared of me."

"Ah." Owen reaches out to squeeze my shoulder. "That's how it was? Before you were cursed?"

I nod.

Owen watches me as he says his next words carefully. "Did Mor tell you about the guy who broke into her house?"

My body goes rigid. "What? When did that happen? Who was it?"

Where can I find him?

"A selkie, believe it or not. Normally, we're pretty tame, but Hamish was a piece of work. He broke in while everyone was sleeping. Used an enchantment to keep them unconscious, but Anthony got to the house after it was cast and wasn't put under. They fought. Anthony almost died."

I'm breathing hard, the heavy breaths like bellows.

Another break-in at the library? I know exactly who sent the selkie. Sev chose a mythic minion who was willing to use violence in a way I never would have against innocents.

"He's gone. The witches rigged up a punishment fitting the crime. But I'm just wondering, if you had walked into the library that night—found Hamish in Mor's room while she was spelled asleep—would you have wanted to scare him?"

The answer requires no thought as I gaze at the thin blue ribbon wrapped around my wrist. "Yes."

I would want to strike terror into his heart. Brand fear onto the man's soul so that he dreams of me and cowers every night.

"That's why I think you could be an asset to this team." Owen pats my chest. "That break-in was out of the ordinary, but the Shellys are sitting on a treasure trove of knowledge. They could be targeted again."

"The house has protections." I know that better than most.

"What if the house isn't fast enough? What if someone tries to accost Mor when she's not inside the library?"

My fists clench and unclench.

Owen sees the signs of my smoldering fury and nods, tapping my chest with his finger. "You don't long for violence. I think that's a good thing. I'm not a fan either. But if someone I love is in danger, I'm going to be ready to help them in any way I can. Even if that means getting uncomfortable." He waves back toward the library. "What do you say, Bo? When danger creeps past the failing wards, is she on her own?"

An image comes to me then—of Mor sleeping in her cozy bed, a moonbeam alighting her pale skin, until the shine is blotted out by a dark figure looming over her bed. Someone who's come to harm her.

Fuck that.

"Never," I growl. "I'll never let her fight alone."

Owen grins and pushes his boat away from the dock. "Great. Welcome to the Oh Shit Team."

41

Mor

Bo is replacing some old boards on the dock, and I'm shamelessly staring at the shirtless monster through our kitchen window. Unfortunately, there's a decent distance between the house and the lake, so I'm only able to goggle a miniature version of the monster.

"Fixed," Jack announces from the room over.

With a sigh, I leave off my staring and join the werewolf at the computer station I have set up for all library-related things.

"What was wrong?" I called in my brother-in-law because the cataloging system he'd built for the Public Mythic Library was creating double records of some books.

"Titles starting with 'the' were listing twice. *The History of Water Beasts* and *History of Water Beasts* comma *The*. My fault. Now they list the second way."

"You're my favorite werewolf."

Jack throws me a smirk. "I—"

He freezes, his eyes going pure black.

And I don't need to ask him why because I spy white

tendrils of light—the same emotional spike he felt—radiating from the front of the house.

Ame is afraid.

Jack launches up, leaving the office chair spinning in his wake as he sprints to the front door, me on his heels. When we burst out onto the porch, the wolf keeps going. Meanwhile, I stumble to a stop, horrified by the sight in front of me.

A Mercedes is parked in the gravel lot. A couple climbs out in tandem—the woman short with pinup curves and shoulder-length blonde hair, the man tall and lithe with a head of dark red hair. They look the same as when I last saw them.

Ame stands as still as the statues in the garden, her face as pale as the fear in her aura.

"What's wrong, Ame?" Jack growls the words as he enfolds his mate in a protective embrace.

"They're here," she murmurs, eyes wide and locked on the couple, all blood leeched from her cheeks.

"Who?" Jack's question is low and urgent. "Who are they?"

"Our parents," I say so she doesn't have to. Regaining my ability to move, I jog down the stairs and try to figure out how to make Helena and Alistair leave and never come back.

Why the hell are they even here?

The Shelly parents seemed perfectly content up in Maine.

Those wards really must be malfunctioning.

"Girls. Look at you." My mother gives each of us a distracted smile as her attention flicks to the house behind me.

The library.

Full of magical knowledge. Endless spells.

"Morgana. Amethyst." Our father's focus stays on us, his grin charming. He's very good at endearing people to him. A skill Anthony inherited, though my brother is also a decent person. My father is missing something fundamental at his core. "It's been too long."

"Why are you here?" The question comes in a hard snap from Jack.

He only ever interacted with the Shelly parents as a cat, but he knows plenty about their version of child raising.

Alistair tilts his head. "What a rude creature you are." Unaware of the danger he's in, my father saunters closer. "I'm allowed to see my daughters whenever I wish. Who are you to question that?"

"My mate," Ame pipes up, her voice strung tight. "This is Jack. He's my mate."

Alistair frowns and glances toward our mother, but she's too focused on the library to notice. "Why didn't you contact us when you were looking for a mate?"

Gods, like she was shopping for a life partner.

"Because you're not a part of her life," Jack states, his voice sharp as cracked ice. He glances down at my sister, his voice gentling with his next words. "Unless you've changed your mind?"

Ame shakes her head.

He turns his attention to me, and I'm surprised by his next question.

"And you, Mor? Do you want them here?"

I feel a warm glow in my chest, knowing that Jack cares about my feelings on this subject. Not that I expect he'd side with me over Ame, but at least he doesn't treat me like a nonentity.

Still, I've never expressly told my parents they are uninvited from my life. Other than the time I emancipated myself, that is. Not sure they even noticed.

But I have a house full of magical books, and they're paying attention now.

"No. I don't want them here," I admit, without a waver in my voice.

My father blinks at me. My mother ignores me, strolling toward the library I've built.

"Wait—"

"No further." So fast that I didn't even see him move, Jack is suddenly in front of Helena, so close that she stumbles back a step with a huff.

"I was told this is a public library."

"Your daughters don't want you here."

"Well then, they should have made this a private library." My mother smirks and steps around Jack, the move possible only because he lets her. She lets out a, "Ha," as if her maneuvering was an accomplishment, and skips up the porch steps.

But when she tries to open the door, nothing happens.

"Why is this locked?"

"It's not," I say, honestly confused, not that I want to help her enter.

"The house doesn't like you." The deep rumble of a voice sounds just before Bo rounds the corner, narrowed eyes bouncing between our tense party.

"The house doesn't know me yet, so I doubt it's formed any kind of opinion." Helena reaches into her pocket and comes out with a handful of red powder, pressing her palm to the thick wood. "Let me in. You have no right to keep me out."

The door doesn't move.

"Ame," Alistair sighs. "Open the door for your mother."

My father makes a mistake then. He places his hand on my sister's shoulder, as if to guide her toward the library entrance.

Ame's aura swamps with white as pure terror condenses in her mind.

The next thing I register is my father's scream of agony.

I throw magic into my shields to keep out the neon blue wave of pain emanating from the man. The move is instinctual, the reaction faster than my mind, as I slowly take in what Jack just did in defense of Ame.

"My hand!" Alistair clasps a bleeding stump to his chest. At his feet lies the severed limb, fingers still twitching.

In front of him stands a wolfman, claws bloody, saliva dripping.

"No," the creature snarls, "touch."

"Get away from him!" my mother yells, running toward her maimed husband, fear finally showing on her previously passive face.

Jack turns and roars at her.

She gasps and raises her red-powdered-covered palms.

Not good, not good—

But Ame is quicker. At some point, my sister dipped her own fingers into the magical assist, and she lunges toward our mother, grasping her wrists in a tight hold. I watch as the red of wanting overwhelms Helena's aura.

"You want to take your husband and go to the healing witch who lives on Peachtree Lane. You want to reattach his hand. And then you want to leave us alone forever."

I can see the struggle on my mother's face. She's strong in her own right, and spells don't tend to stick to other witches well. What helps is that the first two commands Ame gave probably match up pretty closely with protective desires Helena has.

After a stretch, where the only sounds are Jack's panting and my father's sobbing groans, my mom goes lax in Ame's grip. When my sister releases our mother, Helena hurries to collect the hand and ushers Alistair to their car.

They peel off.

Jack, the wolfman, engulfs Ame in his furry arms.

Suddenly, I find myself in a strong embrace as well. And it's only when Bo's arms are around me that I realize I'm shaking.

"They're bad news, huh?" he asks while holding me close.

"Yes."

"Will Ame's magic keep them away?"

"No," the answer comes from my sister. "They'll be back."

42

Mor

NOT WANTING to encounter my parents unannounced again, I seek them out this time. They've booked a room at a bed-and-breakfast on the edge of Folk Haven, the place owned by a selkie, who I'm sure has no idea what type of toxic people she's let into her abode.

When I knock on the door to their room, my mother slips out on quiet feet.

"Morgana, dear." She gives me a wide, toothy smile that has always felt too menacing to me. "You came to apologize, I expect."

Uh, hell no.

"I wanted to talk to you," I say instead of scoffing at her assumption.

"Of course. I saw a bench outside below an oak that is positively vibrating with magic." She heads to the steps. "Your father is sleeping."

"They fixed his hand?" I follow her down the steps and out

the front door, also preferring to converse out in the open. Being inside with my parents feels too much like being trapped.

"Oh, yes. The healing witch here is much better than the one back home. Charges for the skills, but she reattached your father's hand with barely a scar."

"She is skilled," I agree. Maybe I should say, *That's good*, or, *Thank The Dark One he's okay*, or apologize. But I can't manage any of them. All I can say is, "How long are you here for?"

They wouldn't want to stay in a town where a werewolf is ripping off limbs, would they?

"Haven't decided." And as if she read my thoughts of werewolves, my mother begins to pry. "That wolf. He went after your father because he's Amethyst's mate? Are they officially together?"

"Yes." I keep the answer simple and unforgiving.

If our parents ever planned on matchmaking, they need to rethink it. We're all accounted for.

Thoughts of Bo's grin come to mind, and the back of my thighs tingle.

But all through this, I make sure to keep my mental and magical shields in place so my mother cannot pick through and dissect my emotions.

"Is Ame pregnant?"

"What?" I bark the question, almost losing hold of my composure.

Meanwhile, my mother stares off into the distance, in deep thought.

"A witch and a wolf. Their offspring would be fascinating." She blinks and refocuses on me. "You'll need to encourage her to procreate so we can find out what the mixture would bring about."

Horror steals my words momentarily.

My mother speaks about a possible grandchild like a science experiment. And I should have expected this.

Jack will kill them if they try anything, I attempt to reassure myself.

Not that they plan to have kids soon, if ever. I don't know where Ame stands on the subject.

But I do know that Zara—the harpy Anthony mated—is very interested in having a kid and that my brother is open to the idea of being a father.

What would our mother say about that? Or Broderick and Ophelia? Witch magic mixed with a firebird's.

My mind returns to my years of growing up in their house.

The rare times they took interest in me.

What they made me do.

What they took from me.

The idea of my parents attempting the same on potential nieces and nephews has me wanting to rip off a few limbs of my own.

This is not happening. We are not helpless children anymore.

I stand from the bench, towering over her. "You need to leave Folk Haven," I say in an unwavering tone.

"Nonsense." She waves her hands, dismissing my words. "Your father will work on a protection spell to ward off further attacks, and you only need to tell that wolf to keep his claws to himself."

"I don't care about your safety," I snap. No more than wanting them alive so Jack doesn't get punished for murder. "This town is our home, and none of us want you here. You were—and still are—terrible parents. Go back to Maine and forget about us."

Her confused expression turns almost sickly sweet as she tilts her chin up to connect our eyes.

"I don't think we will leave, Morgana." She spreads her arms, palms up. "You do not make the rules. And no matter how you feel, we're still family."

Dread condenses in my lungs until I can't pull in a full breath.

So, I turn, risking giving her my back, and put all my effort into shielding my mind and aura so Helena doesn't catch a hint of how much she scares me.

What am I going to do?

43

Bo

I don't have to be able to read magical auras to know that Mor is terrified by the thought of her parents settling in Folk Haven. My father was a waste of space and did a number on my self-worth, but at least I was never scared of the man.

"Can't The Council deny them?" I ask.

Mor shakes her head. "I went to Selena right after talking to my mother. She said The Council can't even consider expelling someone unless they've attempted to harm a resident of Folk Haven." She blinks her big green eyes up at me. "But by the time they do that, it might be too late to mitigate the damage. And they don't do big things. The pain they dole out, it's small and secretive. Hard to nail down and hold them accountable for." She shudders. "I thought we got away from them."

Fury roils in my chest at the thought of those two toxic witches digging their emotional-damaging claws into Mor and her siblings. I want to shield all of them, but I don't know how.

"I can drive them off," I offer. "Run them out of town. Jack would help."

Hell, Jack would draw first blood.

Mor shakes her head. "Selena warned that if we become the aggressors, it's us who could be banished. We don't get to decide the laws."

My teeth grind together at the unfairness of the situation.

I cradle Mor tight against my chest until, eventually, she slips into a fitful sleep. But I don't slumber, my mind shuffling through possibilities that will keep my new family safe.

There is one I can't deny. A solution that would fix everything.

But how high will the cost be?

Whatever it is, for Mor's safety and peace of mind, I'm willing to pay it.

Carefully, I roll my witch onto her side and slip out of the bed, my steps soft now that I know which floorboards creek. I slink down the steps and out into the chill night. Instead of transforming, I set off at a steady jog in my human form, letting the idea turn around and around in my head. Making sure I've examined all the angles and I'm still satisfied with my decision.

By the time I reach his house, my mind has not changed.

I pause at the edge of the barrier that kept me back last time, but when I step forward, I'm allowed through.

Tonight, I mean him no harm.

My fist is a loud pound on the door, echoing through the mansion the monster built for himself in the far corner of Lake Galen.

He keeps me waiting, but I keep my patience. This is too important to let my prejudices creep forward.

Finally, the door swings inward, revealing a smirking Sev.

"Well, if it isn't my old friend Bosephus. What did I do to deserve this"—he flicks his eyes to how close I am to his front door—"nonviolent visit?"

"I want to make a deal."

He blinks once.

Twice.

Then his smirk curls into a satisfied grin.

"In that case, do come in." Sev turns his back on me—a clear message that he's not scared of me in the slightest—and strolls into the depths of his house.

I follow after, shutting the door behind me and praying to the gods that I am still able to depart at the end of this conversation.

I trail him to a sitting room that's full of furniture that looks like he bought it at a Dracula garage sale. Old, fancy, and possibly hiding bloodstains. He settles onto the most ornate chair, as if perching on a throne, but makes no indication that I should sit. That's fine. I'd rather stand even if it gives the dynamic of a peasant begging royalty for a favor.

"Two new witches came to town yesterday. Helena and Alistair Shelly."

"The parents of your precious librarian," he says.

I'm not sure if he already knew they were here or if he simply used deductive reasoning. Either way, I nod.

And there's no point in being coy about how I feel toward Mor. I don't plan to love her quietly.

"I want you to make them leave town."

Sev raises a single brow. "You don't get along with the future in-laws? This is a drastic step, don't you think?"

"You don't need to know my reasons."

"No, I don't. But I *want* to know. And what I want I get, or you have no hope of convincing me to make a deal."

I clench my fists, then relax them.

"They're cruel. Mistreated Mor and her siblings. Those two weren't parents. They were ... owners. They treated their kids like toys they could play with. Poke at. Hurt, if they found it interesting. And now that Ame and her brothers are mated with other mythics, the Shellys got their eyes on any grandchildren." I grimace at the thought. "More fodder for their experiments."

Sev goes preternaturally still.

"Experiments?" He whispers the word, and I swear the syllables drip with venom.

I can't read the eerie note in his voice, but I really hope it's not interest. Sev tends to have the deadly air of a cat that enjoys batting around their prey.

"That's what they did. Tested different magics on their children. Leeched power from them."

Sev stares out the window toward the dark lake. Silent. Contemplating.

And I wait, holding tight to my patience so I don't ruin this chance.

"I will make them leave and never want to return," Sev announces at last. "In exchange, you will be in debt to me for the rest of your life. I can call on you for whatever I wish."

"Done."

He turns, brow raised. "Just like that?"

"Just like that."

"You hesitated the first time. With your siren."

"She isn't mine. Never was." And thank the gods for that.

I was a fool, infatuated with a selfish woman. Now I know what love truly is.

"What about the witch?" He studies me. "Is she yours?"

"I am hers."

Sev sighs. "Your candor chafes. Don't you know how to keep some secrets?"

"When they count."

He tilts his head, a sharp smirk cutting across his lips. "Does your witch know you are here?"

That has my back molars grinding. "She would if I could speak about you to her."

"Ah, yes. The binding. I think I'll keep that in place. I, for one, know that secrets are power."

"So we have a deal then?"

"Yes, Bosephus. We have a deal."

44

Bo

"WʜAT ᴅᴏ ʏᴏᴜ ᴍᴇᴀɴ, they're gone?" Mor stares at me from where she sits on the edge of her bed.

When she woke up, I told her the good news immediately.

But I guess I didn't think through exactly what I should say.

"I mean, gone. They packed up and hit the road." I rest my hands on Mor's shoulders, holding her eyes so she can see the truth in mine. Hoping she reads the relief and hope and honesty in my aura. And I am confident they're gone for good.

I went with Sev to make sure of it.

Hᴇ ᴅɪsᴀᴘᴘᴇᴀʀᴇᴅ into his house after I swore my end of the bargain and returned holding a small clay jar, filled with a glimmering substance. "Compulsion," was all he explained it to be. More powerful than anything Ame could manage.

A forever kind.

Then I rode along in his sportscar to the bed and breakfast where Mor told me the Shelly parents were staying. The selkie owner watched with wide eyes as we passed through the foyer, but she didn't stop us.

Helena was the one to open the door, expression somehow both curious and cold.

"Is this the one?" Sev threw the question over his shoulder.

"Who are you?" she'd asked the same time I nodded confirmation.

Instead of answering, the monster shoved a handful of whatever spelled substance the jar contained in her face, and she gasped, dragging it into her nose. Her mouth. Her lungs.

Sev pushed past her, toward where Alister lay on the bed, still asleep. Mor's father got the same treatment, sputtering in surprise at the rude awakening.

Then the couple relaxed, gazes vacant, bodies swaying as if buffeted by a strong wind.

"You will obey me." Sev crooned.

"I will obey you," they responded in chorus.

Fear trickled down my spine.

Has he had this all along?

Why hasn't he put the entire town under his compulsion?

"Forget your children. Forget Folk Haven. Return to your former home."

"Yes." Their heads bobbed, and my gut turned with trepidation. Their slack looks remained as they packed up zombie-style, drug their suitcases outside, and drove away.

The monster stood at my side, his focus on the taillights.

"You could do that to anyone you want." My voice came hollow, knowing that my vow to him meant it was impossible for me to warn anyone.

Sev turned toward me then, and I flinched back at the blood dripping from his eyes and staining his teeth as he gave me a gruesome grin.

"God objects have limits." He tilted the jar to show me there was only a tablespoon of the substance left. "And they have a cost." He

waved toward his face. "I'm going to be shitting blood for weeks after this."

"THEY WON'T EVER COME BACK," I assure Mor.

"How do you know that?"

"Trust me."

Mor will have to because I have no ability to explain the bargain I made. No wish to either.

But I should have known it wouldn't be that easy. My witch is too smart for me to maneuver around.

"You did something. Not a threat though. If Jack ripping my father's hand off didn't drive them off ..." Her gaze narrows in thought. "You spelled them in some way."

"Mor—"

"Not another witch. You'd need wealth you don't have even if you could find one strong enough to override their protections."

"The *how* doesn't matter," I insist. "All that matters is that they're gone."

"Not threats," she mutters to herself as if I didn't speak. "Not witches. Not money. But power. It took power to make them leave." Her eyes widen. "Sev."

Shit.

"There's nothing to worry about."

"Did you get help from Sev?" Her green eyes spark with fury. "He has powers. God objects—I'm sure of it."

I keep my mouth shut because there's nothing else I can do. I'm bound to silence.

But Mor doesn't need my words.

"I'm right, aren't I? He used some kind of powerful object to enchant them. To drive off my parents in exchange for ... what?" She looks not quite at me, but more around me.

Reading my emotional aura. "Gods, Bo, what did he demand from you? Is he forcing you to do something?"

"I was never forced," I hurry to assure her. "Trust me, I can't say a bad thing about him."

Once the words trip off my lips, I fight a cringe. They are too revealing. Too literal. Even if I wanted to curse Sev's name through all the dimensions, I couldn't. I am bound to him now more than before. Not only must I keep the secrets of the past, but I am another tool in his arsenal.

Another object in his collection.

Still, I would make the deal again without hesitation. Anything to keep the elder Shellys out of the home Mor has built here for herself and her siblings.

"Bo." Mor's voice is low, ragged.

I pull her into my chest, holding her lush body tight against me.

"Search my aura if you need to. Whatever choices I made, I am at peace with them. I'm happy. With you. And I know that you and your siblings are safe. That is all that matters."

"It's not." Her fingers dig into the muscles of my back. "You matter too, Bo."

My chest expands with the warmth of affection. Of belonging. "Show me then," I murmur, voice deepening with need. "Show me how much I matter to you."

Mor huffs, and then she digs her feet in and pushes me backward until my shoulders connect with the wall. Pinned, I loosen my arms so she can press up on her toes and claim my mouth in a searing kiss.

"This isn't over," she warns, the words hot against my lips.

"Leave it," I murmur back. "I'm happy. We're happy."

Cradling her head with my palms, I tilt her chin at the exact right angle.

Our tongues clash, breaths melding, and I've never known this level of joy.

Mine. All mine.

We spend the day together in the library, and she doesn't say another word about her parents other than to assure her siblings that Helena and Alistair are gone for good.

I'm grateful she's let it go, and I spend the evening using every bit of energy in my body to worship my witch.

When I fall into a deep sleep, I don't notice the touch of magic that holds me there. Only a small instinct, too quiet at the moment for me to discern, warns me that my witch has slipped away.

45

___

Mor

"WHY DOES everyone insist on visiting me in the middle of the night? I'm not a nocturnal creature. I, too, need sleep." Sev smirks at me from where he leans against his doorjamb, arms crossed over his bare chest. He looks paler than the last time I saw him, but maybe that's just the dim lighting of his porch.

"I want to make a deal," I say, guessing they're the magic words for this monster.

He rolls his eyes. "You and everyone else." He flicks his fingers in a *come on then* gesture as he saunters down a towering hallway into what must be the largest home on this lake. "You're lucky I'm curious by nature."

The house is oddly quiet once the door shuts behind me. Almost like I'm in a museum after hours.

If Sev has the collection I suspect he does, the comparison is not far off the mark.

But he doesn't lead me to a room full of treasures. Instead, we come to a dining room with a massive window I bet would show the lake during the day. He settles himself at the head of the table and waves for me to take a seat.

"Might as well be civil about this. You said you want to make a deal? What is it that you want, my dear?"

"Let's discuss what *you* want first."

"Me?" He chortles. "I am handsome. Rich. Powerful beyond what you could comprehend." A smirk cuts across his striking face. "I want for nothing."

"Liar."

"Hmm." His eyes narrow as he studies me. "And you think you know what I want?"

This is it. When I find out if my research led me to the right answer. If the occasional vague mentions of a monster in the texts I've found refer to the creature before me.

"God objects." My voice is steady, my gaze unflinching. "In particular, the golden apple that I have in my possession."

Nothing about his expression indicates if I'm correct, and when I try to get a lock on his aura all I encounter is a fog empty of any true color.

"Interesting." Sev hums. "And why do you believe that I want some silly gilded fruit?"

"You can't come in the library. Which means the house doesn't like you. And the house only dislikes those who attempt to steal from it."

He taps a finger against his lower lip. "This apple is in the house?"

"It was when you first failed to take it. It was when you sent Hamish to get it. And it was seventeen years ago, when you sent Bo to try to find it. I have no idea why he agreed, but I assume it had to do with Georgiana."

"Is that jealousy I detect?"

"No." My voice whips out like a steel dagger, flung with precision. "It's anger. I am *angry* with you, Sev."

"I'll give you a tip, witch." His expression is pure smugness.

"It's never good to let emotions come into play during negotiations."

"Noted. Now do you agree that you want the god object?"

Sev lifts a shoulder and lets it drop, the motion dismissive.

"There aren't many mythics who wouldn't want a god object. So, yes, let's say I'm intrigued by this apple you have. What do you want in exchange?"

"Three things."

"Greedy."

"No. Angry," I correct, and then I hold up three fingers. "First, I want you to lift whatever magical gag you have on Bo and forgive him any vowed obligation he has to you. He has spent seventeen years of his life cursed, and I will not stand aside as he continues to be enchanted and indebted."

Sev stares off to the side, his thumb and forefinger fiddling with his bottom lip, giving the appearance that he's only half listening. "Go on."

"Two, I want a blood oath from you, stating you will never harm me or anyone that I love." He scoffs, and I continue, "I'll even be generous. You cannot harm me or mine, unless we attack you first. Which I think is entirely fair."

"I am on the edge of my seat for point number three." Sarcasm drips from his words.

"Then here it is. Number three. You will also swear that the Mythic Council can call on you one time—that's right, only one—to lend your efforts to protect Folk Haven against a threat."

Owen's proposed plan and my parents' unexpected visit has made it impossible to ignore this town's precarious safety. If I can get a boon from the most formidable mythic I've ever encountered then I'll sleep better at night.

"You want to give The Council that power?" Sev's smile is chiding. "Georgiana Stormwind sits on that council. Cozy in her seat of authority." He drums his fingers on the tabletop.

"The siren who tried to steal from me and then convinced the monster you love to take the punishment in her place."

I blink, taken aback by the sudden reveal.

"Bo hasn't told you, I'm sure. He couldn't. But Georgiana used to be a naughty young woman. Loved breaking rules where no one could catch her." Sev continues to tap his fingers in a repetitive rhythm. "She didn't think I was home. I often wasn't back then. Had other business to attend to. And hadn't bothered to set up a full suite of wards. Thought my reputation would be enough to keep everyone away." His lips curl in a smirk. "But I forgot how arrogant the young are. How stupid. And the little pest crept inside my house, touched my things, and tried to take one with her." Now Sev's mouth stretches into a full grin. "I caught her, of course. And she begged me to let her go. Promised to complete a task for me. One I thought was perfect for a little thief." His eyes meet mine, holding my gaze. "Not even a day past before she found someone to pawn the task off onto. That's the woman you want to give my boon to?"

The monster likely hears how my teeth grind together, the fury locking my jaw.

Now, finally, I have my answer. Why Bo was in debt to Sev.

He was protecting Georgiana from her own stupid mistakes. The selfish siren had thrown him to a dangerous creature to save herself and didn't even glance over her shoulder to see the damage she'd left in her wake.

But this isn't about revenge.

This is about Bo's freedom. And the town's safety.

"Number three stands." And hopefully, another Of the Wing member gets elected to The Council before the favor needs to be called in.

Sev stares at me. Then he laughs. Slow at first, then great bellows of it.

Only to stop abruptly. The transition is eerie in its swiftness.

"No."

"No?" Though I repeat the word as a question, I'm not surprised.

Sev has something I don't.

Time.

But I also haven't laid my final card on the table.

"Your price far exceeds what you offer. But this was amusing to hear. Thank you for the entertainment."

"You still don't know what I offer."

The corner of his lips twitches, as if a frown attempted to take over his sensual mouth. But he restrains the display of emotion.

"You already stated. You offer the apple."

"About that, let me explain." Now it's my turn to lean back, my relaxing posture a power move. Because I know I'm on the verge of a checkmate. "You're not the only one interested in god objects. And while you may have wealth and power beyond my comprehension, you do not have my library. Full of books with the most interesting pieces of information. Fascinating spells. Like one I came across only a few months ago."

His eyes spark, and the cracks in his shield bleed agitation and interest.

"I discovered an incantation that can be wielded on a god object." I lean across the table and hold his gaze with mine. "To destroy it."

Fury blazes hot in his eyes before he shutters them.

"It's never good to let emotions come into play during negotiations." I long to taunt him. But Sev is not one to underestimate. I don't have his blood oath yet.

"Of course my offer sounds unappealing. I bet you've been stealing god objects for years. Decades maybe. I'd bet you're a long-lived mythic and you think you only need to outsmart me in the future or wait until I'm too frail to defend my little treasure." My voice lowers, both coaxing and threatening. "But you don't have that time, Sev. The deal I'm offering is to give you the apple in exchange for my terms, or I'll destroy it. You will never possess it."

I can see murder in his eyes.

"Also, just so you know, I sent a message to a few council members, letting them know where I am. If you kill me tonight, you will be driven from this town. Maybe you'll make your way back once the next generation is here. But the apple will be gone by then."

The monster gazes at me, his expression colder than the metal the man I love was trapped in. Trapped because of him.

Sev has no sympathy from me. And he knows it.

"Clever witch."

46

Bo

I TRACK her scent to the last place I ever hoped to find Mor.

The den of a true monster.

I stand on the edge of the wards in the light of the new day and roar, demanding an audience. Demanding her release.

The front door swings open, and my heart sings at the sight of my witch striding out of her own free will.

"Bo," she says in a calm voice. "It's okay. I'm okay."

Despite her words, I know something is wrong. I can feel it in my bones.

The freedom.

That's what woke me up. The lifting of a weight I hadn't been aware had borne down on me from before I was even cursed into the form of a statue. From the first moment I made a binding deal with Sev, there were invisible chains around my limbs, keeping me bound both to him and from him.

But they are gone.

Which means something happened.

But also, I am free to take revenge upon him.

"What did he do, Mor?" I pace on the perimeter I can't pass because his wards know the violence in my heart. "I'll destroy him!" The declaration rides a roar so loud that no matter the room he lurks in, the villain can hear me.

Owen asked if I could embrace violence for my witch.

Now I know the answer for certain.

"You cannot attack him," Mor tells me as she strides across the yard.

Only when she's over the barrier can I take in a deep breath. One that smells of roses and herbs as I gather her in my arms and inhale with my face buried in her fiery mane.

And as much as I hate disagreeing with Mor, today, she is wrong.

"Yes, I can." I set her down and spread my arms wide, like she'll see the remnants of the bindings that no longer hold me. "The loyalty binding is lifted. I know you did something. Something for me." Gratitude and fear twist painfully in my chest. Knowing that Mor came here for me is both a wonderful and terrifying thing. "But whatever payment he's demanded from you will die with him. Nothing stops me now."

Mor presses her hands against my chest, her touch welcome, but unable to soothe the defensive rage I'm riding.

"I know, technically, you can hurt Sev now. But if you do, then he can attack you back." She slips her hands upward, cupping the back of my neck, forcing my eyes to hers. "Right now, you're safe."

"What does that mean?"

"I bargained the apple for the safety and freedom of everyone I love."

"I ... huh?"

"I love you, Bo!" She digs her nails into my skin, the sting more erotic than painful. "You are one of the people I love, and so you are safe from him. Don't screw it up!"

"And *you're* safe?" I rasp the question, not caring about myself if Mor has put herself in some kind of danger.

Sev is a conniving mythic who's probably only gotten more ruthless in the seventeen years I was trapped.

"I am. All that he gets is the apple." She cups my face and kisses me. "As much as he likes playing with people, he wanted that god object more."

"He shouldn't get to have it," I grumble, not because I want the damn thing, but because it isn't fair Mor has to trade anything of hers on my behalf.

Her thumbs stroke over the stubble on my cheeks. "Items like that are magnets for trouble. Let Sev deal with whoever comes sniffing around for it. The only priceless items I care about are my grimoires." She presses another kiss to my lips. "And the priceless people in my life." Another kiss, this one deeper and distracting. "Do you trust me?"

"I do," I murmur, drugged by her affection.

"And do you want to spend another second worrying about Sev and his deal-making drama?"

"No."

Her smile is wide as she clasps my hand and draws me away from the gaudy house.

"Good. Because from today forward, I plan to forget about him."

My feet don't hesitate to follow, each step lighter than the last as I realize that, finally, I can leave the toxic mess of my past behind.

The future is mine to make what I want from it, with the witch that I love.

47

———————

Bo

MOR SAID the Halloween Ball is a Folk Haven tradition. One she plans to participate in. When I asked Anthony about what I should wear—since he is the most fashionable Shelly—he told me not to worry about it.

I figured that meant that even though it's called a ball, it's not actually a dress-up event. Like maybe I should just put on my newest pair of jeans and make sure that I have an ironed button-down. The Shelly sisters, I found out when I officially moved in a week ago, do not own an ironing board. Or an iron.

Or at least, they didn't. Now, they do.

I showed Mor the closet I stored it in.

"Oh. Thank you. I guess it's good to have one on hand," she said.

Maybe she has a spell to do away with wrinkles, but I, a mere monster, do not. So, the day before Halloween, I made sure to iron my dress shirt—and my jeans, too, for good measure.

But the moment I walk into the kitchen to find Jack leaning

on the counter, dressed head to toe in a black suit as he eats straight from a box of cereal, I realize all my preparation was nowhere near enough.

"It's, uh … black tie?" I ask, hearing the defeat in my voice.

I've never even touched a black tie, much less owned one to wear. Jack might have a spare he could lend me, but not an entire suit. I mean, even if the wolf did, he's a leaner build than I am. I'd bust the seams.

Gods, I'm going to embarrass Mor. If she's dressed half as nice as Jack, I'll still look like a can of Coors next to a bottle of prosecco.

Side note: buy Mor multiple bottles of prosecco to apologize for this.

"Yeah," Jack says in a disinterested tone, definitely not internally panicking like I am. "Go talk to Anthony."

I don't see how that will help. He was the first one I asked. The one who told me not to worry about it. Did the witch just assume I had a suit in my closet? Maybe that's how fashionable the former model is. He couldn't fathom my wardrobe wouldn't have at least one formalwear outfit.

And even if I find the Shelly and explain to him that, no, I don't have anything nicer than jeans because I've only just started to save up enough money to shop somewhere other than a thrift store, it's not like he'll be able to do anything about it before the ball. He and Broderick are also slim, compared to me, as well as shorter.

Mahon's build is like mine, but I doubt that bear shifter has formalwear.

Shoulders slumped in dejected embarrassment, I trudge toward the front of the house, planning on going upstairs and confessing my misstep to Mor.

Will she ask me to stay home?

Not likely. She'll probably assure me this doesn't matter.

Tell me to come in my jeans and shirt. She might even dress down to match.

I won't let her do that. I know her fairy-tale-loving heart is probably all about a fancy ball gown. I should've known …

"Bo! There you are." Anthony hustles toward me, dressed in a perfectly fitted crimson suit. "You need to get dressed."

Once again, I stare down at my perfectly ironed shirt and jeans that I was proud of not too long ago. "I am," I mumble.

He rolls his eyes. "Hilarious. Here. It was a rush job, but Esme helped me out."

Anthony offers me a black garment bag I didn't notice him carrying over his shoulder. Hesitantly, I accept it.

"What is this?"

"Your suit for tonight," he says with an implied *duh*. "I made the family's outfits. Except for Jack. He insisted the suit he wore last year was fine, the heathen. Go put that on and tell me if it fits weird. It shouldn't. Esme has a magicked mannequin. But I like to be sure."

In a daze, I walk to the downstairs bathroom and lock myself in. There's a hook on the back of the door, where I can hang the bag.

When I unzip it, I have to swallow a couple of times.

The suit is a rich, dark blue velvet. The shirt and tie are both black. And when I slip the ensemble on, the whole thing lies on me like a second skin.

There is a knock on the door.

"Let me see!" Anthony demands.

I huff an incredulous laugh, new confidence in my spine when I step out of the bathroom. The witch leans back, running an assessing eye over me. With quick movements, he undoes my tie and redoes it in a perfect knot.

"Good. Do you have any other shoes?"

Our gazes both drop to my work boots.

"Here. I think we're the same size." Jack materializes next to me, holding out a set of black loafers. Not as nice as his shiny black dress shoes, but better than my boots.

"That'll do it. I'm going to go check on my sisters." Anthony jabs a finger at me. "Don't spill anything on that."

"Yes, sir."

He smirks and disappears up the stairs, leaving Jack and me alone.

"You didn't know he was making you a suit," the werewolf says, not a question.

"No."

He holds my eyes. "You've been adopted. You're part of the family."

"I think I'm starting to get that." My throat is tight on the words, as I'm barely able to handle the honor.

"Jack," Ame calls from somewhere above us. "Anthony is making me wear heels. You need to stand at the bottom of the stairs to catch me in case I fall."

The normally taciturn man breaks out into a wolfish grin. "Coming!"

He claps a hand on my shoulder and drags me along with him. And I'm glad he does because after Ame comes teetering down in her dangerously tall shoes and fatally—for Jack anyway—short dress, I get to watch my witch descend in a glorious sapphire-blue gown.

Crystals trace patterns over the rich-colored fabric. Mor has styled her hair in thick curls spilling over one shoulder, leaving the side of her neck exposed—and that is exactly where I aim my kiss.

"I don't know how to explain how beautiful you are," I mutter, struggling even to say that much with her standing before me like a vision.

"That was good." She pats the lapels of my suit. "And I don't know which version of you I like better—fancy suit-wearing Bo or worn-jeans-and-a-flannel Bo."

"Gotta be this one, right?"

"You look good, baby." Her fingers stroke the fabric. "But it's the man in the clothes I love."

I'll never get tired of her saying things like that. "I love you too. So gods damned much."

There's a chittering noise near our ankles, and I glance down to find a raccoon tugging at my pants leg.

Mor's familiar wears a shiny blue bow tie and an expectant expression.

"Charm is coming with us?"

She shrugs. "I'm not about to stop him."

Mor finally settled on a name for her familiar when the creature fell asleep on a book of charms. The chunky critter fully engulfed the book, and Mor didn't even realize it was underneath him until she picked the raccoon up.

All of the Shellys and their mates pile into a limo Anthony booked us for just this purpose. I battle the urge to pull Mor close into my side because I don't want to muss her pretty dress.

When we arrive at the location of the Halloween Ball, there's a crowd of other cars parked in the field and a host of mythics in formalwear, making their way down a candlelit path toward a lakeside pavilion.

When we enter the space, I'm briefly mesmerized—and slightly creeped out—by the golden spiders spinning metallic spiderwebs above our heads. All part of the decorations, Mor assures me.

Lanterns float among the glittering strands, and fog swirls around our feet, matching the curls of smoke that drift from the tops of drinks on floating trays.

The night is pure magic.

"Bo," a musical voice says to my right, and I turn to find the second to last person I want to talk to.

Sev is the first, but luckily I haven't caught sight of him.

"Georgiana," I greet in response, resting my hand on top of

Mor's when I feel my witch's fingers dig into my forearm. I really don't want the woman I love to get in trouble for punching a tit on such a beautiful night.

Georgiana wears a long white gown that is weirdly like a wedding dress. It has me wondering where her husband has wandered off to. Wouldn't mind seeing Dr. Stormwind and thanking him for the glasses.

The siren's smile is tight, her eyes pleading. "I wanted to apologize. For my behavior toward you."

Mor sometimes refers to herself as a bitch witch, and I wonder if maybe a bit of her snark might be rubbing off on me. Because instead of quietly accepting the crumbs Georgiana is offering, I meet her eyes and give her back all the hurt she laid on me.

"Which time? When you used to fuck me in secret and never acknowledged me in public? Or when you stole something and abandoned me when I tried to help you? Or when I was finally free and knew no one but you, and you left me again?" I'm on a roll now and the woman from my past gapes like she's never seen me before. "Wait, no, you're probably apologizing for kissing me when you're married, and I didn't consent. Is it that one?"

Despite my scathing words, I'm truly curious which one of the many ways she hurt me Georgiana finally deemed bad enough to deserve an apology.

But I've stunned her silent.

So, my witch picks up the conversation. "Georgiana, you're going to leave Bo alone, or I will make it my mission to visit every Of the Wing constituent and let them know exactly what you've done to my mate."

Warmth floods my body at that last word. We haven't gone through an official ceremony yet, but there's so much surety in Mor's voice I have no trouble believing we will.

This finally cracks through the siren's stupefaction. "You live in Of the Wing territory by *my* leave."

Mor steps in front of me, towering over the smaller woman. "Try to pry me out of that house and see what happens. That is my home and my roots run deeper than a bird like you could understand."

There's chittering that sounds like agreement, and we glance down to find Charm, paws orange with a substance that looks like pumpkin pie filling, is leaving colorful prints all over the bottom of Georgiana's dress. The siren lets out and unattractive shriek, yanks her skirts away from the familiar, and stalks off through the crowd, multiple heads turning to watch her go.

The raccoon stares up at us with innocent eyes, and I bark out a laugh. "Thanks, Charm."

He babbles something only he can understand then waddles back toward the food table.

"You okay?" My witch asks, eyes creased in concern.

I lift her hand and press a kiss to the back. "With you defending my honor? Always."

Mor smiles, small at first, then wide and bright. "How do you feel about dancing?" Her gaze flicking between me and the dance floor.

"I doubt I'm any good, so you might need to be the one to lead," I admit.

In another lifetime, knowing my feet would fumble and struggle to find a rhythm would have kept me far from the couples swaying to the beat. But I'm done living my life based on fear and shame.

And when my witch's face lights up with happiness, I know I've chosen right.

She twines our hands together, her fingers caressing the webbing I've always been self-conscious of until she kissed the self-doubt away in our bed. I let my heart guide my steps.

Mor gazes up at me. Her brow creasing.

"What's the matter?" I ask.

"I was just thinking of the last ball. And how you weren't here. I'm sorry, Bo. That it took me so long to face the statue garden. That you had to wait so long on me."

I dip my head, breathing in her rose-herb scent and sighing out my contentment.

"Mor Shelly," I whisper against her moon-pale skin, "I would've waited a lifetime if it meant I ended up with you."

"I love you, Bo." She doesn't whisper, speaking the words in a strong voice that is undeniable.

And I'm the luckiest monster to have ever lived.

EPILOGUE

Clementine

On top of all the shitty things that have happened to me in the last forty-eight hours, bleeding on my car's upholstery should not even register.

But it does—because I love this car.

The blood isn't because I forgot to put a tampon in before a multi-hour road trip. No, the reason I'm goring up the front seat of my Prius is because this wound in my side won't heal.

The sucker won't even clot properly.

"Fuck," I mutter, glancing down at the dark stain on my Blink-182 T-shirt.

Thankfully, this rural road in northern Georgia is empty of other cars as I pull off to the side and put my car in park. Tugging up my shirt, I find the gauze I taped on myself is saturated. Carefully, I peel the medical tape off, gasping at the sticky rip of it against my tender skin.

The wound beneath isn't deep, but it's a few inches long, and again, it refuses to clot.

"What the fuck kind of knife was that?" I mutter to myself and try not to panic.

If I were human, I would be in an emergency care unit with stitches holding my skin together and keeping my blood inside my body.

But as a nonhuman, stitches shouldn't be necessary. This should have stopped bleeding almost immediately. I should be well on my way to heeling.

Something is wrong.

Lots of things are wrong.

Which is why I'm on this road in the middle of seemingly nowhere, rummaging through a plastic bag in my passenger seat, searching for alcohol wipes and more gauze and tape.

At least the blood isn't spurting from the wound. Just a slow, ominous trickle. Once again, I patch myself up as best I can, then pull back onto the road and pray to the gods the pain and adrenaline will keep me awake until I reach my destination.

A shaking has started in my body as my headlights flash across a familiar sign.

Welcome to Folk Haven.

I'm home.

Now I need to find *him*.

Hopefully, I haven't brought disaster along with me.

Folk Haven stories will continue!

In the meantime, keep reading for a preview of *Fire Magic & Ice Cream*, Book 1 in the Casual Magic series, where elementals try to find love while controlling their powers...

FIRE MAGIC & ICE CREAM

QUINN

"This is a horrible idea."

I shouldn't have gotten out of the car, but I realized where we were too late. Harley already pressed the button to lock the doors.

"It's my idea, which means it's genius. This is exactly what you need, Fireball." Harley saunters across the steaming parking lot.

With another mighty tug, I try heaving open the car door. My effort is futile.

Cat hovers, dancing from foot to foot. "You told me you wanted to try this place."

Sometimes, I wish my little sister had more evil in her, like Harley. Then I could give her a proper glare for outing my secret longing.

"I said I *wanted* to try it, but that I *can't*. It's too much of a risk."

"Stop being so dramatic. It's not like you're walking into an ammo store, about to set off all the gunpowder," Harley growls at me, already at the front door. "It's an ice cream shop, for goddess's sake."

I know exactly what it is. Land of Ice Cream and Snow. The newest addition to the strip mall where I get my biweekly pedicures. Every time I hobble out of Tulip's Nails with my fresh coat of polish, the acid smell of acrylics clears from my nose, and I get hit with the most delicious scent imaginable.

Waffle cones.

Even though it's torture, I tend to take a roundabout route to my car, just so I can glance in the windows. Not that I ever see much. The interior is dimmer than the blazing Arizona sun.

The easy solution would be to walk into the shop, but I've never done it. Not once.

"I can't go in there!" I lean back on the car, arms crossed.

"Why not?" Harley glares, fists on her hips.

"You know why! The second I step through that door, I'll melt their entire stock. I'm a menace!"

"Oh Quinn. You're not a menace." The distress in Cat's voice almost makes me take the description back. Just to keep from upsetting her.

Harley stalks across the parking lot, coming to stand in front of me. "Listen here, little miss firecracker. You might not be able to control your powers yet, but I can. You start to spark, I'll shut you down. Now get your apple bottom in gear because I'm practically orgasming from the smell of that place, and I'm not about to rush through eating because you're pouting in the car."

We meet scowl for scowl, but I give up first. Probably because this ice cream shop has been taunting me for months.

"You really think you can keep my heat in check?"

My big sister loses her annoyance at my hesitant question, replacing her glower with a saucy grin. "Hell yeah, I can. Could help you out other times, too, if you weren't such a prude."

"Gross! I don't care how kinky your job is. We are *not* that kind of family."

She rolls her eyes. "I'm not asking to be in the room with you like some poorly written porno. I could sit outside your door, read a magazine or something, and make sure you don't burn the house down." Harley tilts her head as she looks me over. "Are you super loud or something?"

"Gah!" I cover my ears and sprint for the front of the shop. "Stay the hell away from me and my sexytimes!"

Through the earmuffs I've created with my hands, I pick up my sisters' laughter. Ignoring them, I take the step I've been holding back from ever since Land of Ice Cream and Snow flipped on their *Open* sign.

I grab the handle and slide in through the front door.

What greets me steals all words from my throat. My nose was already full of sweet scents when I stepped inside, but before my eyes can scan the room, my entire body focuses on the feel of the place.

Cold.

The sensation skitters over my skin, prickling tiny goose bumps and eliciting a shiver.

A shiver.

Shivers and goose bumps aren't for people like me with a constant fire sitting just below the surface of my skin. But here, in this ice cream shop, I experience the sensation of being chilly for the first time in my life.

The bell chiming over my head alerts me to my sisters' arrival.

I whirl around to clutch Harley's shoulders. "This is amazing! I didn't think you could control the fire this much!" I'm so moved that I rise on my toes to press a kiss to her cheek.

She stares at me with eyebrows scrunched together and her lips pursed in a confused smile. "What?"

"Oh my gosh. I've never...this place is so cool!" Cat's exclamation as she dodges around us breaks into my out-of-character thank-you.

Moving past my first experience with the sensation of cold, I finally take in my surroundings. No wonder I was never able to spy much from outside the window.

Most ice cream parlors are all bright colors and delicate furniture. Cute little shops that bring to mind quirky sprinkles or fragile ice sculptures.

Land of Ice Cream and Snow crushes the idea of delicacy under the heel of its heavy boot. This place resembles the homestead of some rugged mountain man or the headquarters of a Viking clan. Solid wooden furniture stretches the length of each wall, and the floor is dark oak. Lights hang from the ceiling, giving off a low glow—small areas of warmth in the stark terrain of the shop. I'm not even sure *shop* is the right word.

More like cabin. A cabin that sells ice cream.

A handful of people sit, talking and eating. I expect, if we came a couple of hours later, after dinnertime, this place would be overrun with sugar-hungry customers. A granite slab serves as a counter in the back of the shop, next to it the one familiar item all ice cream parlors possess—a glass container to view the offered flavors.

I take a single step before realizing the danger behind the counter.

A man.

But not just a man. This man is...well...a *man*.

I think I've found the Viking who pillaged and plundered and built this cabin of a shop with his bare hands. A black T-shirt stretches over shoulders wide enough for me to perch on one side and Cat on the other. His strong, ivory face belongs in a superhero movie. Sculpted cheekbones, square jaw, and enough golden stubble to leave a delicious burn on the inside of my thighs.

Oh shit.

The wonderful cold sensation drifts away as my inner fire senses a rising lust. Heat trails just underneath my skin, pulsing with a life of its own.

"I was right. This is a horrible idea."

But as I turn back toward the door, Harley wraps an arm around my waist. To onlookers, the embrace probably appears friendly and innocent. But in truth, her hold is stronger than steel as she drags me to my doom.

"Focus on the ice cream. Ignore the beautiful man."

"Ignore him? By gouging out my eyes?" I mutter, fighting an onslaught of lust and panic.

The ice cream god steps forward, his frosty gaze locked on the three of us. I watch with fascination as he slips a blue apron, the same shade of his eyes, over his head. The muscles in his biceps flex as he reaches to tie the strings behind his back.

At the display of his glorious muscles, I brace myself for another surge of heat. Instead, my fire remains stoked. The embers are there, teasing me, but they don't burst forth, causing mass chaos.

I guess Harley is as good as her word.

"How can I help you?" The ice cream god's words rumble out like tires across gravel as he watches us.

Not us, I realize. *Me.*

Being the middle child, I've often silently longed for a little bit more attention. But right now, I'm considering hiding behind my curvy older sister or picking up Cat to use as a human shield. All in the name of self-preservation.

As if sensing my cowardly plans, Harley gives me a shove forward, so I end up stumbling into the granite counter. My hands land flat on the surface to steady myself.

Cold shocks through my palms, racing over my skin, practically extinguishing my fire, if not my lust. To my utter embarrassment, my nipples tighten with a shiver, and my bralette does nothing to hide the reaction.

When ice cream god's eyes drop to my chest, I'm torn between crossing my arms over my boobs and attempting another escape or ripping my shirt off and asking if he has a bed in the back room.

I settle on the happy medium of staring up at his gorgeous face and losing the ability to form a coherent sentence.

Maybe, if he were a creepy perv, I'd be able to collect myself. Unfortunately, ice cream god almost immediately removes his stare from my overly excited nipples to look me in the eye again.

"Do you know what flavor you'd like?"

I begin to thaw with a shake of my head. The Viking man turns his back. Steady again, I drag my hands off the frigid counter, rubbing my palms on the sides of my jean shorts.

Not that I mind the cold. In fact, I find the sensation fascinating.

I'm never cold. I was beginning to think I'd have to be dropped in glacial waters or launched into space to truly experience such a low temperature.

But apparently, I just needed my big sister to crave ice cream. Despite her borderline bitchiness earlier, I throw a grateful smile over my shoulder.

In classic Harley fashion, she pokes me in the back. "Stop ogling the man candy and figure out what you want."

Feeling less generous, I stick my tongue out at her and then glance forward, attempting to kick my brain into gear so I can remember what flavors I like.

But I'm thrown off track again when I find a mini wooden spoon in my face.

"Flavor of the day: blueberry pie." Grumbly voiced ice cream god holds out the offering.

On pure instinct, I reach for the spoon. The tip of my finger brushes the edge of his thumb.

At the brief contact with the gorgeous man, I fully expect the utensil to burst into flames, forcing me to pretend I'm a street magician and my sisters are my camera crew and that everything has a weird but still plausible explanation.

But instead of heat, there's another trickle of coolness.

Harley is going to be exhausted after tamping me down. She'll probably pass out in the car on the way home.

Ice cream god continues to watch me, and I realize I'm just standing, holding the sample, and staring at his expansive chest. To my amazement, the sample hasn't melted. However it's headed in that direction with one and then two drips falling from the spoon onto the counter.

Desperate not to reveal my detrimental effect on frozen treats, I shove the flavor of the day into my mouth.

When I smelled waffle cones outside the shop, I kept my composure. When I set sights on the mountain of sexy behind the counter, I had a brief internal freak-out, but overall, I held it together. When cold visited my nerve endings for the first time, I kept my reactions on lock.

But this? It's too much.

"Oh, fuck me," I groan, not caring if there are children around, being corrupted by my involuntary reaction. In my opinion, no one under eighteen should be allowed in this shop. This ice cream is too sinful for young innocents.

I want to fashion a man out of this ice cream, marry him, and then devour him for as long as we both shall live.

The Viking ice cream man clears his throat in a glorious deep rumble as he crosses his arms over his chest, all the while watching me. The pressure of his eyes sits cool and heavy like the chilled treat currently melting on my tongue.

Would he taste just as delicious?

Continue reading Quinn & August's romance in Fire Magic & Ice Cream!

NEWSLETTER SIGN UP

Get another Folk Haven romance for FREE! Sign up for my newsletter to receive *A Selkie's Secret,* a novella that tells the story of Isla, a selkie, and Finn, the human she refuses to fall in love with...

ACKNOWLEDGMENTS

Before writing Mor and Bo's story, I took a long break from the world of Folk Haven so I could write a few other books. But I missed this small magical town tucked away in the woods of Georgia!

Thank you to my fantastic editor Jovana who always polishes up my messy manuscripts. Special thanks to Claire who help smooth out some bumps in Mor and Bo's story.

And as always, thank you to my readers. I hope you had another fun romp through Folk Haven!

ALSO BY LAUREN CONNOLLY

Find a list of all of Lauren's books on her website:

https://www.laurenconnollyromance.com/book-list

ABOUT THE AUTHOR

Lauren Connolly is an award-wining author of contemporary and magical romance stories. She has lived among mountains, next to lakes, and in imaginary worlds. Lauren can never seem to stay in one place for too long, but trust that wherever she's residing there is a dog who thinks he's a troll, twin cats hiding in the couch, and bookshelves bursting with the stories written by the authors she loves.

www.ingramcontent.com/pod-product-compliance
Lightning Source LLC
Chambersburg PA
CBHW060658190726
48289CB00002B/467